This Charming Dilemma

By Sharon Gartner

Facebook/Sharon Gartner Author

:

Copyright © Sharon Gartner 2018

All rights reserved

Angelwords Publications.

This Charming Dilemma

IBSN: <u>978-0-6481619-0-5</u>

Cover Design

Leo Fairclough

Insta : @themiscvault

Editing Janine Ogden

Also Available by Sharon Gartner

This Charming Shack

This Charming Angel

This Charming Guest

Bare Feet

This Charming Dilemma

For you Louise

This Charming Dilemma

1

Oh my god I feel like such a tart.

Millie is staring at me in disbelief, and if she doesn't say something soon I shall be forced to end this discussion and leave the room.

It's been 4 months and 1 week since I found out I was pregnant and I have only just worked up the courage to tell Millie.

It's so unfair and I cannot believe the universe did this to me. Okay yes, I did want babies before I turned forty and shrivelled up like an old prune, and yes, I will have just slid in to home base to become a mother before the big 40 but that was before I was offered a chance to become a TV celebrity.

You see we had a guest called Brendan came to stay at the Bed and Breakfast to make an amateur documentary about boring old social interaction in the bush, even though technically we're not in "the bush", only a couple of hours drive from the outskirts of Sydney. So that *was* his plan, until I convinced him to invite a bus-load of men for an amateur dating show so I could find a man and have babies (even though the show was hijacked by controlling friend Millie, and turned into more of a promotional documentary that went horribly wrong in my opinion).

This Charming Dilemma

And after Brendan went back to the city and showed footage of the week-long event to a reality TV director, they realised my true talent and invited me to have my own reality TV show which starts filming next week. I mean, how cool is that, and I don't have to do anything, just be me.

With a bulging belly.

Oh god!

'You're having Jake's baby?' Millie finally asks still in disbelief, exhaling a loud sigh through her nostrils.

'Um... kinda.'

'So you're not having Jake's baby?'

'Yes I'm having a baby.'

'And he is the father?'

'Um, well I haven't decided that yet,' I said in hoity tones.

I knew the question would present itself so I decided to take a new age woman attitude and choose who is worthy to be the father of my baby.

'You haven't decided yet?' repeated Millie again in disbelief, 'so Jake isn't the father?'

Okay, so it's not all about being a new age woman. Truth is Jake came back into my life and I realised there may still be a tiny flame there and what was I supposed to do, ignore my feelings?

9

But there was also my drunken encounter with local stoner Damo, or Damien as a normal person might call him, when I felt sorry for myself after finding out Daniel, my business partner, is gay and not into me as I thought. So I got drunk and somehow ended up taking Damo's virginity. So it could be either.

'Oh god Lisa!' Millie said as she slumped into a chair, 'please tell me you know who the father is.'

'Pfft, of course I do,' I said.

'Then whose?'

'Well… there is Jake,' I said.

'And…?'

'And, well, there was someone else, but I didn't know what I was doing so not sure if I really did it or not.'

Didn't want to tell Millie it was stoner Damo, I'll only get a lecture followed by more judgemental noises.

'Oh for the love of god,' Millie said, covering her face with her hands, 'please don't tell me it's Damien?'

My god Millie can be freaky sometimes with her psychic behaviour.

'How did you know it was Damo?'

'Because you went on a date with him.'

This Charming Dilemma

'Oh yeah. It happened before that.'

Okay wrong thing to say, as now Millie is rubbing her temples and looks pale.

But it's not like I'm proud of the fact I do not know whose baby I'm carrying. The doctor could only estimate how far along I am as I don't keep a record of my menstrual cycle, I mean it normally just turns up. And believe me it wasn't easy keeping this from Millie, she's my best friend and well, she lives with me, gotta tell her some time.

So far thank god I haven't been sick or anything, just not eating Daniel's mint cream biscuits he normally keeps at work and am totally off coffee. Besides, it's not like I *planned* it, what did they expect me to do, keep a diary of who I did it with and when.

'So are you planning on telling Jake and young Damo about the up and coming special event?' Millie said in her sarcastic tone.

Okay you may think Millie is being mean with her tone of voice, but this is Millie's way of showing support. Millie's not the soft, it will be fine, type. Millie's more of a, I'll interrogate you until you break and then help with a solution, type.

'What event?' Sid asks, catching the last of the conversation as he enters the kitchen. Sid is Millie's terrified husband and I have to admit, he has been great these past few weeks when I announced that I will be staring in my own TV show.

He was a bit frazzled to begin with, okay, frazzled is an understatement, as he ran and hid under the bed and it took ages to coax him out. But he slowly came around to the idea after I pointed out that he would be able to showcase all his hard work around the place including the ant race track he was hoping to build. He finally saw that this would be a good thing for all of us as it would give great exposure to the B&B business we all run together and it's not all about me.

Well it is all about me, but Millie, Sid, and baby Amy are family so... it's also about them. But only a tiny bit.

Which reminds me, I'd better tell Mum and Dad.

About the show I mean, not the pregnancy, pfft, not telling them about *that*.

'Nothing!' I quickly said to Sid before Millie opens her mouth, 'I mean, err, not nothing, obviously there is something, um Millie is talking about the event of the TV series.'

Millie's mouth is hanging open in mid air, I dare not look at her again.

'Oh okay, I just wondered what you had to tell Jake and Damo about?' said Sid in neutral tones as he collected the toilet supplies for the bathroom, 'I thought you may have heard some news about the Crankshaw's and who burnt down the farm buildings and house, that was all.'

Ever since Sid has became a house husband he is always probing for a bit of gossip.

This Charming Dilemma

'Oh no, Millie just meant we have to tell them about the TV show, you know, keep them in the loop.'

Sid stopped what he was doing and looked at me puzzled, 'I thought they already knew about it. Damo was talking about it the other day?'

When Sid's question met my blank stare he shrugged and left the room, love Sid, he knows when to stop talking and leave.

Shame about Millie.

'Okay why are we not telling Sid?' asked Millie, 'are you waiting until you're a bit further on?'

'No, I'm not telling Sid because I have decided not to tell anyone,' I beamed, hoping Millie will be on board with my plan, 'well, you know, not until the baby is born.'

I figured that if I told Brendan, the director of my up and coming show, about me being pregnant then he will go back and tell the producers of the show. And then they may rethink the whole reality television series and I would have to go back to my old career of being an event planner. I mean, so unfair, I have been waiting my whole life to become famous and what happens?

'Lisa you cannot hide a pregnancy!' Millie scorned, 'how far on are you?'

'Well I found out just after I found out about the TV show,' I said, hoping Millie wasn't that good at maths.

'You've known you're pregnant all this time and you're only telling me now!' she said, her voice taking on a scary tone, 'so what does that make you, around 10 weeks?'

'More like 16,' I mumbled. So turns out she isn't really good at maths.

'Oh good fucken lord,' Millie said, rubbing her brow once again.

God I am soooo starting to regret telling Millie, I mean it's okay for her, she was married when she had Amy and didn't have an up and coming reality TV show to deal with when she was pregnant. If she doesn't come around to my idea soon I shall be forced to yell 'just kidding!' at her, then she can just be surprised with the rest of them when the baby is born.

'Well Neroli did it,' I wailed in my defence.

'You are not planning to pull a Neroli,' Millie said, frustration building on her face.

Neroli was an old friend that came to stay. She was living here a whole month before anyone found out she was having a baby. Neroli's not exactly a big woman or anything, I mean we didn't even know there was a baby until, well you know, she had a baby.

'Lisa you cannot do that,' Millie sighed, 'Neroli didn't tell anyone cos she was in denial and couldn't cope with the prospect of having another child on her own.

This Charming Dilemma

You don't want to tell anyone because you don't want to miss out on your big television show chance.'

Not sure what to say, as per usual, Millie is trying to see things her way so I just fold my arms in a huff.

'Look,' she said, her voice softening, 'you know I will support you whatever you decide to do. And for now I will keep my mouth shut because it's blinken obvious *you* are in denial. I'm pleased you told me but think about what is more important, your well-being or a TV show?'

Typical Millie, tear you to shreds then tell you the good stuff afterwards, don't know how Sid puts up with her, no wonder he is timid and hides under beds!

'Here,' she said, taking Amy from her playpen and handing her to me, 'you start practising nappy changes while I go help Sid with these beds, the production crew arrives tomorrow.'

'Okay but don't tell Sid,' I said to Millie's back as she exits the room at a fast pace, which could only mean one thing and that is, that she's dying to tell Sid. God why did I tell Millie?

Okay I told Millie cos the truth is I have no idea what to do now and thought that if Millie knows then I won't feel so alone, but I don't want anyone else to know.

God this baby stuff is confusing.

'Sup?' Matt appeared wearing a dark suit and dark glasses, looking like something from Men in Black.

15

Matt is nearly 20 and barely out of puberty. I first meet Matt when I woke up from yet another drunken night to find him in my bed, but let's not go there. He has been hanging around since.

'Man what's the stink?' he said, covering his nose.

'Oh it's Amy,' I said, pulling myself from my thoughts and coming back to reality, 'she needs changing. Matt what are you wearing?'

'It's my bodyguard outfit,' he said 'I've come to see what you fink?'

Oh god, doesn't matter how much I've tried to discourage him, Matt still has it in his head that if he is seen in the reality television show as a body guard then a celebrity might see how good and well dressed he is and offer him a job.

Apparently it's Matt's dream to become a bodyguard for a famous celebrity (a real celebrity as Matt puts it, not me).

'So which one are you, Z or J?'

'Huh?'

'Never mind,' Matt doesn't get Men in Black references, it's before his time.

I lay Amy on the change table but my stomach is turning with the stench, I have changed Amy before without a hitch but today it's bothering me.

This Charming Dilemma

'So you haven't told me what you fink,' Matt said as he does a half turn in his suit, 'cost me $100 bucks so had better be a good investment.'

'Depends on what you are trying to achieve,' I said, trying not to bring the contents of my stomach up while I wipe Amy down, 'if you're trying to say you are a youth dressed up in a cheap suit, then I think you're there.'

Oh god, I really am going to be sick, not sure what Amy is eating these days but it's really not agreeing with me.

'This suit wasn't cheap, $100 bucks Lisa, that's almost three cartons, so seriously, what ya fink?'

He looks proud as he adjusts his cheap tie so what can I say.

'Oh shit, hold this,' I said, holding out Amy's soiled disposable nappy, 'I think I'm going to throw up.'

'I can't hold dat,' he says, 'I'm in my suit.'

'Matt seriously, I'm not kidding, get rid of it.'

'You've done it before, what's your problem?'

'I... um... have a stomach virus, just take it.'

'Just put it down.'

'No! I cannot stomach the smell. Here, finish Amy off then.'

'I can't, I'm in my suit.'

Too late. I open my mouth to protest at Matt's stubbornness and expel the contents of my stomach.

My first official 'morning sickness' should be a memorable moment but instead I have Matt yelling at me while Amy is lying on the change table crying.

'You frew up all over my new shoes, oh man you even got the bottom of my pants, $100 bucks Lisa.'

Millie, upon hearing Matt's rant, came to Amy's rescue, giving me a half-hearted pat on the back as I stood bent over in my moment of shame.

'So you're still not over the first trimester maybe,' she quietly mused, handing me one of Amy's wet wipes to clean my face as I contemplate dying. I hate throwing up, it's on my top ten list of worst things to endure, listed just below childbirth.

Oh god, oh god, maybe I *should* call Brendan and inform him. We could do an episode of fear factor, because fear just kicked in.

'Have you eaten anything this morning?' Millie continued, kicking into her caring mother mode, 'and Matt why are you undressing yourself in my living room?' Millie asked puzzled, trying to address the two of us at once.

'Cos Lisa spewed on my new suit so now she has to take it to the dry cleaners,' said Matt, removing his pants to expose his heavy work socks.

This Charming Dilemma

'Just give them to Sid, he will deal with them,' Millie said as she continued to rub my back gently as I remain bent over the bile I had just deposited on the floor, 'so have you eaten anything?' she pressed again for an answer.

'She better not eat anything if she has a spew bug,' said Matt, 'she might spew it back up.'

'Oh dear!' said Sid, making an appearance as I straighten my back up, catching the pained look on his face at the mess before him. I know he is dying to yell, "for god's sake I just cleaned up in here!"

'Only a cup of tea,' I answered Millie. I couldn't handle my normal breakfast of toast with peanut butter that I crave most mornings.

If I wasn't pregnant this vomiting would be a great way to lose weight for my production. Now I have the opposite problem, I'm only going to get bigger, why universe, why!!

'You should probably eat something,' said Millie fetching one of Amy's cloth nappies to put over my pile of spew, 'might make you feel better.'

'I just said she shouldn't eat anything wif a spew bug,' protested Matt as he stood there wearing his fluorescent undies and the top half of his suit. 'My mate had a spew bug and he had a big iced coffee and in like 2 minutes it all came back up.'

'If you've got a virus then maybe you should head to bed,' said Sid all concerned and sounding slightly alarmed, 'we have a lot of people arriving tomorrow and the last thing we need is everyone coming down with it,' he said pained, like he envisioned himself dealing with a never-ending pile of laundry.

I shot Millie a look and by the looks of her returned gaze she hasn't told Sid and her eyes are pleading with me to give her the go ahead to tell Sid.

Ignoring her silent pleas and acknowledging Sid's advice with a nod and accepting his offer to clean up, I gathered up my phone and the bottle of water Millie handed to me and head off to bed, not only because I feel poorly again, because I need thinking time.

As I turn I'm met with a blast of aerosol mist in my face!

'Argh! Matt what the hell?'

'Anti spew spray,' he said, holding a can of spray disinfectant in his hand, 'I don't want ya spew bug!'

2

I really do not know what to do.

On the one hand I did want kids so I am kinda happy about it, on the other I really, really, want to be a celebrity. I mean imagine the opportunities this will bring me, I can move out of here and be able to afford a big grown-up house all by myself. It would give me great pleasure to give Millie and Sid this house, after all Sid loves it here and they have done so much work around here, they deserve it.

I'm lying here under the covers of my bed recovering after having my first real bout of morning sickness before Matt drowned me in disinfectant spray contemplating how I am going to pull this off. Matt questioned Millie's statement about me still not being over the first trimester but lucky for me, Matt's dumb arse is a few tools short of a tool shed as according to Matt he thought Millie meant I have the 100 day flu, hence why the whole house including the back of my throat and eye sockets smell like pine fresh disinfectant spray.

Millie came to check on me earlier and suggested I tell Brendan sooner rather than later, but I tend to disagree.

I have no doubt that as soon as I tell Brendan and Daryl Loft, the producer of the show, that I am pregnant, they will pull the idea for the show as fast as Millie's ability to jump to conclusions every time I open my mouth.

Okay well she has just cause to jump to conclusions most of the time, but this is my opportunity to make something of myself. All I need is a little time to get myself out to the world, get recognised, and when I become a celebrity sensation then I will showcase my belly.

I mean celebrities have babies all the time, doesn't stop them from being famous.

Millie insists I will get bigger any time now so I have assured her I will tell Brendan and the producers about my pregnancy, but this was just to get her off my back, I am now contemplating how I am going to prevent Millie from talking to Brendan the whole time he is here!

I'm sure a solution will present itself.

So tomorrow is the big day when filming starts on *'Tales From The Lemonade Stand',* a production crew of three will be here. We have a camera operator, a sound person, and a director. The idea is a reality television show of life in a small town with the focus on me a single ex-city girl in a small town and the trend of young people getting out of the rat race and making a living and blah, blah, they will follow me and the groups involved like the CWA.

As the title suggests our town's Lemonade Stand has made headlines around the nation, the tall tales from many people stopping to visit is the drawcard. We don't just sell lemonade,

This Charming Dilemma

we sell baked goods and souvenirs made by our local ceramic class and wood-turning club. And if Fran's arthritis isn't playing up, ugly knitted creations. The stand was originally put up by the CWA members when Betty suggested we raise funds to help out the Crankshaw's after their family farm house and sheds burnt to the ground in a suspicious fire.

The Stand started off as a fold out table under a pop-up marquee, but now it's a permanent structure made from the local timber with a very English thatched roof made by locals. Our main custom is the bus-load of workers heading out to the mines in the west, as well as passing tour buses. Our town has become a central refreshment shop. Although we have many cafes and a bakery somehow the Lemonade Stand seems to be the most popular, with people from all walks of life. Seems a bit strange considering we don't actually sell a lot of lemonade, or ugly knitted creations, or ceramic mugs come to think of it. But Betty is head of marketing and don't ask me why, but she always seems to make ends meet. In fact it's more than making ends meet, the Lemonade Stand brings in more profits than any other fund-raising activity the CWA has done since the fiasco of the marijuana filled eye pillows (the CWA was cleared of any wrong-doing due to having no knowledge of selling illegal substances disguised as eye pillows). Betty even moved a motion to get the go ahead to purchase two mobile phones so the members can communicate with each other while tending the Stand.

As the president I didn't see the need to purchase mobile phones as I didn't see how they could be useful for such a thing given that all they do is sit behind the Lemonade Stand

and chat all day, it's not like they are running a corporate business that requires communication at all times, but since they weren't roping me in to baking goods or making ugly knitted creations or really involving me at all (and the fact I was outvoted) the motion was passed and the CWA is the proud owner of two iPhones.

But all my problems aside I really am excited about tomorrow. So I guess I will just have to put the pregnancy aside for now and concentrate on winning my audience over. I have come up with the following plan.

. Meet and charm the Director and crew.

. Pretend I'm not pregnant until I convince Director and crew of my celebrity potential.

. Once my celebrity status has been established then I will reveal that I am with child.

Then I will be the most talked about rural ambassador/business owner/single mother to hit the women's magazines.

Perfect.

Except for the single mother part, that kinda doesn't feel good.

Oh god! I throw myself under the safety of my bed covers again, the excitement dulling as I go into depression mode over my expected bump.

This Charming Dilemma

I am convinced this must be Jake's baby, it cannot be Damo's because that only happened once, well Jake only happened once too but because Jake's more mature I think there is a better chance it would be him than Damo, and of course the fact that I can remember my night with Jake so I definitely know the deed was done. But I guess the million dollar question is, should I tell Jake? Because it's a big deal, I need to be sure. I mean it would be terrible if I told Jake and he got down on one knee to finally declare his love and propose marriage only to find out when baby arrives that he/she has Damo's blond locks not Jake's dark complexion. I mean how awkward would that be.

But if I tell either of them now, then they will definitely have a much lower opinion of me then they have right now, I mean this skeleton in my closet could potentially ruin my proposed clean-cut celebrity status.

Groaning at my revelations I roll over under my covers, I cannot believe I ended up as one of those people who will have to have paternity tests to reveal who my baby's father is. Where did my life go so horribly wrong? It's not only Damo and Jake, I also had a drunken encounter with Matt when I first moved here. When did I get so promiscuous? I mean I was brought up in a stable environment, okay I was an only child but I was never spoilt. And Mum made sure I always had my cousin Mark around for company, even though he was obsessively into Dungeons and Dragons, wore heavy green knitted jumpers and ate his own snot, he was still around like a brother would be, so I know I don't have men issues.

I was never like this in the city, in the city I was always a one-man woman, and never ever would I contemplate going to bed with any of them until the relationship was established. Yes I admit I shouldn't drink alcohol due to my ability to lose memory as soon as a glass touches my lips but I was never promiscuous when that happened either. In fact when I did drink too much, I always had Millie around to throw me in a taxi and send me home alone so the chance to make drunken mistakes was never there.

No, this only started when I moved to the country, and Millie became preoccupied with the house renovations, getting married and having babies. And considering that it was Millie that convinced me – no – forced me, to move here in the beginning to face my tiny mistake of buying a rural property (out of love I might add), then it's all her doing!

Millie and the fresh country air has forced me to drink more and sleep with random men!

Oh speak of the devil.

'Are you okay?' Millie asked after knocking faintly before entering, 'I bought you some tea and dry crackers.'

'It's all your fault Millie!' I mumbled from the depths of my bed covers.

'What's my fault?' she asks as I feel her fluffing up my pillows.

'That I am such a drunken free-giver when it comes to men. If you hadn't forced me to move here none of this would happened.'

This Charming Dilemma

'And that's my fault?' said Millie, 'wow and it's only 9.45 in the morning, now sit up and try this,' she said peeling back the covers from my head, 'it's ginger tea, it may help. Let's see if you can start the morning over again.'

Despite myself, I sat up and took a sip of her tea, the aroma settled me down straight away, its times like this that I can almost forgive Millie for turning me into a country hussy.

'So what are you blaming me for now?' asked Millie clearing a space on my bed to sit down, 'your drunken free-giving ways?'

'What have I become?'I sniffed to Millie, wrapping the corner of my bedsheets around my finger, 'I'm pregnant and don't even know who the father is. It wouldn't have happened if you didn't tell me to move here,' I said in a tiny voice to lessen the impact of blaming Millie.

'Oh my god,' Millie laughed, 'okay I've heard it all now, drag you off into the fresh air of the countryside, take my eye off you for a second and you go and accidentally have sex.'

'Well when you put it like that Millie...' I said.

'Lisa, your problem is, that you just get too passionate with the moment and don't stop and think about the consequences of your decisions,' said Millie, picking up the heaped clothes on the edge of my bed and beginning to fold them, 'yes you shouldn't go near alcohol with a ten foot iron stripper pole, I had spent countless nights putting you into a taxi whenever you had a epiphany to change the world, that was the cue you'd had enough to drink. But you're a big girl now,' Millie said in her sarcastic tone, 'so stand up, face the wrath of your poor drunken decisions, and look at the positives.'

Bloody Millie's answer to everything. Look at the positives.

'Well I didn't ask to get pregnant!' I said, resisting her positive attitude and folding my arms across my chest.

'Yes you did,' Millie scoffed, 'that's all I've heard for the past two years, how much you wanted a baby, didn't you even write a letter to the universe requesting one? Well now you are having one, which is fantastic, and the best bit is you won't have any more drunken sexual encounters for the next five months cos you won't be able to drink,' she beamed.

Oh my god that's right, another whole five months to go of no alcohol, my life *is* definitely over.

'You also have helped build this place into a working B&B and built a successful business with Daniel,' continued Millie, ignoring the look of devastation on my face. 'And tomorrow you have a camera crew coming because for some reason they find you an interesting drama queen.

This Charming Dilemma

So if you are still telling me all that was all my fault then I am truly humbled Lisa, you are so welcome but I really cannot take all the credit for your success.'

I don't know what to say as I know Millie is right, so I just fold my arms across my chest tighter.

'Anyway, drink up,' said Millie, getting off the bed and smoothing the covers out where she sat, Millie's such a mum. She never used to be like this, but ever since Amy came along she does things like… folds washing, brings me tea and fluffs pillows, 'remember you have a CWA meeting in half an hour.'

Shit, bugger, damn! I totally forgot about that, god, of all days it's when I'm having a self loathing and morning sickness day.

'Well you have to get prepared for tomorrow,' said Millie reading my facial expression, 'the CWA are a big part of this reality show as well, as their president you have to make sure they know what is going on.'

'Can't you go for me?' I moan, slumping back into my pillow feeling fragile.

'Nope your deal, your dealings,' said Millie, making her way to the door, 'Betty just phoned, said to pass on to you that Jake's bringing down the old banners that Mrs Crankshaw had in the old shed, the one that didn't burn down, so he needs someone there to meet him to let him in.'

Driving frantically towards CWA meeting place.

I feel so much better after Millie's tea, I leapt out of bed before Millie even had time to leave the room and of course Millie also made things easier by having folded my clothes so it made it so much easier to find stuff to wear, which cut down a lot of time. Gotta love Millie even though she commented about my speedy interest in getting to the CWA meeting by stating there was nothing like the prospect of a certain male presence to motivate me to get to the meeting, but that's not why I'm keen to get there!

Okay, it's a tiny bit of the reason I am keen to get there.

I haven't really seen Jake since the Crankshaw farm burnt down.

Yes we slept together and it really looked like we would be getting back together as he seemed really keen to build a relationship, I mean hell, since he came back, we spent a total of three nights together and two of those nights we did nothing but play scrabble! Not to mention the text messages and late night phone calls in between, and the fact he was the only applicant to apply for my dating show, so you know, there was potential there for a relationship. But since his Aunty and Uncle's farm burnt down, Jake has been withdrawn and apparently not really talking to anyone except his brother Rick and Mr Gough from the hardware store when he gets his gas bottle refill for his caravan.

Not that I have been stalking him or anything,

This Charming Dilemma

 but it's been almost five months since our big love-making night and the fire and I cannot understand why he's withdrawn like a hermit? I know he was a bit annoyed that his Aunty and Uncle, Mr and Mrs Crankshaw, decided to split, leaving Jake to deal with the investigation and with no chance of any insurance payout due to the fact that it seems the Crankshaw's may have burnt down the farm themselves, but he is also ignoring offers of support from everyone. I gave up on Jake when he didn't return my calls, or text messages, or answer the door to his caravan which he has parked amongst the charred remains of the farm.

Rumour also has it that he had to sell off some of the dairy herd too, so by the sounds of things poor Jake is left holding things together and I really wish he would let me come out and see him. Thank god I had the up and coming reality show to distract me from becoming obsessed with seeking answers from him.

I see him around town occasionally and I do get a wave or some form of acknowledgement, but I haven't really had a chance to "bump" into him. I mean I don't know if he even knows about the reality TV show.

Pfft, who am I kidding, of course he would know, I did a mail drop after all.

And then of course there was the local paper.

But if I am going to declare to him that there is a fifty percent chance I am with his child, then I am going to have to break the ice somewhere, sometime.

I arrived at the CWA building, which used to be the old scout building. Jake's ute is already there, parked at the side of the building near the back door. I'm also grateful I am the first one here, well I know I'm the first one here cos I passed Fran in her Nissan Micra four blocks ago.

I waved out to him when he acknowledges my arrival by climbing out of his ute. Signalling to him that I will have to go through the front door to unlock the back door for him, my knees are starting to go shaky with the prospect that I would be able to – you know – well, talk to him again. I unlocked the heavy door and made my way through the musty hall towards the back. Okay now whatever I do I must be poised calm and not act like I may be carrying his baby and need to pin him down so we can arrange a wedding date soon. No, I must treat him like an old friend that I have had many naked relations with, hmm no, I need to treat him like he is on the ten most wanted list, no that's not going to work either, too cautious, okay I need to treat him like he is my father.

Oh god, no, no, no, abort mental image.

I got it, I'll just treat him like he is a random delivery person.

Whom I want to jump all over.

Oh god I hope that is the hormones talking and not actually due to Jake's intoxicating presence.

Actually I think I'm going to be sick again. Okay no big deal, it's only Jake waiting patiently behind that door.

This Charming Dilemma

'Lisa,' barked Fran, coming up behind me causing me to almost deliver an embryo right there on the spot, 'what is with you? I was driving down Lake Road heading here when you sped past me on the inside lane, could have caused an accident if I was turning, and the speed you were going!' Fran huffed, 'honestly Lisa where did you get your licence?'

'I wasn't going that fast,' I scoffed.

'And what was up with you beeping your horn at old Errol as he was trying to get his push bike across the road?' Fran continued, 'almost ran over him, honestly you young ones have no respect for the road, not to mention wearing your tyres out. Were you late for an important date or something, if I didn't know any better I would say you were quite keen to get here.'

'I just wanted to um... make sure the door was unlocked you know, so you people are not standing round outside cos you know, brrrr is a bit chilly out,' my face is burning red at my lies.

'What are you talking about? It's 27 degrees out there now. Are you going to let poor Jake stand out there all day?'

'Um no,' I said, fiddling with the key in the old lock.

Bugger Fran for turning up so quickly. The only reason I sped past her was so I could get a chance to break the ice with Jake first.

I opened the door to Jake standing there supporting a long wooden sign under his arm.

Slapping the sweetest but "seeing you is no big deal" smile on my face as I greeted him, I almost threw up when he gave me a soft and friendly greeting back.

'Ah perfect,' said Fran as she observed the sign Jake carried past her to place it at the front of the room, 'I was hoping Barb still had that.'

'Another couple to go,' Jake said, 'I also found the original you were after Fran.'

'Such a good lad,' said Fran, marvelling at Jake's news as he gave her a smile and headed back out to his ute. I'm standing there like a dummy not sure what to say or do.

'Is that the signs?' exclaimed Betty, as she made her entrance, clapping at the sight of a wooden board, 'oh hurrah, look girls it's the signs.'

Equal amounts of joy were expressed as Mary, Gloria and Maggie also made appearances.

Not seeing the need to express joy in an old wooden sign it dawned on me that I should offer Jake a hand with the rest of them.

'Did you need a hand with those?' I asked, fluttering my eyes as I made my way out to Jake's ute.

'No it's all good thanks,' he said pulling the last two off the back of his tray with one hand.

This Charming Dilemma

'Okay, yeah sure, no probs... so... how you been?'I asked as casually as I could, deploying my plan operation ice-breaker.

'Yeah good', he said, 'and you?'

'Good, good,' I said nodding to express how good I have been, 'bit excited, you know... with the TV thing and all.'

'Oh yeah that's right,' said Jake, making his way up the rickety ramp towards the door, 'I think I read something about that. Aren't you going to be in the star role in something?'

Oh my god, he does know about my up and coming celebrity opportunity, I wonder if he is put off by the whole idea and that's why he has been avoiding me! Better play it down a bit.

'Well yeah there's me, but it's mainly about the CWA and the area,' I said, extending my arm to gesture to include the greater area, not that he was looking at me, too busy trying to negotiate the door.

'Yeah well it should be good for the area,' he said, like he was making polite conversation with his dentist and not the possible mother of his child, not that he knows that yet. 'Shame I'm not going to be around to see it all happen,' he said, struggling with the length of the sign through the door. 'Probably a good thing, no-one would want to see my ugly mug on TV,' he chuckled at his own joke as he disappeared inside the building.

My ears rung at the news that was just delivered to me by Jake himself. What does he mean he is not going to be here to see it all happen? What is he doing? Where is he going?

Alarmed, I bolted up the rickety ramp in the faint hope he would explain why he won't be around! Is he suicidal? I mean it's not like he can leave, he has a dairy farm to run, what about the cows, who would feed and milk them?

Jake had placed the signs next to the other ones and joined the marvel over the stupid boards. I sidled up to the group in the hope I can get Jake to elaborate on what he meant.

'Ah Lisa,' said Betty, 'you're here, that's good, we better get this meeting under way, lots to discuss before tomorrow.'

'Oh it can wait,' I scoffed, hoping that Jake didn't take that as a cue to leave. God we are the CWA, why aren't we offering this man a cup of tea?!

'Lisa you're looking very pale, is everything okay?' asked Maggie, concerned.

'Yes fine, just a bit tired,' I said, stifling a fake yawn.

'I bet its nerves,' mused Gloria, 'our big celebrity girl here Jake,' she winked, 'going to put us on the map.'

'Oh not really,' I said, waving my hand in an absurd manner.

This Charming Dilemma

'Lisa you really aren't looking good,' said Maggie again, 'your colour has faded more since we have been standing here. Did you get enough sleep last night?'

Actually come to think of it I'm not feeling great at all, my stomach feels like it's on a roller-coaster ride, it's also not helping standing next to Fran as she smells like a fruit cake.

'its fine,' I said, 'I did have a little tummy bug earlier so it could have taken a bit out of me.'

'Is that why you sped past me at a great rate of knots in your desperate haste to get here dear?' said Fran, 'you should have told me you're not feeling well.'

'No, no it wasn't... well err, sorry yes, yes it was that yes, but I'm okay, just need some fresh air, so how about I walk Jake out to his ute and catch a breath while you ladies get...'

'Ohh sure you're not pregnant rather than sick there Lisa,' joked Betty, giving Gloria a teasing nudge in the ribs.

'Well if she is,' Gloria mused back, 'she must be stashing him in a closet cos I haven't seen a hair of a man there since the busload of men disappeared.'

'Oh hahahahahahaha, hahahaha,' I laughed very loudly causing Betty and Gloria's little chuckle to cease at my overreaction to her little joke. I didn't dare look at Jake.

'Well ladies, better make tracks,' Jake said, rubbing his hands together.

Maggie immediately turned to give him a hug. 'Take care young Mr Crankshaw,' she said as Jake acknowledged her sentiment.

'Yes,' said Mary, also giving him a sad hug, 'send us a postcard.'

Postcard?

'Haha, if I can find one,' Jake joked politely as he acknowledged the thanks and well wishes, waving as he made his way to the door while I stood there like a dummy not knowing what to do. And if I wasn't mistaken I swear he gave me a suspicious look in his two second gaze in my direction, I mean he was quick to leave after Betty made a joke about me being pregnant. Did he take Betty seriously?

It would have been great if he did, saves me an awkward conversation, but I swear he couldn't get out of here fast enough and it does sound like he is leaving the area and going far away. I hope that it's not because he went to Angela the tarot reader and she gave him a heads up that I'm pregnant and he has decided to get out while he can!

God I need to catch him.

'Oh um… I'll just go and get some fresh air,' I said, preparing to bolt towards the back door hoping to catch Jake and find out where exactly he is going, my god how irresponsible is he!

This Charming Dilemma

I'm trying to walk fast but my stomach is shooting me warning pains to slow down and I'm having a very hard time holding it together.

'Lisa, sit down if you're not feeling well,' said Gloria, grabbing a chair and making me sit down, 'you look like you are about to throw up.'

'Nerves,' said Fran.

'I think she just needs to slow down,' said Gloria, 'your heart is racing, must be the adrenalin of the big event coming up. How about we get this meeting done quickly so you can go home and rest up before tomorrow.'

'Yes good idea,' Mary said, throwing a desk and a bit of paper in front of me. Just as I heard Jake's ute start up and drive away.

Why oh why do I let old people control me!

'So Lisa,' Betty said, settling on her seat as the sounds of chairs being placed on the wooden floor indicate the start of the meeting, 'is this an official meeting or a sub meeting?'

I really wanted to scream at them all that I don't care what type of meeting it is, someone tell me where the hell Jake is going! Then I realised that I am sitting in a room of five women who know exactly where Jake's going so all I have to do is swing the subject around somehow.

I usually bring my gavel to meetings like these as they can get unruly, well not unruly as such, normally they are either chit chatting about council rates or something boring like that or they are laughing at me over something that is really not at all funny, and it's hard to get their attention, honestly old woman are worse than toddlers. But today they are sitting ready and keen to get on with this meeting

I better get on with it.

'So the 172nd meeting of the Taromeo division of the CWA is underway, present are Mary, Fran, Betty, Gloria and Maggie.' I started.

Not present due to 5 old women scaring him off without even offering him a cup of tea and a piece of fruit cake, is Jake.

'So first item on the agenda,' said Betty, 'is the 100 year celebrations. So I just want to touch on this very quickly before we get to the main item on the agenda which of course is the documentary, but as you all know we have our 100 year celebration of CWA coming up, and I must also add, 100 years of service to this community and the wider community, is quite an achievement so let's give a big round of applause.'

Sounds of applause all around, god knows why, it's not like they have been present for 100 years.

Apart from Fran.

And possibly Betty.

This Charming Dilemma

'So it's only appropriate we have some sort of community event to showcase the CWA, after all, it is important we keep the community support for the CWA alive, especially now we have the lemonade stand, so any suggestions are most welcome.'

Betty sits down and the room fills with silence.

Oh that's right, it's my cue.

'Okay, um thank you for that Betty, so yes any suggestions are, well accepted. Right, moving on.'

'Hang on there Lisa,' said Fran, all purse lipped, 'aren't you going to open the floor to suggestions? Tch, so hasty to get on with things you are, you should slow down a little you know.'

'I think it's the excitement of tomorrow,' suggested Mary.

Murmurs of agreement all around.

'Okay then,' I breathed, trying to find my inner patience, 'any suggestions for the 100 year celebration?'

Betty stands up again, honesty, why did she bother to sit down in the first place, why didn't she say something before when she was rambling on about the 100 year celebrations. Seriously I swear they do it to me on purpose.

Betty starts talking and I try and think of a way to incorporate Jake into the conversation without raising suspicion, I should just ask them straight up why Jake is leaving the area, seems like the easy way to go but it would never be easy for me after that. Old people have this way of sniffing out what is really going on and if I let on that I have an interest in Jake, it won't take them long to figure out why, then there will be a small chance that I wouldn't be able to get anywhere near Jake due to fact that there will be 5 old woman showering him with knitted baby booties and baking fruit cakes for the up and coming wedding.

I mean no wonder he is leaving before the fact.

Betty is talking about some competition and I need to start probing into finding about Jake.

'Ahem, excuse me Betty,' I said, 'maybe that is something Jake Crankshaw could help us with?'

I figured if I say his full name it sounds official and not personal.

Puzzled silence fills the room.

'You think young Jake Crankshaw could help us with knitting the longest world record breaking scarf?' said Maggie filling the silent gap.

Okay, maybe not.

'I think it would be a grand thing to do,' continued Betty moving on from my little interruption, 'it would be like all our knitted efforts over 100 years all coming together.'

This Charming Dilemma

'I think it's a fantastic idea,' said Gloria, 'the only thing I would be concerned about is the time factor, are we going to get it done in time?'

'Yes, and not to mention the wool needed,' sighed Mary, 'I mean I think Spotlight's annual sale runs out Monday.'

More murmurs of agreement all around followed by more silence.

'Maybe we should enlist the help of outside influences,' I said, seizing the moment to mention Jake again, 'I mean why don't we ask the locals what they would like to see, oh I don't know, someone like um Jake Crankshaw for example.'

'Oh I've got it,' cried Fran, jumping in her seat, 'why don't we ask young Brendan what he would like us to do? I mean after all it's his production crew that will be here tomorrow and they are making the lemonade stand the focus of his documentary so why not put it to him, as you all know the 100 year celebration will fall in the middle of his proposed filming. I think it would tie in nicely.'

'Brilliant idea!' shrieked Betty, 'maybe we could suggest to Brendan we have a Mardi Gras, you know like the gay people do in Sydney!'

'Oh what a fantastic suggestion,' clapped Gloria, 'if we could get the whole community involved and maybe have a parade wearing nothing but their favourite knitted garment.'

Shrieks of laughter all around, except me, I'm not laughing.

'Yes Fran, maybe you could knit some of that bondage gear and get someone to wear it on the float while you whip them with your walking cane,' exclaimed an amused Mary.

More shrieks of laughter all around.

'Who would wear it?' roared Betty, trying not to wet herself.

'How about old Mr Johanson from the antique store,' snorted Maggie, thumping the table at her own joke as the room continued to fill with shrieks of Kookaburra sounding laughter.

I am not really that amused and really should rein in this meeting and get it back under control before Betty loses her bladder control yet again. Honestly the amount of incontinence pads needed in the room right now would support the national economy, but I don't have my gavel with me, so I shall take this opportunity to mention Jake.

'I know right,' I said, running with their convulsive bursts of laughter and pretending to join in on their side splitting joke, 'we could get Jake Crankshaw to parade down the main street wearing nothing but Betty's tea cosy,' I roared, banging my hands on the table in amusement at my own joke and throwing my head back in a howling chuckle.

Sounds of laughter dying down as the room looks at me with sudden blank stares.

'We can't ask Jake Crankshaw Lisa,' said Betty in a serious and puzzled tone, 'he's not going to be here.'

This Charming Dilemma

Back home.

And still no information concerning Jake! Betty insisted I get hold of Brendan to put forward our idea, and after arguing amongst themselves whose phone I was going to use since the CWA have two iphone's in their possession, I whipped out my own phone and put to Brendan the ridiculous idea of a CWA Mardi Gras showcasing knitted garments. Brendan thought it was a great idea and stressed to everyone on speaker phone that it's our reality show and reality shows are about everyday life so if this is the sort of thing the community normally does then that's what we should do.

I'm pleased I am home after Fran brought out her mushroom soup to have for lunch while we tediously tried to nut out the finer details of the event. The smell was that much I almost didn't make it to the door to express my need for fresh air. So after much fussing and Betty's home-made cool pack slapped on my head, they sent me home to get over my "stomach bug".

It was good that I didn't have to stay for the organisation of the old people Mardi Gras, as I would rather poke knitting needles in my eyes, but not good as now I had no more chances to find out why Jake was leaving.

'You going in to work this afternoon?' asked Millie, entering the kitchen where I stopped to sit down on my way to the bedroom due to the fact that I couldn't be bothered to go any further.

'I have to,' I moaned, placing my head on the cool top of the kitchen table, 'I promised Daniel I would get the store set up to maximise advertising since I will still have to go to work.'

I mean pfft I'm not a celebrity yet.

'Still not feeling good huh?' said Millie.

'No,' I mumbled, 'stomach settled down but just so tired.'

'Well it's not going to get any better so maybe you need to have a word to Brendan when he gets here tomorrow.'

Oh god Millie is still on her "tell the whole world" rant. I really want to ignore her but I know she will just keep pressing the issue.

'I really think he should know,' Millie continues, 'I mean after all, if you are going to be sick for the filming then you cannot fake the flu for the next few weeks.'

'Millie,' I started, trying to be assertive with her as I know she won't stop and I am a big girl now and she can't tell me what to do! 'I will not tell Brendan because I err… haven't even told the father,' I said with a full stop to my voice, jeez that was quick thinking, maybe having baby brain is a good thing.

'And who is the father?' Millie said in sarcastic tones, 'listen, I think you are missing the point. You don't have to tell everyone just yet, talk to Brendan in confidence, then he can pass that onto the producer.

This Charming Dilemma

Maybe then if you are having a bad day they can edit some of it out until you *are* ready to tell people.'

'Well I can't tell Jake because apparently he is leaving,' I said, trying to get Millie to see reason.

'Leaving to where?' she asked.

'I don't know, just leaving,' I said, trying to get her sympathy, 'the CWA girls were giving him goodbye wishes,' I said with a small teary voice.

'Well that's good then, go and see Jake as well and tell him there is a possibility you are pregnant with his baby before he leaves, that way he can decide before he leaves what he wants to do and you won't feel guilty when you tell Brendan.'

Grrr why can't Millie see my point, she always has to be so practical.

She is looking at me and I can see she will keep pressing on about it until I tell Brendan, and if I don't then I know she will. I can't tell Jake, not until I'm sure it's his baby, and I can't tell Brendan because it may ruin my chances for more opportunities on TV.

I don't answer her, hoping she will get sick of the subject but she is looking at me for a response.

'Lisa?'

'Okay, okay, I'll tell him,' I said, deflated.

'Both of them?' she pressed.

'Yes, both of them.'

Satisfied, she left the room before she could see my face burning red with the white lie I just told. Of course I'm not going to tell Brendan or Jake, but I now have to convince Millie I have done exactly that, so the next few weeks are going to be tricky. But no time to think about that now as I am already late for work, 6 hours late in fact and I cannot ignore Daniel's text messages any more.

Arrived at work. Cannon and Collins Event Planning and Photography.

I still get a kick every time I see that sign, it used to also say "dating agent" but Daniel recently had that removed due to many of the older locals mistaking it for a "drop in" dating agency if you know what I mean, wink, wink, kind. It's still part of the business but it's more of an online sideline.

'Did you have a big night?' Daniel asks as I slump into my chair.

'No I had a CWA meeting,' I groaned, 'sorry I'm late.'

'Oh really, well you look terrible.'

I leave the comment hanging due to the fact he is right, I do look terrible.

It's really a shame Daniel is gay, we get on so well, and I can never get mad at him, not that does anything anyone would get mad at anyway, and he also leaves me alone and doesn't ask too many questions.

He has already started rearranging the place for a new look, and it looks great, he has placed more emphasis on his photography business by putting more of his shots on the wall and a display of past events we have done. Of course this is for the cameras, even though we are not allowed to advertise. It won't take long for people to see how efficiently we, I mean Daniel, run the business and google us. Well, they will google Daniel, I'll be too busy being a celebrity.

Daniel has always had this special way of making the shop look fabulous with minimal effort, it's a gift he possesses, even his house looks like something out of a House and Garden magazine.

I first met Daniel through my ex fiancé Rick, who happens to be Jake's twin brother. I didn't like Daniel at first, think we got off to a little misunderstanding when I accidentally flashed my half naked sexy self at him when he answered the door to Rick's house one day, and then tried to blackmail me into buying his shitty merchandise when I was planning Neroli and Matt's doomed wedding. But once we got past that and Daniel proposed we set up *Cannon and Collins Event Planning and Photography,* well, it was a marriage made in business heaven. It also means we share the rent on the building so overheads are minimal. I mean he is so understanding even when I mistaken his magnificent terracotta pot for a toilet one morning after a big night at the B&S ball and vomit the contents of my stomach into it, well I didn't mistaken it,

I just got lost finding the toilet and the huge vase was the closest thing. And that's not before I woke up in Daniel's bed with no clothes on and a very fragile stomach.

Which seems to be the story of my life. Anyway, that may or may not be the night of the "big conception", unfortunately, and I say this with a heavy heart, not by Daniel. But by Matt's stoner mate Damo who also happened to end up in Daniel's show home in Daniel's designer spare bedroom. But let's not go there.

I carry out my general tasks in silence, busy converting the organised chaos on my desk to one of a more professional and in control look for the cameras tomorrow (and also upon Daniel request). As the hours ticked by my tummy feels much better, but emotionally I feel the weight of the world on my shoulders. I'm trying to think of a plan to be fabulous for the camera, you know, like the next hottest thing to come out of the rural scene but physically I just don't have the energy and I really want to tell everyone to naff off while I have a big long sleep.

Even though there is an underlining buzz of excitement in the air about tomorrow, it's been business as usual. But thank god Daniel has been dealing with the walk-in customers and phone enquires, not only is my phone manner a bit off, I think Daniel was just making sure he got to the customers before they took one look at me and run in the other direction.

'Here,' said Daniel, pulling me from my thoughts and handing me a tall orange beverage.

This Charming Dilemma

'What's that?' I asked.

'Vitamin drink,' he said, 'looks like you need it.'

I take it from him with a nod of acknowledgement as he sat down opposite me with his cup of Earl Grey tea in his favourite china cup. Daniel is a cross between a man's man, you know the type, loves beer, V8 motor cars, footy and a big plate of all you can eat steak; to this softer guy who... well, drinks Earl Grey tea from a china cup and saucer.

'I think we are there with the shop,' he says, looking around with satisfaction, 'we also scored a couple of photo sessions today, a 21st birthday to organise, and a christening for the 25th of next month, so not too bad for a quiet day.'

'Good, so I can go home then,' I said, trying to come off sounding upbeat but mainly coming out sounding like a depressed sloth.

'You excited about tomorrow?' Daniel asks, like he is trying to read my mood.

'Can't wait,' I said, trying to muster an excited face and letting out an extremely uncontrolled burp at the same time.

'Well you wouldn't know,' he chuckled at my half hearted attempted to convince him otherwise, 'what's up?'

I pretended to drop my pen to give myself a moment. Shall I tell Daniel? I mean Daniel knows a lot about me already and I have a feeling he already suspects something due to me going off certain foods in the past couple of months, he probably knows more about me then Millie truth be known and he has never once tells me "he knows best", or "he told me so".

But it's not so much not wanting to tell him about being pregnant, it's about Jake and what to do as far as the Jake situation is. But then again, telling Daniel will be a good thing as I know he will have my back as far as Brendan and the film crew goes you know, if I ever have to throw up I'm sure he will be there to hold my hair back and tell them I've just had bad Chinese food, but I'll have to have his guaranteed silence on the matter.

Making my decision, I pulled myself up off the floor, pen in hand. I run my fingers through my hair for a more dramatic start to the conversion.

'I have something to tell you, but you have to promise on your whole gay life you won't tell anyone,' I said.

'Sure,' Daniel agreed.

'No, you have to really promise,' I pressed.

'I promise,' he said, placing his hand on his heart in a half amused gesture.

'No, really, really, like not a single soul,' I should draw up a contract as I'm not liking his verbal commitment here.

'Lisa!' Daniel exclaimed, 'stop being an arse and just tell me.'

'Okay! I'm, ummm, what do you call it,' I said, rubbing my brow, trying to find the right word.

This Charming Dilemma

'I'm pregnant.'

Daniel's expression suddenly changed to stunned and his face crinkled slightly as he stared at me. It's like someone had hit him in the face with an invisible cast iron pan and he can't figure out why.

'You're pregnant?' he eventually whispered barely above his own breath.

Un-oh, I can recognise that sound anywhere. The sound of five approaching old woman nattering, coming towards the shop door.

I closed my eyes and braced myself.

'Lisa dear,' exclaimed Betty as the sound of the shop bell rings, announcing the presence of the members of the CWA, 'glad we caught you at work, we're here to talk business, and you as well Daniel.'

Daniel tore his stunned gaze away from me slowly, to address Betty as she stood over him.

'Oh, okay, yes, sure,' he said, trying to locate his fancy tea cup from the desk in front of him and find his feet, 'okay well um... take a seat,' he said, barely functioning and acting like he is trying to pull his thoughts back from the edge.

'I'll um, just get more chairs.'

'Now Lisa dear,' Betty said, planting her backside in the empty chair Daniel had just occupied, while the rest of the members took the seats Daniel was individually handing out before taking a seat himself, his expression unreadable.

'We have just had a bit of a rethink on the 100 year celebrations signs that the lovely Jake dropped off this morning, although they hold a sentimental value and have a historical appeal to them, we are thinking we may have to upgrade them, especially if we are going to hold a knitted Mardi Gras event.

'Yes, the termites have got to the original ones,' Fran said with a sigh.

'Yes, so after you left this morning we had another small sub-committee meeting and decided that we need to come up with new signs, so can you help us?'

I looked at Daniel, as this is normally his department, but Daniel doesn't look quite with it just yet.

'Oh, um, yes sure,' he said finally snapping out of it when he was met by the gaze of five old women, 'do you have a particular design in mind?' he said, raising from his chair and grabbing the display book.

'Well something funky,' said Betty.

'Yes something that represents CWA *now*,' said Mary.

'Something that coincides with our Mardi Gras.'

This Charming Dilemma

'You're holding a Mardi Gras?' asked Daniel, gazing at them like a school teacher looking over the top of his glasses, but not wearing any glasses.

'Yes, for the 100 year celebration of the CWA,' said Gloria, holding her pen and paper waiting to write something down, anything, 'we decided at a meeting this morning that a Mardi Gras festival parading erotic knitwear would be the go, we are trying to bring the new world lifestyle to combine with our old traditions.'

Daniel looked at her like it was the queerest thing he had ever heard, and that's coming from him.

'Yes,' said Betty proudly, 'and we have also voted unanimously that Lisa should be the parade queen.'

'Pardon!?' I spluttered.

'Yes dear, it will be perfect since well, it's your reality TV show and you are young. And besides, Fran has already started on your outfit.'

'Please don't tell me that hideous ball of mustard yellow wool she has on her knitting needles is destined for something I will wear?'

'It's not hideous Lisa, seriously, no gratitude, it's a lovely colour and will suit you. Besides this is just one colour of a multi coloured outfit.'

'Not that there is going to be much of the outfit,' sniggered Mary.

Murmurs of sniggers all round.

'Yes and you have a nice firm midriff Lisa so you would look lovely in a two-piece outfit, it seems that you are the obvious choice to be the face of the CWA for the future and all.'

I should be flattered, but quite frankly I have never wanted to be swallowed up by quicksand in my entire life as much as I do right now. I stare in horror at Fran's clacking knitting needles, feeling like I'm in a bad dream.

'Oh and another thing,' Mary added, 'we need some help planning this event,' she said as she turned to Daniel, 'it's all very well us doing it but we really don't have the numbers, and of course there is the question of actual manpower, so we thought maybe local business can sponsor their own floats and make them, I mean after all we are only a few members and with Lisa here being occupied with her TV show and Maggie having to look after her grandchildren at the moment, we just don't have the time or the resources... or the money.' Mary added with a hint of sombreness to her voice.

'I thought the lemonade stand was doing well?' said Daniel in his teacher voice again, sounding suspicious.

'Oh it is,' said Mary in a convincing voice, before dropping her head again in a sad manner, 'but, well, we have never done or planned anything of this scale before and, well there is lots to think about and...'

'Okay, okay,' said Daniel, trying to calm Mary down with his hand,

This Charming Dilemma

'I get it, we can sponsor the Mardi Gras with a couple of signs and I'll provide the necessary expertise needed to run the event, police to handle traffic, insurance and the like.'

Hmm, I swear I just saw all the members secretly high five each other at Daniel's offer of handling the big stuff, well played with the sob story Mary, well played.

'But I need a firm decision on a date and event signs and fast,' said Daniel with a hint of annoyance to his voice. This took me by surprise, it's not like him to snap or get impatient. Especially at a bunch of senior citizens.

'Well if you're not busy now we have come up with a few ideas,' said Betty retrieving a folder from her bag, 'nothing special but we were thinking more of a rainbow sheep as a logo, you know, suits the knitted theme and well the whole fiesta thing with the colours.'

'The only thing we are disagreeing on,' said Fran in mild frustration, 'is do we put the sheep in lingerie, you know, to go with the whole erotic thing.'

Murmurs of agreement combined with disagreement all round.

'So what do you think?' Mary asks Daniel as five sets of hopeful eyes suddenly look in his direction.

Daniel looks like he'd rather be somewhere else.

Me? Well I'm still constantly sidetracked by the hideous thing that Fran is knitting and willing her stitches to drop.

'I think the rainbow sheep on the banners will work just fine on its own,' said Daniel with an amused look on his face. Well at least his expression has changed from the stunned mullet look he had since I broke the news of my pregnancy to him.

'I think we need to have something on that banner that says eroticism,' said Fran in her firm, no nonsense tone not looking up from her knitting.

'It's not necessary,' said Maggie, 'after all you know how I feel about this!'

'But you are not involved,' says Fran, like she is reminding Maggie about an old argument.

'Okay maybe it's not necessary,' said Mary, 'just thought it may be appropriate, keeping the whole CWA on the same page.'

Whoa! I'm confused and I am getting the feeling that this is not about the sheep any more.

Oh my god, Jake's just walked past the shop.

'Um, let me go and get a second opinion shall I,' I said, hastily jumping from my seat and bolting towards the door.

My brain has snapped into gear and I have a brilliant plan on how to find out where Jake is going.

And it happened in three seconds, things are definitely looking up with this whole baby brain thing.

This Charming Dilemma

'Jake!' I called out from the shop door, grabbing his attention and then his arm, 'we just need to borrow you for a second,' I said as he complied with my invitation to step inside the shop. God his arm is so muscular, I forgot how strong his arms are.

'Now we just need your opinion on something,' I said, trying to cool my tingling hand down after touching his hot skin. My god if my baby is a boy and Jake *is* the father, I'll definitely have to get an iron bar to beat any bitches off him if he ends up with Jake's looks and body.

I hope he'd have my personality though.

'We were just wondering what would work better,' I said.

'Yes,' interrupted Mary, stealing my thunder, 'which one would you prefer Jake?' she asked, holding up two sketches that Gloria had drawn up in the short time of discussion, love Gloria, she is such a good artist.

'Would you prefer the sheep dressed in the black lace lingerie, or the sheep without the black lace lingerie?'

Jake looks astounded as he shoots a look at Daniel for support.

Daniel returns it with a shrug and a look of dull bewilderment.

'Um... without I guess,' he said with caution, not knowing where this was going.

Fran looked annoyed while Maggie looked relived.

'Okay, without it is,' said Mary, giving him a little pat on his arm.

'Is there anything else?' asked Jake, his eyes darting around the faces looking for an explanation.

'No that will be all thanks young Jake,' said Betty with a fond smile.

'Well no, that's really not all is it Betty,' I mused, trying to stall Jake long enough to find out where he is going, 'I mean don't we have any other matters that we may need Jake's opinion on, I mean we haven't even discussed background colours.'

'I would love to help ladies,' Jake said bolting for the door before we start showing him pictures of cows in bondage gear, 'but I must catch the bank before it closes.'

Tch, lame excuse, I mean it's only... oh wait, it is nearly closing time.

My god the day has gone quick.

'All the best mate,' said Daniel giving him a wave, 'stay out of trouble.'

'Yeah thanks,' Jake called back.

Wait even Daniel knows where he is going.

'Keep safe,' waved Betty, 'have a nice flight.'

Flight! Is it international? Is he really skipping the country?

This Charming Dilemma

I can't stand this any longer.

'Wait!' I cried, extending my arm out like an officer of the law directing traffic to stop.

Jake stops in the doorway waiting for me to say something, along with the others in the room.

I can't find the right words, come on Lisa, just come out and ask him.

'Um live long and prosper,' I said, quoting Star Trek.

What the hell Lisa!

Jake laughed, 'I'll try,' he said, before giving the room a wave and exiting.

No, not good enough, I can't just let him go without knowing, I just can't.

'Jake wait!' I cried again.

'Lisa he has to get to the bank,' Betty scolded, 'he only has a few minutes to catch them, let him go.'

Jake is looking at me impatiently.

Okay Lisa, go for gold, make something up.

'I'm having a, um, pre-drinks thing tonight for um, the new, um, show, well documentary, everyone will be there,' I said, incorporating the CWA ladies, 'and since, you know, you gave us your valid opinion about the sheep was wondering if you wanted to join us?'

'Oh, um thanks for the offer but sorry Lisa I'm flying out for the mines in a couple of hours.'

'Mines?' I asked, puzzled.

'Yeah, I'm working out there. Okay so goodbye everyone,' Jake said, 'have a good night.'

Jake disappeared into the street leaving me to process that information.

'Lisa dear,' said Betty, annoyed, 'we can't have a celebration drink later, its bingo night down at the hall!'

3

It's the day of the film crew's arrival and I can feel the buzz of energy from here.

Or maybe it's just Millie stomping around while Sid does his best to stay out of her way.

I really should get up but I'm not sure how my body is going to respond so thinking I should just get up at lunch to avoid morning sickness.

I ended up staying a bit longer at the shop with the CWA ladies yesterday, mainly cos we couldn't get them out the door, but after a painful consultation over the signs, a date has been set, the sheep will keep some of its dignity and the colour of the banner has been decided.

Daniel did the order and it looks like we will showcase to the nation that the town of Taromeo is the home of not only the lemonade stand, but the host of the only knitted erotic parade in the world!

Daniel looked like he really wanted to speak with me, but I couldn't stay long due to Millie needing me home to look after Amy while her and Sid have *date night*.

I could have invited Daniel over to elaborate on my news to him yesterday, but I really wanted time alone to process the fact that Jake has gone out west to the mines to work, I mean for how long and is he coming back? What if he meets someone. Then what? My baby will have a weekend dad only.

Okay, not jumping the gun yet, it could be stoner Damo's baby.

Oh god!

After Jake left the shop yesterday, Daniel must have caught a glimpse of my disheartened expression and when I met his gaze, Daniel had a look of sadness on his face, I couldn't quite read it but if I didn't know any better I would swear that Daniel has cottoned on to the fact that it may be Jake's baby and is feeling sorry for me.

But I have decided to put all of this behind me, as I have been waiting for this day to come for such a long time, it would be a pity to miss it over a guy and the fact that I'm pregnant.

I'm suddenly starting to feel the excitement, I mean thank god, cos it's taken a long time to look forward to this. Even last night I didn't feel the excitement like you would if you were on the eve of your wedding or the excitement you feel on Christmas night. I'm finally going to be a celebrity, how cool is that.

The film crew are expected to arrive in a couple of hours to get settled in. Then they start following me around tomorrow. Brendan says they have already put together a pilot series

This Charming Dilemma

from some of the film he took on his last visit when we invited a busload of men to come and compete for a date with me, but it didn't end up like that, it was more of a documentary of social interaction for the area, which I'm sure people would find so boring, I mean I'm not sure what footage he had to put together for a pilot but I can guarantee it would be stuff that would make you stifle a yawn.

God I hope that doesn't put the ratings down right away, I mean how devastating would it be that the show got cancelled on the first episode.

Better have a word to the producer.

'You getting up?' Millie banged on the door.

'Way ahead of you Millie!' I said as I bounced out of bed as she entered the room.

'Woah, maybe a bit too fast.'

'How you feeling?' she asks as I pause to let the nausea pass.

'Great,' I beamed, trying to send a message to the baby that I would not be entertaining any distractions while this filming is going on. I mean discipline must start in the womb!

'I was just bringing you up some tea,' said Millie, placing a cup beside my bed, 'maybe you should try something in your stomach before you get up.'

'I think you're right' I said, sitting back down on the bed and taking a sip of the tea.

Millie has changed to a good mood so I'm going to agree with everything she says, you know, to not rock the boat and keep her on my side.

'Oh *what*? You still got da spew bug!' said Matt as he made his dramatic entrance in my bedroom wearing his suit and dark glasses, 'better not spew on me again Lisa.'

Trust Matt to turn up when I'm fighting nausea, he only makes it worse.

'It's just the end of it Matt,' I lied, 'and if you would stay out of my way you would be fine. Why are you wearing your suit anyway?'

'Cos we're being filmed Lisa, don't you know nuffing.'

'Yes but not until tomorrow,' said Millie fussing with some throw pillows I have on a chair.

'Then what's happening today?' asked Matt, 'everyone be like, going crazy and tidying shit.'

'The film crew arrive today,' Millie said, as I continue to sip my tea and stare at the floor like it's a horizon on a rocky ocean.

Okay maybe it's not good to think of an ocean.

'So they're not doing the camera shit today?' asked Matt.

'No.'

This Charming Dilemma

'Well no-one told me,' Matt whinged as he turned away, 'and we should be informed of these things, us being security all dat. Come on Damo.'

Shit Damo is here. Great just what I need, potential father number two hanging around outside my bedroom.

'Where are you going?' asked Millie, 'you can hang around and meet the crew,' she says, which is code for Millie saying "stick around, I'll find a job for you to do".

'To get changed,' said Matt, 'this is a good suit, don't wanna get stuff on it, and besides Lisa is still spreading germs, she could spew on it again.'

Managed to look up in time to see Damo give me a wee wave and smile.

God what was I thinking?!

That's it, no more alcohol, ever!

'So you're good?' said Millie when Matt left.

'Actually yes, I think I am,' I said, finishing off my tea. Which surprisingly did make me feel better.

'Awesome,' she said, 'so before they get here, I think we may need to have a bit of a sit down and nut out some boundaries.'

'Who?' I asked.

'You, me, Sid, I don't want too much personal stuff showcased to the nation. Business yes, but limits on family and what Sid has for breakfast is off limits.'

'Millie, I'm sure a lot of people would find it cute that Sid eats his bacon and eggs with Darth Vader lightsaber cutlery.'

'I'm sure, but I do not want the nation to know I married a 38 year old child. So, at the kitchen table in say half an hour,' she said, looking at her watch.

Millie will run this whole thing with military precision, I just know it. She never used to be like this, well she was a bit but it's only gotten worse since she had Amy and discovered the benefits of a strict routine. Even Sid has his whole day mapped out for him, down to the last second, Millie doesn't like to call it routine but more like being efficient. She has even thought about creating an app for it.

I don't think Millie realises it's going to take me more than half an hour to get ready, but I will just nod in agreement cos I don't want to rock the boat, especially since she hasn't mentioned telling Brendan about my pregnancy since yesterday, I'm hoping she will forget.

She left me to get dressed, I have had my outfits planned for each day. I have been working on it for a while, so today it's just meeting the crew day but it's still an important day as I have to present myself as celebrity material. So I left the important stuff like washing hair and painting nails until today.

This Charming Dilemma

I thought about having a manicure and stuff but with me being under the weather, those nail salons smelling like a meth lab, and my stomach being a tad fragile, best I DIY.

I sit at my vanity table and set out for myself every type of foundation and every shade of lipstick I have, which I got through the local makeup lady in preparation for my everyday filming. I wanted to put one of those star signs on my door that states my name, you know like the celebs have in front of their dressing rooms, but Millie told me point blank that is going too fucking far, when Millie starts swearing, that's when you know you have gone well… too f'n far.

I thought it might be a good idea to have a test run of makeup before I jump in the shower, that way if the foundation isn't the right colour I can start again with a fresh face and not one that has traces of makeup remover on it.

Yes I know it sounds pedantic, but who knows what the camera will reveal with close ups etc, I mean you don't see celebrities with crap all over their faces, it's always flawless, so I must get it right. And besides my foundations and lipsticks only arrived yesterday due to the backorders that my makeup distributor Jenny had to do, so it's not like I have had a chance to try them all out.

I have to say I don't look too bad today, my skin doesn't look as pale as yesterday and so far no pimples. I think the universe is working in my favour today. As I apply the Honey Beige #2 foundation to my face I can't help but think that Jake is missing out on so much.

I mean if he isn't interested in pursuing a relationship with an up and coming celebrity who is okay looking, with medium size breasts, not a bad figure, and owns her own business, then there will be no pleasing him. I don't know why Jake and I run hot and cold. It wasn't that long ago it looked like Jake and I were going to get back together then all of a sudden it's like he doesn't even know me, not once, but twice.

Okay Honey Beige #2 is too light. I might try #3.

So maybe it's a good idea I don't pursue Jake, I admit I may have a tiny bit of a flame there for him but having his baby is not going to fuel that flame, is it?

I contemplate this as I discard my makeup remover wipe in the bin beside me and start applying Honey Beige #3 foundation to my face.

But then again, all relationships start with having a tiny flame and it grows over time, it's not like Jake gave me a chance to show him what a great girlfriend I can be. I know it's obvious he's just not that into me, but come on now, there must be something wrong with him not to be slightly interested. I was engaged to his brother for crying out loud you would think he would want to find out why Rick worshipped the ground I walked on for a while.

Maybe that's it, maybe Rick told him all my bad habits and he wouldn't be able to live with me putting mayonnaise in my mash potatoes to make them creamier.

This Charming Dilemma

 Or the fact I leave cupboards doors open causing the next person to injure   whatever body parts that happen to be at appropriate height, it's not like I do it on purpose, I mean I'm just too busy to think about these things, who has the time.

Nah, Rick wouldn't have told him anything like that, Rick's a gentleman. Besides it's not like they are bad habits, just different preferences to things.

Oh no, I've just realised this isn't Honey Beige #3, it's my Honey *Bronze* Fake Tan #3. See this is what happens when you allow men to distract you from life.

God I hope this stuff comes off easy.

'Lisa, you ready?' asked Millie, banging at the door, 'Sid and I are waiting, we've just made coffee.'

Ready? I haven't begun. Seriously it's only been 10 minutes, Millie can be so... oh wait, it's been 40 minutes.

40 minutes, really?

Okay my face looks orange.

'Lisa?'

'Yes, yes I'm here, but I'm nowhere near ready Millie, can't it wait, I still have my nails to paint.'

'Lisa the crew will be here in an hour, I really want to go over some rules with everyone, Matt has arrived and Daniel is here, so I think it's a good idea we have a quick meeting now.'

Oh god, why does everyone have to be here when I'm trying to get ready in peace.

'I'll be out as soon as I finish doing my nails,' I said in a medium tone that said "Millie I won't let you push me around but I'm trying not to get on your bad side as well" voice.

'Lisa, bring your polish with you and get your arse to the kitchen now.'

I poked my tongue out at her from behind the door in defiance and gathered up my ten bottles of nail polish.

Making my way out to the kitchen I can hear Daniel's upbeat voice making light conversation with Sid.

'Here she is,' said Sid as Millie came pounding up behind me to abruptly take a seat at the table.

'Morning,' greeted Daniel.

'What happened to your face?' asks Sid.

'Oh, yeah that, don't worry I haven't had a shower yet,' I said, forgetting that I had fake tan on my face.

Daniel took a seat beside me, as I pile my ten bottles of nail polish on the table.

'Okay Matt can you hear me?' Millie asks, placing her phone in the centre of the table after putting it on speaker phone.

'Yep,' said Matt's voice coming through the phone.

This Charming Dilemma

'Okay can everyone hear Matt?' Millie sighed, handing Amy's juice bottle to her as she attempts to pull herself up on Millie chair.

'I thought I saw Matt's car outside?' said Daniel.

'Yeah you did,' said Millie, 'he's out in the car, he's not coming in.'

'Why not?' asked Daniel, puzzled.

'Cos Lisa's contagious,' said Matt through the phone, 'she's still got a spew bug, better watch out that she doesn't spew on you. Damo's here as well, he don't want it.'

Daniel went to say something then he stopped when he realised he may be the only one in the room that knows about my pregnancy. He isn't, Millie knows of course, but Daniel doesn't know Millie knows and Millie doesn't know Daniel knows and I would rather it stayed that way for now.

Millie let out a sigh at Matt's absurdness while I met Daniel's glance in a secret squirrel knowing glance.

'Okay I thought we should just make ourselves clear in this group about what the boundaries are as far as privacy goes,' said Millie, 'even though they may edit it out, I don't want to give the film crew a reason to argue about what will or won't be in, so for a start I think everyone agrees that Amy is out of bounds? Yep thought so,' said Millie when everyone agrees without hesitation, while Millie writes it on an agreement she has drawn up for us.

We have already signed an agreement with the producers though a lawyer, along with a waiver as far as the filming goes, but it was a standard contract about disclosing of information and privacy and what we allow and don't allow etc. But this is between us, in house, I think this is Millie's way of making sure no friends will embarrass her on national TV, especially me. Bit rich considering she's married to Sid.

'Of course Amy will be introduced and in the background, but her bath and bedtime routine and stuff are off limits to the cameras. Okay, obviously no financial earnings to be disclosed,' continued Millie, 'um personal routines. I know I've said it before, but I really don't want it to be revealed how often I brush my teeth,' said Millie in an amused voice. Daniel has a little chuckle in agreement.

'And of course *really* personal activities if you know what I mean,' added Millie.

'Now Matt doesn't want anyone to know he and Damo smoke pot or play golf with the oldies. Well that's a given Matt. Daniel, you have agreed to come out on camera but not straight away, to give the rest of your family time to adjust, so no disclosing Daniel's preference for men. And Lisa,' she says as she rubs her brow, 'no… oh god never mind, the list is too long, just be you but don't involve me okay.'

'Or me,' said Sid, piggy backing on Millie's comment only because Millie is here. If Millie wasn't here, Sid wouldn't have the courage to tell me himself.

This Charming Dilemma

'Or me,' whinged Matt, 'like when you made us do that stupid hippy stuff in the paddock that morning.'

'Oh if you are still doing the mediation I'll be keen on that,' said Sid as an afterthought.

'Meditation?' asks Daniel.

'Yeah Lisa did this stupid thing where she made us flap our arms around in our undies in front of the cattle when the busload of miners were here,' whinged Matt. 'I got it on video, I'll show ya later.'

'It wasn't like that,' I scoffed too, 'it was an early morning thing that Jamie started, I just joined in.'

'No it wasn't,' continued Matt on his rant, 'she only did it cos she was sneaking back home from that wanker Jake's place. Lisa never gets up that early, got that on video too, Lisa sneaking home.'

There is a sudden silence around the table, Millie shoots me a sympathetic look at Matt's comments.

'Oh I didn't know you were seeing Jake,' said Sid all innocent and upbeat,

'I'm not. I wasn't,' I scoffed, 'Matt is just being an arse,' I said loudly into the phone.

'Just stating facts,' he retorted through the phone.

'Actually Millie, I would like to add something to that,' I said pointing to her list.

'I would like to add that Matt should zip his mouth through the entire filming and not reveal anything about me at all! In fact maybe he should just not be there.'

'I'm a bodyguard remember Lisa, Brendan said I could be, me and Damo. Bodyguards don't talk unless you ask them a question so I'll already be doing that, but not because you told me to.'

I can see Daniel is working out something in his head and I bet all the tea in China that he is trying to work out my baby's conception date. Yep, now there is a flash of sadness across his face, the same expression as yesterday. And his body has gone all stiff and rigid, oh my god I think Daniel is upset.

'Okay enough Matt,' said Millie, 'I have an incoming call so if you want to continue with this you have to come in the house.'

Millie disconnects from him and answers another call and moves away as Sid picks a noisy Amy up from the floor and puts her on his knee.

'You okay?' I asked Daniel, curious of the rigid expression on his face. I'm still feeling a bit embarrassed with Matt's outburst but I suppose people are bound to find out eventually who the father of my baby is, that is, when they eventually find out that I'm having a baby. And I suppose if I look on the bright side, if Jake does deny it then at least Matt has it on film me sneaking back from his place,

This Charming Dilemma

truth be known that was the morning after the great conception. Well one of them.

God why do I have to keep constantly reminding myself that Damo may also be involved, gotta stop doing that.

'Um, can I just have a quick word?' Daniel said in a gentle voice.

'Yeah sure,' I said as we moved off. I don't mind Daniel's "quick words" cos they are exactly that, quick words, not drawn out lectures like Millie's "quick words".

'Lisa, sorry to ask,' he said when we moved off into the living room. 'But your pregnancy...' he said, his eyes darting to my tummy.

'Yes?'

'Is everything okay, you have been to a doctor?'

'Yes,' I said, 'apart from being a bit sick, but apparently they think I am around 16 weeks on, well according to the estimates I provided the doctor cos you know, can't always keep track of these things, I'm okay.'

'Good, good. Well I hate to ask but, who is the father?' he said, like it was very difficult to ask, 'it's just that, I wasn't aware you were in a relationship,' he said quickly like he was trying to justify the question.

'I wasn't,' I sighed, 'I had a one-night thing with Jake,' I said, hanging my head in shame.

'Oh so it's Jake's?' Daniel said, sounding deflated.

'Yes and well, maybe someone else's,' I said with all the shameful tone I could muster.

'Someone else's?' Daniel asks surprised, his eyes widening like saucers.

'Yes, but I'm a little shamed to say,' I said with my head down like a naughty school-kid.

'May I ask who the other was?' he said, like he was holding his breath.

'Okay but you promise not to judge,' I wailed.

Daniel looked at me as if I should know better than for him to judge me on anything.

'It may be Damo's,' I said quickly, exhaling as I say it.

'Damo, Matt's Damo?' Daniel said in surprise, looking a bit taken aback and puzzled.

'Yes and as I said, don't judge but it was the night we all stayed at your place after the B&S ball and somehow I managed to end up doing it with Damo,' I said in my silly me voice, 'not that I can remember, well don't have to tell you how drunk I was...'

'And who told you this if you couldn't remember?' Daniel asked like he was trying to put together a mystery.

This Charming Dilemma

'Damo,' I said, 'apparently, and don't say anything, but I took his virginity.'

Daniel is standing there looking at me like he has just been told the human race was nothing but an ant farm to a higher source of life, like the absurdness about how that could be possible.

'We better wrap this up,' said Millie poking her head into the living room, 'that was Brendan on the phone, they have just arrived in town a bit early so they will be here in 10 minutes.'

Didn't mean to bowl Daniel over in my haste to get to the shower, but he was standing in the way and I really, really needed to get into the shower before the film crew turns up and sees me with an orange face. Bloody Millie, why did she have to tell Brendan and the crew to come on over this soon, she knew I was nowhere near ready. Millie said not to fuss, just throw something on cos it's not like they are filming anything today but she just does not understand one bit about grooming yourself to be a potential celebrity, I mean Daryl the producer is coming, he is the one that will have the final say about everything, does he really want to see his star looking like something that the Kardashians threw away years ago!

Thank god I had a leg wax two days ago otherwise there would be blood on the floor, literally. But I still have to finish washing hair, blow dry hair, straighten hair, put on makeup. I still haven't decided on what foundation would suit best and to top it off, because I have a cute stylish skirt to wear, have to apply fake tan to legs.

Arghh!

'They're here!' said Millie, tapping on the bathroom door.

'Of course they are!' I scowled loudly to Millie, as I shut off the water.

'Out of the way!' I growled to Daniel, as I sprinted past him in a towel dripping water all over the carpet. Daniel obviously learned from the last time as he jumps out of the way immediately. Back in my room and I am frantically trying to dry myself off with my hair-dryer while applying moisturiser to my face. The fake tan has left a slight residue on my face, but you really can't tell that much unless you really look so that was lucky, finished off drying and ran to throw clothes on. I quickly glanced out the window to see how far away the film crew was from entering the house. Millie has greeted them at their minivan, which has a big enclosed trailer attached, I take it that's where all the film equipment is. Another 4WD has turned up towing a caravan and another sedan, which I gather is Daryl Loft the executive producer, who is not staying but only down for the day to oversee the set up apparently. Matt is there in his best jeans helping unload luggage from the back and so far, I can only recognise Brendan as they take in their surroundings.

Which is perfect, still gives me at least five minutes.

Okay, so ditched skirt for jeans due to skirt now being a bit tight. I'm wearing the cowgirl outfit, the one Daniel dressed me in when he did my shoot for the website

This Charming Dilemma

The Country Girl Wants a Husband. I wanted to wear this outfit tomorrow but I mean, have to swap them around due to the fact that I have no time to apply fake tan in an even manner and skirt suddenly shrunk overnight.

Back to blow dryer, this time on actual head hair, not body, as I apply foundation to my face at the same time. Went for Honey Beige #2 as I think it would give me a better flawless look, hadn't chosen colour of lipstick yet but shall just go with Cherry lip gloss, again, the time factor.

I can hear approaching footsteps towards the door, so better wrap this up because Millie wanted all of us standing at the door like military men when she makes the introductions.

'Lisa you in there?' came Sid's quiet and meek voice from the other side of the door, 'Millie said to um... Millie would like to...'

'Yeah I get it Sid,' I called back, 'Millie wants my arse out front so we can line up like military personnel.' I said cursing the fact only one side of my hair is dry.

'Yes and not in five minutes Lisa, now,' shouted Millie from behind the door causing me to jump.

Bloody hell, can she not trust Sid to do a job.

'Jeez Millie, just a joke,' I called back hoping to stay on the right side of her.

'Um... she's gone,' called back a nervous Sid, 'so um, we'd better...'

'Coming,' I called back in an irritated voice.

I quickly grab my black mascara and dab it across my eyelashes. My hair looks terrible due to the fact I forgot to put product in it to keep it from fizzing under the hair-dryer so I think I'm just going to have to hide it underneath my hat.

Fuck where is my hat?

'Lisa, now!' said Millie through gritted teeth, abruptly opening the door, 'I'm begging you,' she said in a lower voice, 'just come and meet them, they are all waiting and I cannot stall them.'

'But Millie,' I wailed, 'I can't find my hat.'

Millie's look tells me I am about to cross a line.

'You look fine,' she said in a lowered evil tone that I wouldn't dare disagree with.

Panic is starting to rise as I haven't even given myself a final look in the mirror to see if my hair is on point, so I grab a hair band to tie it back.

Oh my god should have thought about that before, too easy.

'Hmm or maybe you shouldn't,' said Millie with a slight awkward look on her face.

'What?'

'...oh never mind, it'll be fine,' she said grabbing my hand before I retreat to the safety of my mirror.

This Charming Dilemma

I step out the front of the entrance with Millie while Daniel is making conversation with Brendan and a relaxed looking Daryl Loft.

Matt sees me coming and moves to the other side of the verandah. Damo gives me a tiny wave and makes a rubbing gesture on his face at me.

Don't know what that is all about.

My attention is soon diverted as I felt my hand grabbed by Daryl Loft as he greeted me. Wasn't sure what to do as a curtsey is a bit over the top but a hand shake is a bit informal considering this will be the man responsible for my stardom.

He makes small talk with me like 'really great to be back in the area' and 'nice day' and blah, blah, his eyes keep diverting to my face, especially around my lips. God I hope he doesn't think I need collagen.

'Hi Lisa,' greeted Brendan after Daryl's attention turned to Millie and Sid as he clucked over Amy in Sid's arms.

'Excited?' Brendan asks me after I greet him back.

'Oh immensely!' I said with great enthusiasm as Daryl Loft pauses to look at me. Great, my use of big words has grabbed his attention.

'Awesome!' Brendan said clapping his hands together.

'Okay so let me introduce everyone, well Daryl you all know, he's not staying but I'm sure he'll hang round for lunch,'

Brendan muses. 'Our cameraman John Kirk,' Brendan continues as a heavy set man steps forward, looks as solid as a brick house dressed in denim shorts cut off at the knees. Not much hair on top I think it's all on his legs, but looks around my age.

'You will get sick of the sight of him by the time this is over,' Brendan chuckles at his attempt at light humour. Millie, Sid, Damo, and Daniel greet John with a handshake, he goes to shake Matt's hand but Matt seems entranced with something. A big turnaround from the staunch presence he attempted when they first arrived. Now he looks like his spirit has left his body and there is nothing left but a shell of a spotty youth.

'And this is Marline Tui,' Brendan continues, as a pretty looking lady with long dark locks dressed in pale jeans and a t-shirt, that is supported with a kind of figure that rocks the dusty jeans look. She steps forward to smile and shake our hands. Brendan continues around introducing everyone, again leaving me out of things.

Matt looks like he is about to have an accident in his pants when she got round to him, well that explains why he has been on another planet for the past five minutes, it seems Marline has caught Matt's attention. Hope that means with her around, Matt will continue to stay the way he is, unresponsive and not talking at all.

I'm slightly offended that he hasn't introduced me to anyone just yet. I mean I am the main attraction and they are fobbing me off!

This Charming Dilemma

'... and finally, the star of this little production, Lisa,' beamed Brendan.

Okay I take it back, obviously they like to keep the best till last.

'Ahh so you are the lady that's been giving us the laughs,' said John the cameraman, 'I look forward to working with you.'

Laughs?

'Okay well lunch will be served in about half an hour,' said Millie, 'it will be served out here on the front verandah since it's such a beautiful day,' she says in her best hostess voice. 'Sid here will show you your rooms, except of course Brendan, who brought his own,' Millie said, referring to the big caravan parked out front.

'It isn't your company I promise,' Brendan joked back as murmurs of giggles went around the circle. 'Yes, we will get settled then we shall have a chat over lunch about how things are going to work,' Brendan says.

'Oh Lisa, we should probably find someone to help you with your make-up,' he said as he picks up a bag and heads inside.

Grrr, why didn't Millie tell me that my foundation is the colour of volcanic clay and highlighted all my lines and wrinkles.

So embarrassing.

Anyway, after a quick fix up and half a packet of makeup removal wipes we are finally sitting down for lunch. It's a nice atmosphere out here on the verandah, I have to remind myself how far this old house has come from the day I first arrived. Well the day Millie forced me to move here after I brought the place on impulse trying to impress my alternative boyfriend at the time. I don't know why I thought we could make lots of cheese and babies while pioneering off the land, especially when we never really wanted to leave the city, but that is now a distant memory I would rather live without. And besides look at me now, about to become a celebrity single mother, funny how things work out.

Thank god I'm over doing stuff like that.

Buying houses that is.

Okay, stop thinking now.

Millie and Sid have done an amazing job transforming it from a run-down old shack to this grand country style B&B (complete with its own petting zoo), you could almost forgive her for not telling me how silly my makeup looked this morning. Maybe just a little bit.

I purposely sat down beside Daniel because I know Daryl Loft wants to discuss the 100 year celebration now, on account of Brendan opening his mouth and telling him what the CWA is

This Charming Dilemma

planning but because *Cannon and Collins Event Planning and Photography* (and occasional dating agency) is planning the event.

He is asking Daniel all the hard questions like how much emphasis he is going to expect on advertising as it may create a conflict of interest and there seems to be a big grey area with a reality television show in which the business is involved because it's part of my daily life and showcases the business. It sounds confusing but once again Daniel has got it sorted, he informs Daryl that they are going to focus on the small town activity and the CWA recruiting a small country business to help, which of course is the whole idea of small town country living and local support. So he is suggesting that the business will not be named but mentioned as a non entity. And there is no agenda to promote the name and he will take precautions not to stir a conflict of interest with the production. Daryl seems to be satisfied with the answer.

I would have said all that but I'm busy trying to hold my grace.

Matt hasn't said anything since the crew arrived, in fact I have never seen him so quiet.

But really, he should stop staring at the sound lady Marline.

And close his mouth, it's embarrassing.

The crew are discussing going into the village this afternoon for a look at the different venues and places that will be mainly featured so they are familiar with everything.

I have also been on the phone with Betty about arranging a meet and greet with the CWA this afternoon at 4pm with the crew so everyone is familiar with one another. I wanted to make it 5pm but as Betty informs me, that that is dinner time and Family Feud is on at 5.30pm so dinner dishes have to be cleared away by then so they can all sit down to watch it and what was I thinking. Didn't want to tell Betty that I'm thinking she is not making getting old sound very appealing but couldn't be bothered.

The buffet of pumpkin soup, three types of salad, cold meat and rolls prepared by Sid were consumed, as the clutter of empty plates and condiments were exchanged, ending lunch. Brendan explained that a voice over introduction and commentary will be added in later in the editing process. They are so confident the first season will go well based on the pilot that they have also submitted an application to the station for season two. My stomach leapt into my throat when I heard that. Season two, oh my god, they can see potential stardom in me already and we haven't even starting filming. I glanced at Millie to share my expression of excitement but Millie doesn't look excited, in fact Millie looks burdened and stressed at the thought of season two.

Brendan goes on to tell us that after the second episode is filmed and edited then they will launch the pilot. I'm so excited my heart did a little leap at the prospect of this coming together so soon.

Or it might be reflux.

Yep it's reflux.

This Charming Dilemma

I couldn't control the burp that escaped my mouth, causing everyone to look in my direction.

'So, ahem, I take it this pilot episode you are talking about will be the one that is filmed tomorrow?' I asked trying to cover up my outburst of reflux.

'The pilot has already been done,' said Brendan, 'it's edited and ready to go on air and I have to say it's going to be great.'

Murmurs of agreement from the crew all round.

'Soon?' asked Daniel, although his question wasn't a metaphorical one.

'Yes, we launch during filming, that way if the ratings are not good the series can be wrapped up before any more funding is spent,' Daryl said, 'but if a series is filmed in advance and the executives pull the pin after a couple of episodes it's a waste of funding. It keeps the investors happy,' he added taking a sip of his orange juice, 'always a risk when you launch a new TV show.'

'Yeah I suppose that makes sense,' agreed Daniel.

Marline, the sound girl, excuses herself and asks Millie where the ladies room is. Matt wasn't sure whether to rise from his seat or stay seated, the result being he just ended up looking like he was pelvic thrusting the edge of the table.

'Um, what footage for the pilot show are we talking about?' I asked, bringing everyone back to the subject at hand.

Oh great, now I have the hiccups.

'The footage I took when we did the tourism video with the visiting miners,' Brendan interjected, 'it was edited and made into a pilot, Daryl used it to sell the idea to the executives.'

I'm a bit confused, surely they don't mean all the stuff Brendan was filming when the busload of men were here after they hijacked my idea of country girl wants a husband and turned it into a boring amateur documentary about small town life and the lack of a decent dating scene. I mean as I recall all Brendan got was some footage of the area, hardly reality TV show material.

Oh and I think he got some of the morning mediation we did after I was trying to sneak home from Jake's and got caught so said I was meditating to explain the fact I was trying to sneak through a barbed wire fence at 5.30am.

And that visit to the olive grove when I thought the crazy French lady was coming after me with a gun.

And the Crankshaw's house fire.

And come to think of it, I'm sure I recall Matt mentioning that he was at the B&S ball where I had orange hair, got drunk and tried to hit on gay Daniel but ended up with Damo!

Oh my Lord!!!

'I need to see a copy of that pilot,' I exclaimed, letting out a big hiccup before dramatically taking a swig of my water trying to suppress the next hiccup.

This Charming Dilemma

'Are you going to spew again?' asked Matt, moving his chair away from me even further.

'Yeah sure,' said Brendan, 'I have a preview of it on my ipad, I'll fetch it for you later.'

'That would be great,' I whispered dramatically, letting out a slow calming breath and taking another swig of water.

'Spew again?' asked Daryl, looking at me for confirmation.

'Yeah Lisa's contagious,' said Matt, 'she's got a spew bug.'

'She hasn't got a vomiting bug,' Daniel said, gesturing calm with his hand towards Matt, 'Lisa had a touch of nerves this morning, she is fine now.' Daniel said, addressing the nervous looking crew.

Matt didn't say anything more due to the fact Marline has just returned from her comfort break.

'Well that's understandable,' said Daryl smiling at me, 'but don't worry Lisa in a couple of days you won't even know we are here.'

'Yeah cheers,' I said, quickly swigging down a mouthful of water as I felt another hiccup rising.

Love Daniel, I knew telling him about my pregnancy would be a good thing.

So all I have to do is keep Marline and Daniel around and between Matt taking an involuntary vow of silence due to the fact he seems to be smitten with Marline, and Daniel coming to my defence the way he just did, I should have a peaceful few weeks of filming with no hint of anyone even suspecting I am pregnant.

I'm a bit worried about this pilot episode though, I mean I wasn't exactly my best back then, okay yes it was only 4 months ago, but still, I feel like I have changed since then, and I feel it would be better if they showcase my life from right now, not weeks ago where everything around me was out of control due to Jake coming back into my life as well as playing host to a busload of men.

But the worst part is, Brendan decided it would be much better to wait until we see the CWA ladies later and then he will show all of us the preview of the pilot. So unfair, as I should be the first one to see it, you know, to make sure there is nothing in that footage to lead the millions of potential fans in thinking that I'm always like that, I mean even celebrities have off days and after many attempts to distract Brendan long enough that I could swipe his ipad from the depths of his bag, he had it constantly on his shoulder now. I now have Marline the sound lady watching me after she caught me with my hand almost in Brendan bag.

It has been a good day so far though, I'm still grateful that Daniel came to my rescue after Matt opened his big dumb mouth. And apparently reflux is a part of being pregnant,

This Charming Dilemma

so Millie informed me, as I tried to get her on board with the whole hijack Brendan's ipad thing (which she wouldn't buy into), so that's just great, another thing I have to manage while trying to be poised and in control.

Daryl Loft left after lunch and after the crew got settled we all piled into the minivan and headed for town. Daniel followed in his car as he needed to go ahead and open the shop. Matt opened the van door with the same lovestruck expression he has been wearing all morning. Honestly I wish he would just get it out of his system I think it's starting to freak everyone out.

All the shops look fantastic with their sparkling clean windows and fresh displays. The town has certainly pulled out all stops to impress the crew and I felt a little tang of pride at the effort the locals were putting into the area. Mind you that was the doing of the local real estate agent who had dollar signs in his eyes as soon as he heard that a production company wants to film in the area, he put out notices to all local business about our little village being showcased on national television and the potential that has to bring more buyers into the area to kick-start us out of a real estate slump.

But now we are at the dreaded CWA meet and greet and it's been such a long afternoon, I am completely worn out and in desperate need of a nap. I caught a glimpse of myself in the window of the bakery while the crew brought coffees earlier and I have to say anyone who said pregnancy makes you glow needs to reassess their beliefs cos I look the colour of a tub of humus at the moment with my pasty complexion.

Thank god my hair is hidden under this hat as it is still sporting the unbalanced combination of frizz and dampness since this morning.

Good thing filming doesn't start until tomorrow, as tomorrow I shall become a new woman with goddess like looks.

All I need right now is 20 hours of sleep.

The CWA ladies cannot control their excitement and I had concerns at one stage that Marline, Brendan and John were going to be crushed in a senior citizen stampede. Matt and Damo have gone home after I convinced Damo that maybe Matt needs to go and have a cold shower and the fact that he just needs to leave before Marline takes out a restraining order on him for stalking. Damo agrees due to the fact that it's me and at the moment he appears to be slightly over friendly to me again. God why, why me?

Oh, maybe because I took his virginity and am pregnant with what may or may not be his child.

Okay let's not go there, positive thoughts!

The CWA didn't provide too much in the way of afternoon tea due to the fact we arrived one hour after their regular afternoon tea time and one hour before their regular dinner time. The meeting was an informal one, it was so the committee can meet the crew, of course they filled them in about the idea for the 100 year celebrations, including the idea of the erotic knitwear.

This Charming Dilemma

I swear I saw John the cameraman scream help from the depths of his soul to the universe as his eyes widened in horror. Brendan filled them in about how the whole thing works and stressed that it's a reality show so just carry on your normal daily activities as if the cameras weren't even there. And of course they reminded him that they don't need any coaching as they have had a lot of experience with carrying out their daily routine.

'Lisa are you having a look?' scolded Betty, as she nudged my arm which was being used to prop up my head as they all gather around Brendan to see the preview of the first pilot episode on his ipad. I tried to get a front row seat but I got pushed out by Fran and her knitting needles. I was going to force her to move by pulling her and her chair to the back of the crowd but Marline the sound lady is still watching me with sight suspicion so best I don't, after all she already thinks I am a pick pocketer, don't want her thinking I also inflict elder abuse on the CWA members.

And besides Fran will just kick up a fuss and then it will be all about her and not me.

I strain my neck to see over the top of Betty's head and I can only just see the screen of Brendan's ipad. It's only a preview so we are just getting snippets of it, not the actual whole show. I can't really see due to the reflection, I state this to Brendan and his reply is that he will pass it around after. Great, still going to be the last one to see it.

Lots of ohhh and arrgh-ing escape the group and from what I can make out it's a great shot of the gardens of the B&B with the old home glistening in the morning sun, there is a close up of the sign at the entrance way that says Abby'toir B&B complete with a voice over giving an introduction.

Then it moves to a shot of all of us having dinner under the coolness of the verandah with the busload of miners, I have to say I look pretty good, but I suppose at that stage I thought we were filming *The Country Girl Wants a Husband,* just before I found out that the idea had been scrapped due to lack of applications and the reason the men were here is because Matt intercepted a busload of mine workers coming back from a two week shift and bribed them with free food and accommodation for a week so we didn't end up with a lawsuit. So no wonder I looked so elegant and charming

...And I'd only had two wines at that stage.

Shrieks of laughter rang out around the group and I quickly strained my neck further to see what they were laughing at. I felt the warmth of my blood draining my body. There it was. All the snippets I had been dreading so far. Cannot see much but from what I *can* see, it captures the moment I stole Betty's scooter to go and tell Jake how much I love him, the moment I hung on to Daniel's trouser leg after I thought I was in danger of being shot Mafia style by Italian woman after giving her husband marriage advice. And what the hell? There is even footage of me sneaking back from Jake's through the depths of the thorny lantana bushes.

This Charming Dilemma

It looks like Matt's amateur footage, the stuff he threatened me with after he suspected I was seeing Jake again, and bribed me that if I didn't go out on a date with Damo, he was going to show Millie.

That little turd. Wait till I see him. I cannot watch any more, Fran looks like she is going to lose control of her bladder and Betty is holding her sides like they are about to split.

All at my expense.

Comments of joy exploded from the members, accompanied by applause as the preview came to an end. This is a disaster. It is nothing like I imagined it to be. Okay so yes, it is reality television and that was real footage. But I wanted a reality TV show based on what I want in it, not what actually happens.

'So any questions?' asks Brendan, 'okay so the full episode of what you just saw will be aired several Tuesdays from now at 7.30pm,' he continued when no questions were asked. 'But this won't be its regular timeslot, once we launch the program, it will be moved to its regular slot which will be at 5.30pm weeknights.'

Silence fills the room. Brendan and the crew all exchange glances of puzzlement until Betty finally broke the silence.

'Well I'm sorry, we are not going to be able to watch it!' Betty snapped.

'Um... because?' asked Brendan.

'Because it is going to clash with Family Feud, that's why!'

4

Day of filming 5.17am.

God I feel terrible.

And so much for an early night. After the CWA ladies wrapped up their meet and greet, the crew headed back to the B&B while I went to the shop to sulk to Daniel over the footage on the pilot episode. I managed to watch it all while the ladies were cleaning up and I have to say it's really not what I wanted showcased to the world. Being a new television network it is obvious the producers and executives have no vision into what a reality television series should be. And after asking Brendan if they can do another pilot episode (this time without the unnecessary drama), and my request was met with a blank and awkward stare, I threw my hands in the air and ended up venting to Daniel for an hour and a half.

Daniel had already seen the preview when we visited the shop earlier. Brendan caught up with him while I was convincing the rest of the crew about signing up to my dating site (well Marline is single and John is divorced), so even though Daniel doesn't think there is anything wrong with the first episode, in fact he thinks it's going to be a winner as it adds a touch of character and humour, there was much relief as he still listened with sympathy as I vented non-stop. Love Daniel.

This Charming Dilemma

He also wanted to talk about my pregnancy but managed to divert away from that subject. Not that I didn't want to talk about it. I just didn't want to remind myself every second of the day, there is more to life than being pregnant!

Like staring in your own reality TV show.

I am really excited and after talking to Millie when I got home from Daniel's and after two hours of her rubbing her temples in frustration at my "unnecessary and ungrateful" rant (as she put it), she also reminded me that I have a chance to turn things around and the pilot is there to grab attention from its viewers! She then went on to say if it was a boring old fart show from the beginning, no one would want to watch it and it would be off the air quicker than anything I have ever done on impulse.

Love Millie (sometimes).

And she is right! The Universe *is* working in my favour. I mean the universe obviously had it in the plan all along. That wasn't the real me in the preview, that was the universe working with me so I would have a successful preview to showcase to the world.

Brilliant!

I feel the urge to jump up and start my day but my unfortunately my body is saying no.

John said last night that filming will just start randomly, there is no set time and just go about our normal day.

So I'll think about what I could do today that is not out of the ordinary but something that will set me apart from other celebrities. I mean I am no Kim Kardashian (nor do I want to be) and Mother Teresa owns that type of role (and rightfully so), I'm not very musical so trying to be like Madonna is a push, hmmm it's going to take some thinking.

'Do you think that Marline chick is into me?'

'Argh Matt!' I exclaimed, whipping the sheet covers off my head to find him perched at the end of my bed in his suit. 'how long have you been there for?'

Shit, how long *has* he been there for, was I talking out loud?

'So do you fink?'

'Matt,' I groaned, 'how long have you been sitting there for?'

'Since like 4.30am and you sleep talk by the way.'

'Oh god Matt, why are you here at all?'

'So answer my question.'

'What question?'

'Do you fink that Marline chick is into me?'

'What? God I don't know, have you spoken to her?'

'No.'

'Has she spoken to you?'

This Charming Dilemma

'Nope.'

'Then I would say if you never open your mouth then she would be totally into you.'

'Don't be a smart-arse Lisa. I came to you for advice cos you might know about this stuff, you know woman's instincts and that stuff. You don't have to be mean about it!'

'Mean! Well that's rich coming from you considering you sold me out to Brendan."

'How did I sell you out to Brendan Lis-a?'

'By giving him your videos of me on your phone'

'He asked, and if I didn't you wouldn't have your stupid TV show, he said that you know.'

'If it's so stupid then why are you here? In fact, Matt, why are you in my bedroom at 6 in the morning?'

'5.30, and cos I'm your bodyguard Lisa. And besides Millie's up so I thought you would be.'

Oh my god that doesn't even warrant a reply. I kick my blankets off and jump out of bed. Matt's got me so wound up I may as well get dressed.

'So serious now,' Matt pressed on, oblivious to the mood he has just put me in, 'do you think I have a shot?'

'Yeah I suppose,' I said, not really caring, 'she is single so guess that's one tick off the list.'

'How do you know she's single?' asked Matt.

'Cos I signed her up for my dating site.'

'Ohhh what'd ya do that for,' Matt whinged, 'now I have competition.'

'Your last girlfriend was very similar so you never know,' I continued, ignoring his whining.

'Neroli? She's nothing like Marline.'

'Yeah she was,' I argued, picking out the outfit I had planned to wear yesterday, 'for a start they are both island girls,' not that I care, I just want Matt to go away.

'Marline is not from Ireland and besides I wasn't the one that went out with twins.'

'What are you talking about?' I said as I headed towards my underwear drawer.

Shite, I'm starting to feel a bit light-headed. Oh god not now.

'When you went out with both Rick and wanker Jake,' Matt whinged on, 'you only went out with Rick cos he reminded you of Jake, I know cos Rick told me.'

'Oh my god, that is so obscure!' I exclaimed, my face turning red.

'But true,' said Matt, 'and besides Marline is from like Fiji or something, not Ireland,

This Charming Dilemma

she talks normal Lisa so she can't be.'

'I said islands Matt you idiot, not Ireland,' my patience wearing thin and my head feeling like it's detached from my body, but glad Matt didn't press on about the whole Jake/Rick thing, 'I think she is from Hawaii or something.'

'Nah,' he said, 'she's definitely from Fiji.'

'Hawaii,' I mumbled one more time. Far out, I better get some ginger tea into me and stat!

'Actually neither,' smiled Marline from the bedroom door as her and John stand there with the camera.

Argh filming has started and I'm in my PJ's arguing with a spotty obnoxious know-it-all youth!

'Sorry,' she said to John as he stopped filming and gave her a teasing "what did you do that for" look.

Oh god I'm going to be sick.

After empting out the entire contents of my stomach.

Okay I have learnt some things.

Try not to make it obvious you're about to spew.

Be prepared for a camera in your face at all times.

But thank god I had my best pyjamas on though.

And the look on Matt's face was priceless.

So funny that it wasn't me putting my foot in it for a change. Even though Matt brought up the whole Jake/Rick thing, I don't think the conversation will be shown thanks to Marline not containing the urge to say something, which means the whole scene had to be cut.

But now the cat is out of the bag about Matt's intentions I'm surprised Marline is still here and has not put in for a transfer of job.

So funny.

But now I am sitting at the breakfast table with Millie and the cameras are rolling. I'm feeling a lot better since I threw up and so far no-one, including Matt, has mentioned the fact that I ran off towards the bathroom looking like the Grinch so dodged that one. But I'm cautious about what I'm eating so it doesn't happen again, ginger tea and rye toast it is. I hadn't thought of anything yet that is going to set me apart from any other celebrities, so for the moment I have decided to show my intelligent side.

I can't see Millie wanting to discuss the situation in the Middle East over her eggs and coffee so I brought a set of reading glasses and ordered the morning paper to be delivered, you know, for a more sophisticated look.

'What are you doing?' asked Millie with a slightly screwed up face.

'Catching up with current affairs,' I said, looking at the camera as if to say "tch I do this every day".

This Charming Dilemma

'Are you sure those glasses aren't going to hurt your eyes?' she said, getting up to clear the dishes off the table.

'So what are you up to today?' I quickly asked Millie to divert the focus away from the fact that Millie is being a bitch.

'What I normally do,' she said abruptly, piling dishes into the sink. I can see Millie is not going to make celebrity status with that attitude.

'Also I've got to pop down to the shops later,' she continued, 'so I'll grab some of those ginger lollies I was telling you about earlier for your…'

'Oh my phones ringing, that must be Betty,' I said in a loud voice to drown out Millie. My god what is wrong with her, she has no tact!

'I didn't hear it ring,' Millie said in a puzzled voice.

'Oh hello Betty,' I said to the no-one as I put my phone to my ear, 'yes, yes,' I mused, followed by a little laugh for effect, 'okay I'm on my way.'

'Well I'll be off,' I said to Millie while I gather my dishes, 'can't keep Betty waiting, we have the 100 year celebrations to organise, lots to do,' I mused at the camera.

'So that was Betty on the phone was it?' said Millie in a dry tone.

'Pfft, yes,' I scoffed.

'Okay, well that's funny cos Betty is standing right outside that window.'

'What?' I spun around and yes, wouldn't you know it. There is Betty holding her scooter helmet under her arm, tapping on the kitchen window.

Oh for the love of god...

'Tch not that Betty,' I said rolling my eyes, 'another Betty,' I added in a small voice as I made my way outside to see what was going on.

'What are you doing here?' I hissed at Betty, low enough so John and Marline don't hear.

'Lisa I just came cos I'm a little bit concerned,' Betty said, giving the camera a coy smile and wave.

She hands me a bit of paper and it's a flyer containing information about a proposed open cut mine. Honestly, any excuse to get in front of the camera.

'I haven't got time for this,' I mumbled at Betty, forcing her to take back her bit of junk mail.

'No you don't understand,' Betty insisted, pushing the brochure back at me, 'read it!'

Oh god I'm not going to win this one without a scene from Betty.

This Charming Dilemma

I take the paper from her again and pretend I'm taking in its contents while Betty continues to smile at the camera. It's a short two page flyer about a coal mine. It contains a picture of a woman in a hard hat with the words "jobs" and "growth" and blah blah, and printed on the back is a website address containing more information. Seems legit, don't know what Betty is going on about.

'Yes, well um... very *concerning* Betty, thanks for sharing, I must be going,' I said handing her back the paper.

'So you think it's what I think it is?' asked Betty.

'Oh definitely,' I nodded, making my way back inside to retrieve my car keys, stuffing the unwanted brochure in my bag. 'Well must be off Betty, 100 year celebration meeting, don't forget 10am,' I reminded her like a boss.

I think Betty must have got the hint as I heard her scooter start up. God I can see this is going to be a long meeting with the CWA ladies, they will be pulling out all stops to get the limelight.

John met me at the door as I retrieve my car keys and suggested that him and Marline will travel in the car into town with me while I talked about the 100 year celebration and what it's all about.

You know like they do in reality TV series like Cops.

Matt appeared out of nowhere in his suit and insisted he drive, seeing that he is my bodyguard assistant (his dumb words) but after realising he couldn't because he didn't have a spare pair of provincial driving plates that his licence required, and after ten frustrating minutes of him trying to work out how to prise off the ones super-glued to his ute's exterior, which he'd done so they wouldn't come off when he was driving at the speed of light (again his dumb words to impress Marline), he piled in the back-seat with a very anxious Marline while John sat in the passenger seat to film me as I drove into town.

Honestly I don't know why Matt didn't just take his own vehicle.

I almost had this driving while talking to cameras thing down-pat, if Betty hadn't pulled out in front of me on her scooter when we caught up with her, causing me to quickly veer left to avoid her. My wheel must have got caught in a rut on the gravel road or something cos next thing I know, my car was fishtailing down the road as I fought to gain control.

We came to the safety of a sudden stop but not before Betty rang the local police from her CWA owned iphone and reported the car for hooning and almost running her off the road. So after being pulled up at the edge of town and fined for reckless driving, I arrived in town with my very nervous film crew and Matt ranting that from now on he is driving.

Putting that all behind me as I walked towards the shop, I am beginning to feel like a real celebrity with my camera crew in tow. The local people are coming out of the shops to look and people driving past in their cars are rubbernecking. It's so cool.

This Charming Dilemma

'Good morning,' I chirped to Daniel when I entered the premises of *Cannon and Collins Event Planning and Supplies.* I'm not sure of the protocol with the door when you have a camera crew following you. I can't exactly hold the door for them both, that would interrupt the flow of filming and unless you write instructions on a wet fish and slap it across Matt s face he wouldn't think of holding the door open, as it is, he seems to be on Marline's heels like a love sick puppy.

I did give Matt a list of duties a bodyguard does one night after he was annoying me, like bringing me food and fetching me cups of coffees etc, but I didn't specify "hold office doors open" so I may have to sort that out later. But good old Daniel came to the rescue anyway and held the door open for John as he struggled with the heavy door while I strolled in and took position at my desk like a pro.

'How are you feeling this morning?' Daniel asked, handing over a cup of herbal tea. My god, any more herbal tea today and I'll turn into a hippy.

'Fine, never better,' I beamed, 'so what is on the agenda today?' I asked, opening my diary to look busy and important.

I still haven't found my celebrity angle yet, but I'm sure that will come to me soon.

'Don't you have a meeting in half an hour with the CWA ladies, the 100 year celebrations?' said Daniel, puzzled.

Trust Daniel to bring up the obvious.

Matt finds a chair on the other side of the room and opens a newspaper, pfft like *he* is going to read.

'Can you tell us about your working relationship,' John interrupts.

He was addressing Daniel thank god, cos I didn't know how to answer that considering there are a lot of grey areas about mentioning too much of the business workings, and besides even though I am part owner, I really am just winging it. But then again, he wasn't really asking about the business per se, he was asking about our "working relationship", better tune in.

'So Lisa and I set up Cannon and Collins Event Planning and Photography about a year ago.' Daniel started, shoving his hands in his pockets and leaning up against my desk. 'Lisa is the event planning side of the business and I am the photography side of things.'

Grr he forgot to mention the dating agency.

'And how did you two meet?' John asks Daniel as I studied my reflection in the stainless steel pencil holder that Daniel brought me so it blends in with the decor. Hmmm, not liking this brand of lipstick I choose this morning, it's only been an hour and it's already faded, better apply some more.

Oh shit, now I have it on my teeth.

'I first meet Lisa when I returned from the UK. I was working for a food magazine over there photographing dishes,'

This Charming Dilemma

Daniel went on, 'I decided to return to my home town to settle down, Lisa was engaged to my best friend…'

This lipstick doesn't seem to be shifting when I rub it with my finger, I might try a bit of tissue dunked in my tea.

'Lisa?'

'Huh?' I jumped, suddenly hearing my name as Marline let out a little giggle from behind John.

'You were engaged once?' John asked.

'Oh, um… yes,' I said, realising that suddenly all eyes were on me, 'to an um… guy.'

'But you never got married?' pressed Brendan from behind that camera.

'Uh, nah,' I mumbled tight lipped, shaking my head to try and conceal the lipstick still on my teeth. I shrugged my shoulders to answer the next question which no doubt would have been "what happened", then raised my hand to excuse myself as I made my way to the bathroom to remove my lipstick stain from my teeth. Okay not a good start to my professional television career. I was not prepared for them to start asking personal questions, especially about the past, I mean what happened to the here and now, but I suppose they have to build some type of background profile. I mean look at the Kardashians, I'm sure one of them fell for some guy before being dumped then finding out his twin brother was living in your ceiling so you get engaged to him but end up not getting married then the other twin brother comes back in your life and you end up with a strong possibility that you may be carrying his child! And look how successful they turned out. But still, the less information is better.

I can still hear Daniel talking to the camera, I can hear bits and pieces and it sounds like Daniel is talking about himself which is good, as I think it would be better to remain a woman of mystery. That way I will keep my audience interested, they can't know everything about me on the first take.

After a quick visit to the loo which seems to be happening more often since this baby appeared, I fixed my makeup. Satisfied with my look I took a deep breath and now I am ready to go take the world by storm.

I opened the door to a flurry of voices, it looks like the CWA have arrived for our meeting about the 100 year celebrations. Typical, they are all crowded around John like a pack of vultures.

'Oh yes, Lisa is a very good president,' I heard Betty say as John's camera seems to be focused on the group hovering around him, 'do you remember the time we had our Kinky But Nice Party?' Betty asked the hovering group.

'Oh yes, Lisa dressed up in that dominatrix outfit,' said Fran, 'we raised lots of money that night,' she said, giving John a little pat on the arm.

Oh crap!

This Charming Dilemma

'Then there was that other time when she got herself in the paper after saving that local politician from falling on a BBQ. Fell on top of her he did,' laughed Betty, letting out a little snort.

'Was it for that?' asked Gloria, 'I thought it was for the time she wrestled a ghost in the main street, claiming it was old Larry remember? Margo's daughter filmed it on her phone…'

Arghh.

'Okay ladies!' I exclaimed, 'no time for um… spreading fickle rumours, let's all get seated,' I said in my best authority type voice.

'Okay so as you all know we have the 100 year celebrations coming up so we have a lot to organise. This is our chance to really showcase our town as a welcoming, open-minded community,' I said, glancing at the camera and owning the meeting like a boss.

'So first things first, Daniel has got a couple of samples of the designs for the signs you proposed,' I handed the floor to Daniel hoping to buy enough time as I quickly opened my laptop documents to try and find the meeting's agenda that Gloria had emailed to me the night before. I was so wrapped up in worrying about the preview episode I completely forgot about the agenda, I have to show leadership in all areas. Okay, the Country Woman's Association is not exactly the United Nations but still, I am the centre of this reality television show, I have to demonstrate at all times I have what it takes.

Oh here it is, I quickly scanned through it as Daniel continued to show them some designs of rainbow coloured sheep, I glanced at Marline and she looks like she is trying not to burst at the seams with laughter. Grrrr why are old ladies insisting on embarrassing themselves with outrageous signs!

Hold on a minute, item four on the agenda is proposed mine, what proposed mine? Oh god it's probably the same thing Betty was panicking about this morning. I bet you she has forced Gloria to put it on the agenda.

Daniel ended his painful discussion about the sign and got confirmation about which sample to go for, I really didn't see what the outcome was, I just nodded in agreement. Daniel moved off to sort the ordering of the sign as Gloria satisfactorily ticked that one off the long list she has in front of her.

Item two was just as tedious as Mary was running down the list of sponsors and local business willing to put a float entry into the parade. Even though I looked official and nodded in all the rights places I couldn't help but glance at the film crew occasionally to see if any of them had fallen asleep. Marline seemed to be concentrating on a device attached to the sound microphone and I couldn't really see John's face behind the camera. Matt is pretending to read but his eyes are fixed on Marline. Hmm I really should get a spray bottle to remind him to stop staring, it's embarrassing, thank god Marline hasn't noticed. I shot a glance at Daniel after I wrap up item two and read out item three on the agenda,

This Charming Dilemma

the advertising, which I hand over to Maggie. Daniel is looking straight at me like he is contemplating something, in fact his gaze is really intense. I cannot work it out, in fact it's so strong I quickly tore my gaze away.

This meeting is going really well, in fact it's one of the best ones yet, no interruptions, no outrageous suggestions, this is the quietest I have seen the CWA ladies during a meeting for a long time. The fact that they are all glancing and waving at the camera may have something to do with it, Gloria gave me a little nudge with her elbow.

'Oh okay, sorry, which brings us to item four,' I said, coming to, 'which is, oh god, the coal mine, who brought this up?' I asked in my exasperated voice.

'I did!' snapped Betty, 'remember Lisa, I came to see you about it this morning, you said you also had concerns about this, honestly, between this and trying to run me off the road, anyone would think you have baby brain.'

I swear I just heard Daniel swallow hard as my insides stopped working for a split second.

'She has to have a man first to have baby brain,' giggled Mary to Fran.

'Yes okay Betty,' I said quickly before they all wind up in a game of "why Lisa doesn't have a man", 'but what has a proposed mine got to do with the CWA?' I pressed, feeling a headache coming on.

'Well it involves one of our members,' Betty said, trying to say it in such a way the camera wouldn't hear her.

'What member?' I asked.

'I thought Betty showed you the proposal,' Gloria said, also keeping her voice low, 'the proposed coal mine on a property of a certain ex member of ours.'

'Pamela?' I queried, as I saw Daniel take a brochure Maggie handed to him.

'Lisa honestly,' scolded Betty, 'why do you tell us you know these things when it's clear you're not really paying attention.'

'Well I think it's disgusting,' Fran said, 'what will become of our community with a great big gaping hole at the edge of the town!'

'Do you think that's why... you know?' whispered Mary.

'Oh definitely!' said Fran firmly.

What the hell are they all carrying on about? And it's obvious they don't want the camera to hear as they are all whispering and making sure their backs are turned to John and Marline. Honesty if they didn't want to talk about it in front of the camera, then why put it on the friken agenda.

God I wish they would stop beating around the bush and come out with it. I'm over guessing.

This Charming Dilemma

Oh that's right, I still have the brochure in my bag from Betty, I glance at Daniel again and he is reading the flyer with such concern on his face it must be important. I reached in my bag and pulled it out, it fell open to the map of the proposed mine site.

I studied it for a moment before it hit me.

The mine is proposed right across the Crankshaw's Farm.

~~~~~~
~~~~~~

5

Back home, still with John and Marline in tow.

I'm exhausted. I have to be on my "A" game at all times cos I never know if John is filming me or not. One minute I am in the zone feeling good and putting on a star performance only to turn around and find out he hasn't even got the camera out, but the second I am doing something uninteresting like making a cup of tea and checking my spam folder on my emails for any special shopping deals I may have missed, he is all in my face with the camera.

But still, whatever I do I have to do it with grace and style. Even after learning about the proposed coal mine going across the Crankshaw's farm. We got through the meeting without too much drama, until, of course, the subject of the mine came up and all of a sudden old women's opinions were flying everywhere. Daniel ignored the hysteria that was item four on the CWA agenda to look up the website of the company who put out the information. And sure enough, there is a coal mine being proposed for the area, at this stage it seems it's still in the early stages and they have only just put in a permit for samples. I'm a bit surprised that they have gone over the Crankshaw's farm, and can't help but wonder if Jake knows.

Well he must do, it's his Aunties farm still, I think.

This Charming Dilemma

The Crankshaw's farm house and sheds burnt down only a couple of months back, this was back when Jake and I well... were... kinda dating again. It was horrible and they lost everything except the dairy shed and a couple of smaller out buildings. Apparently it was started by an electrical fault, then spread by fuel catching alight, which would be plausible, except for the fact that the buildings damaged were nowhere near each other really so it seems a little strange that the fire was started in one building but managed to damage the sheds. Of course one of the buildings was the Crankshaw's family home which had been in the family for two generations. The CWA did a collection for them through the now famous lemonade stand, after rumours went around that they were not insured, on the day of the presentation and after they received their cheque, the Crankshaw's left town with their shiny new caravan in tow leaving behind a bewildered Jake and a suspicious community. Of course everyone pointed their finger at Jake deliberately starting the fire to begin with but after Jake's Aunty and Uncle bolted, leaving him behind to deal with the police and the community, everyone's suspicions turned to the senior Crankshaw's themselves.

Hmmm, so I wonder if this mine has any links to the farm's "accidental" fires, maybe the Crankshaw's refused to sign over the farm so someone from the mining company did it to scare them off.

But still, it's not like it's going to happen, the mine that is, it's just an idea, no reason to get knickers in a knot over it.

But anyway I haven't got time to worry about some stupid mine as I still have to find my celebrity talent.

It wasn't a bad first day of filming, wasn't exactly riveting stuff either, I did manage to get a small break in the day when John and Marline went to film Betty and Fran at the Lemonade Stand while another busload of tourists stopped to use the public amenities and buy refreshments. It was kind of set up that way as the local information centre informs the CWA committee of when a tour bus is due so they can be there when it stops. The sign on the lemonade stand reads *CWA, here for all your need*s, with the word *all* being emphasised. I didn't have anything to do with that, that was the bright idea of Betty and Fran. God knows it just sounds silly, it's the Country Woman's Association, what possible things can they offer besides homemade goods, tea and scones. Oh and lemonade of course.

But it's not really homemade lemonade. Well it started off being homemade but after a small reminder from the CWA head office (and the local police) that this branch has to have a permit to sell anything "homemade" unless it has a certificate after the fiasco with the garden club fund-raiser where we accidentally sold eye pillows stuffed with marijuana. We now just sell commercial cans of lemonade along with cakes and the ugly knitted ware and goods (all approved by authorities of course).

This Charming Dilemma

The local cafes and bakery kicked up a stink when Mary brought along her coffee maker from home and started making everyone cappuccinos, so we banned that idea. I don't know why the Lemonade Stand came to get such a reputation so quickly, it originally got set up to fundraise for Crankshaw's then stayed to serve the busload of miners that used our small town as a halfway stopping point when they were bussed out to their jobs, another bright idea by Betty and Fran, and it seems to be doing alright, as it has paid for two iphones, a new commercial kitchen for the Scout Hall so we can make all our cakes, a new laptop for Gloria to do the minutes on (even though she still brings along her notebook and pen) and there is even talk of a trip to Fiji to personally hand over items collected to help out after their recent cyclone. Seriously, the stall has only been going for the same amount of time I've been pregnant.

Oh that's right, I'm pregnant. Keep forgetting about that.

Matt was around for most of the morning but seemed to disappear after lunch, haven't seen him since so I'm hoping he just got bored or came to the realisation that Marline isn't into him and decided to get a life. Damo was also meant to be Matt's sidekick bodyguard but due to work commitments, he had to give that idea up before it started. Thank god, as I really don't need the constant reminder of that mistake in my face every day, especially when I am trying to wipe the slate clean and make a fresh start as a celebrity.

I mean what kind of celebrity do I want to be here?

One that portrays herself as a strong business type entrepreneur woman with poise and grace admired by many in her community, or one that will be known for drunken promiscuous behaviour and outrageous dance moves.

The first option I think.

But even though the day was okay, it wasn't exactly Summer Bay either, I guess the highlight of the day was the CWA outburst over the mine, I mean it got so heated at one point between Fran and Maggie I thought it was going to turn out to be an episode of the Jerry Springer show, Fran of course was accusing the Crankshaw's of selling out while Maggie was defending them, saying she has known the Crankshaw's her entire life, there was no way they would have sold out.

John was filming the whole outburst as sides were taken over the opinions of both parties, but I seriously doubt they would have that in the actual episode because as soon as the outburst happened Betty jumped from her seat and lunged at the camera, covering the lens with her hands like she was in an episode of Cops, ranting to John to turn the camera off and almost knocking him to the ground.

Me, well I was busy on Google, but not chasing information about the mine, finding out celebrity tips and hints so I can stun the crew with my personality.

Daniel slowly emerged from behind his desk and coaxed Betty back to her seat in a calm manner before I declared the meeting closed and Gloria reminded everyone about the donations to be collected for our monthly raffle,

This Charming Dilemma

before they all set off for the Lemonade Stand with a nervous John in tow to have a nice cup of tea and bit of cake as they wait for the tour bus to arrive to offer them their services.

I can see that I will have to come up with something quick as I'm sure it won't be long before John will have had enough of filming me at my desk surrounded by old people discussing knitted underwear for a celebration of 100 years of baking cakes for the community.

I'm concerned cos it is now night fall and Brendan is in the dining room of the B&B, Marline and John are at the local bingo night getting familiar with the night life. Brendan is looking at the footage of film of the day so far and his expression is reading blank and uninspired.

'I got you your ginger tablets,' Millie said, throwing them into my lap, 'oh and this,' she said handing me a copy of What to Expect When You're Expecting, 'I found it earlier when I was cleaning up.'

'Millie!' I hissed quickly tucking the book away behind me as Brendan briefly diverted his attention towards Millie's entrance before returning his attention to the task at hand.

'Not in front of you know who,' I whispered nodding my head towards Brendan.

'You haven't told him yet?' asked Millie in a loud voice, collapsing into the seat beside me.

Oh that's right I told Millie I was going to tell Brendan. Better tell her I did before she tells him.

'Yes of course,' I mumbled in my firm voice, 'but you know, I don't want them to know everything, it's kinda personal... you know, having sex and becoming pregnant... so um, how did you go with your interview?'

'Oh that's right,' said Millie, excitedly reaching for her bag, as I breathed a sigh of relief that I managed to divert her attention.

'Went really well,' she said, opening her resume to show me the literature on the company. You see Millie thinks she has found her calling and answered an advert about becoming a private detective, there is a new PI company starting up that is interviewing for recruits. It's not like stalking your spouses to find out if they are playing around or anything, well it is, but the main work is finding misplaced funds or looking for relatives type stuff, bit boring really, but Millie loves snooping so it's right up her alley, and they tell her she can do the majority of work from home so she can be around more for Amy instead of being in the city all the time for work.

'They seem like a really good company,' said Millie, 'and I get to work from home mostly.'

As long as Millie is excited about the prospect of a job that requires snooping, she is not snooping into my business.

'So how was your day,' she said after about twenty minutes of going through the entire interview word for word.

This Charming Dilemma

'Me… oh it was okay, a bit non-eventful,' I said so Brendan could hear, 'bit unusual around here isn't it Millie, for a day to be as boring as today.'

'Meh, not really,' said Millie, shrugging her shoulders, 'so what is this about a mine opening here? Sid said it's meant to be going right across the Crankshaw's farm,' she said, tucking her legs under her like she does when she is ready for a full-blown gossip session.

'Oh that,' I groaned, 'Betty seems to have a fixation on that. How did Sid know about it?' I asked.

'Daniel and Rick were talking about it in town earlier, Sid caught up with them.'

'Rick?'

'Yes Rick, he knows nothing about it apparently. Mind you, he is not really a part of that farm any more is he, but still… bit rude if you ask me.'

'Well I don't think it's a big deal' I said, 'if Rick doesn't know about it then it can't be happening,' I said, a bit put out that Rick is back in town and Daniel didn't even mention it!

Rick is Jake's twin brother and for a while, was living in my ceiling without my knowledge, this was before the attic was converted into a bedroom for the B&B. We dated for a whole year before getting engaged, but unfortunately Rick may have had Jake's looks but... well... I just wasn't that into him. Shame, as he is such a nice guy. Rick has moved on with another girl but we not really on talking terms. Something we better get over if this baby turns out to be Jake's, you know, family and all.

'What's this about a mine?' Brendan piped up from the depths of his footage.

'Oh nothing,' I said waving my hand to back up my sentence, 'it's really just some rumours going around about a hole they want to cut in the area, no biggie.'

'Well the CWA ladies don't seem to think so,' Brendan said, turning the screen of the camera around to show us Betty's outburst.

I rolled my eyes.

'Well, you know what they are like, kick up a fuss over anything,' I tutted.

I'm getting the impression that Brendan is not impressed with today's take, I mean you have to admit, for a reality television series, it wasn't that interesting. I really have to think of something interesting, and quick.

'Um... so Brendan, since today was an unusually quiet one, maybe tomorrow we could you know, start showing the world what really goes on around here...'

'Such as?' he asks.

This Charming Dilemma

'Oh well you know… um…' god, I really can't think of anything, are we that boring?

'Lisa, it's your life, just live it how it is,' Brendan said, yawning, 'well I've got to hit the sack,' he said gathering up his things, 'I'm stuffed.'

Murmurs of goodnight were exchanged as he made his way out toward the caravan and I'm now extremely worried, Brendan doesn't seem too happy, okay he said he wasn't unhappy but he didn't comment on it which normally means he has nothing good to say. And he would be right, it's my life just live it, well yes, but seriously, what is my life. I really didn't think this through when the opportunity came up. Yes reality TV is all very fine but there were not really any guidelines of what I was meant to do. Be myself… hmmm all very well but every time I try to be myself, it always ends up in disaster. Research, that is what I need, research.

'You going to bed?' Millie asked, stifling a yawn.

'Nope,' I said, lifting the lid on my laptop to download episodes of Sylvania Waters, 'I have research to do.'

'Yeah okay whatever,' Millie, said removing herself from the couch, 'don't forget to take one of those ginger lollies before you get up tomorrow,' she said.

'Yeah, yeah,' I waved at her as she left, I think it's probably best to start at the first episode.

Sylvania Waters was a reality TV series back in the 90s my mother was addicted to, so best I download the first episode and see what made my mother burn dinner when it came on TV.

I didn't really get into it, but because it was based near where I grew up, it would be the closest thing to compare to what is trying to be achieved here. Well without the bickering and arguing which there seems to be a lot of, so far, and I'm only two minutes into the first episode. I mean nothing like that goes on around here, the odd disagreement yes but nothing like that. In fact, I don't think this is my cup of tea at all, I'll watch a little bit more but to be honest with you, I don't think it will take my interest.

I can hear Marline and John in the kitchen which means they have returned from a riveting night at bingo. I should go in and see them, get a feel for how they think the day went but it's so comfortable here and I'm onto episode two. Still the same old stuff, arguing, going on about their nice house and how they worked hard, blah, blah, apparently this show was quite popular, goes to prove how far we have come cos no one would be interested in a show like this anymore. Which means I need to step up this reality television show idea, somehow I need to take this into the new millennium. I mean if Sylvania Waters was the show in the 90s then I need to make "The Lemonade Stand" the show of this decade.

Starting with the name – The Lemonade Stand. I mean who thought of that. Okay Brendan did, and he is the producer, and Daryl loft the executive producer. But seriously, doesn't exactly scream excitement, screams... well lemons.

This Charming Dilemma

I've probably been sitting here for an hour or so, I grabbed a pen and paper to start jotting down my ideas as they come, starting with the name change. But then had another thought that it'll be too late to suggest a change because the first episode has already been advertised, grrr I should have gotten onto this when the idea first was pitched to me, but I was too busy thinking about other things, like finding out I'm pregnant.

Speaking of that, I'm starting to feel a little sick, and really, really, tired, I think it's a mind over matter thing cos I wasn't feeling like this an hour ago, it's only when I think about being pregnant that I start to feel sick so I think the trick here is to not think about being pregnant at all. But I'll just watch a little more of this Sylvania Waters, even though it's not turning me on but I need to know what not to do, then I'll go to bed. Not that it's a big day tomorrow just the same old work routine. I have a client at 10am to discuss her wedding, but not sure how I can make that exciting. I'm hoping John and Marline might focus on something else tomorrow, maybe they need to pop across to Tim at the bakery.

Okay maybe not Tim, he is more boring than Fran's knitted bed-socks.

'Sup?' entered Matt, pulling me from the depths of my laptop. He looks dressed for work, well not work, as he is an apprentice mechanic and he is dressed in his suit, so he is dressed in his "let's annoy Lisa in her reality TV show" clothes.

'Whatya watching?' he asked, planting himself on the sofa next to me and leaning over to look at my laptop.

The impact of the sofa bouncing under Matt's weight stirred my fragile tummy, it's not going to be good. Better get myself to bed. And have one of Millie's ginger lollies.

'Just some old school reality TV show, trying to get some ideas.'

'Boring,' Matt said, fiddling with the sofa cushion behind him, 'you should watch Game of Thrones, everyone is doing it.'

'It's not about entertainment,' I said frustrated, 'it's about research. Okay be honest with me,' I said turning to face him, 'if you were watching a TV series would you want to watch a bunch of people discussing knitwear?'

'Depends.'

'On what?'

'Like who is in it, I mean if it was me and Damo, then yeah I'd watch it, Damo's a pretty interesting guy you know, not that you care about Damo, since you won't go back out on a second date wif him.'

'No I mean what kind of stuff would you expect from reality TV?' I said, rubbing my brow in frustration and ignoring his last statement.

'Probably some action stuff,' said Matt giving it no thought, 'maybe some hot chicks, and maybe some punch ups.'

God why did I even bother to ask.

'Why? Do you fink you're boring?' asked Matt.

This Charming Dilemma

'A little,' I said, 'well not so much boring, I just… well, don't have much of a life. Not one that people would be interested in, I mean if I was to find something that seemed like my life was more exciting…'

'So you want to make stuff up?'

'Well not exactly make stuff up…'

'Cos you can't you know, that means it's not reality TV, it will be made-up TV.'

'Yes I know that Matt, it's just…'

'And you do heaps of funny cool stuff,' said Matt, still trying to adjust the back cushion on the sofa and making me more and more nauseous with every movement.

'Like what!' I scoffed.

'Like the time you dyed your hair orange and started head banging on the table at the wool shed ball. And that time you got stuck up the ladder when we found all that weed in the ceiling. And that time we went to kill the rooster and it died of fright then you found it the next day tied on the clothes line. And that time you ended up a mental case cos you made friends with a ghost, and that time you…'

'Okay, Matt enough! I don't mean *those* type of things, those things were like… accidental, I meant stuff that makes me … well, more me.'

'But dat is you.'

'No it's not.'

'Yes it is.'

'No it's not, I want to contribute something worthwhile, I need to find my, you know… god never mind! What are you doing here anyway?' I said feeling fragile, this baby is really knocking me around this evening.

'Ready for another filming day as your bodyguard,' said Matt.

'I mean what are you doing *here,* don't you have a home to go to?'

'Yeah and I've been there already,' said Matt, trying to get comfortable on the sofa. I don't dare move now in case I lose my stomach, not in front of Matt. If I'm sick in front of him again then he might suspect something, so far he still thinks I'd had a stomach bug.

'No I mean why are you staying here?' I said in desperation, just wishing he would piss off, 'shouldn't you go home and come back tomorrow?' I discreetly opened the ginger lollies that were in the pocket of my jumper and popped one in my mouth hoping it would calm things down and distract me.

God, even sucking on the lolly is making me nauseous.

'And miss a whole day?' Matt said. 'If you don't want me to be your bodyguard just say so Lis.'

'Matt I don't want you to be my bodyguard.'

'Well too bad cos Brendan said I could.'

This Charming Dilemma

'Stop being sensitive, anyway Matt I meant what are you doing here now, at this time? Shouldn't I be seeing you in the morning?'

'It is morning.'

'No its no.'

'It is, look,' Matt said, showing me his phone to reveal 5.46am.

AM! In the morning! God have I been up all night?

'Have you been up all night?' asked Matt, looking at me with fresh eyes.

'I must have,' I said shutting my laptop down on which appears to be the start of episode nine of Sylvania Waters!

Was I that engrossed in it? Can't have been, it's not that interesting.

'That explains why you look like shit,' said Matt, 'and you fink I'm crazy.'

'Matt will you sit still,' I scolded, feeling a lump stirring in my throat.

'I can't get comfortable, Matt whinged, 'it's like there's something hard in your sofa.'

'Morning,' Brendan greeted, 'ready for another day? Lisa, you okay? You look pale.'

'She's been up all night watching Days of Our Lives or something, for research cos Lisa finks she's boring,' Matt said finally bouncing up from the sofa. He lifts the cushion to reveal Millie's What to Expect When You're Expecting book. 'Dat's what the hard fing was,' he said in a not so discreet way.

Shit! Forgot that was there.

'Tch Millie,' I scoffed, rolling my eyes, 'leaves her stuff everywhere.' God I hope Millie doesn't walk in here about now, I can hear her in the kitchen, think I better leave the room now.

'You should go get some sleep now even if it's just a couple of hours,' Brendan suggested, 'I have asked John and Marline to focus on you today,' he said, 'follow you around, getting your thoughts on everything. Yesterday was pretty much about the community, today it will be about you.'

Nooo not today. Not when I haven't prepared anything remotely interesting!

'Okay, no problem,' I said, trying to get up out of my seat without causing too much trauma to my fragile self, but trying to be upbeat and in control at the same time.

'I'll just um… go to bed shall I.'

'Lisa, you sure you okay.' Brendan asked, concerned, 'you're clutching your stomach.'

This Charming Dilemma

'Oh fine,' I said, breathing through my mouth and waving his concerns away, 'just you know, been sitting in one spot for too long, muscle spasms,' I said, stumbling away like the Hunchback of Notre Dame.

'Okay, well sleep tight,' Brendan said, 'I'll wake you up in a couple of hours,' I heard him faintly say as I made it to the safety of my bedroom door. Thank god, cos I wasn't going to hold out much longer, lucky Millie had put a bowl in my room for such occasions and after relieving myself of my morning sickness, I pushed the bowl under the bed and crawled amongst the covers.

I'm too tired to think of something remotely interesting, but I know if I don't I will miss my opportunity. Especially since Brendan said today will be all about me.

~~~~~~
~~~~~~

6

'I fink Millie is pregnant again,' Matt pipes up from the drivers' seat as we drive into town.

'Why do you say that?' I yawned from the passenger seat.

'Cos she's reading dat book again, the one dat tells you what to do when your preggo, da one I sat on this morning, and I fink she spewed in your room, it stinks in there.'

I don't recall falling asleep but I must have for Matt to come in and rudely awaken me and even though Matt's driving sucks, it's really good that he is driving cos I can't be bothered doing anything physical.

Not a good start to the day of being fabulously interesting, not that I have come up with any ideas on how to be original. I didn't answer Matt's comment on him thinking Millie is pregnant, in fact the more he suspects Millie the better.

And to top it off, I forgot to charge my battery on my phone so I can't access the several messages Daniel has left me. Well I could but Matt doesn't have a phone charger in his car, just loud thumping music.

This Charming Dilemma

'So whatya doing today?' Matt asked, over the top of the thumping base which is a combination of heavy metal music and Irish jig.

'Oh you know, work stuff,' I shrugged.

'Boring,' Matt said.

I opened my mouth to remind him of the conversation I had earlier but let it go. I'm really getting sick of repeating myself to Matt, but if he has his music this loud all the time then no wonder he is deaf, and arrogant.

We turned in to the main hub of town and Matt parks up. Brendan, John and Marline are waiting for me outside the shop as I walk towards the door. As usual, Matt hovers behind me like a shy child upon seeing Marline and despite that fact I am feeling like a zombie in an apocalypse, as soon as I see John roll the camera, I get a second wind, man I must be a natural at television stuff.

Opening the shop door feeling fabulous as John tracks my moves while Brendan takes notes on his tablet for the voice over to be edited in later, I quickly retracted my steps, knocking John and Marline backwards.

It's Rick! Rick is standing in my shop!

With Daniel.

Rick, the man I almost married, Jake's twin brother.

Shit now what am I going to do?

'Errrrr,' I stalled, looking at the puzzled faces looking back at me as I am trying to come up with something quick. Not that I have a problem with seeing Rick it's just that...

Okay, I have a problem with seeing Rick.

'Hey shit man, it's Rick,' Matt said, digging me in the ribs forgetting his vow of silence around Marline and pushing past me to go and greet him like cavemen do.

I know, I'll just nip down to the lemonade stand and have a quick word with Betty, that should fill in an hour.

'Lisa!' Daniel said, catching me before I made a hasty exit.

'Your ten o'clock is here.'

Oh that's right I have a 10am client.

Gaining my fabulous, I strolled into the office taking a sideways look, oh god he looks good, he looks more like Jake every time I see him.

'Hello Lisa,' Rick greets me in his deep muscular voice that sounds similar to Jakes.

'Oh, hi Rick,' I said, trying to sound surprised, as if I just saw him for the first time. My client is sitting on our guest lounge, very pretty lady with blond natural curly locks and pure blemish free skin, the kind of lady you will find perched under a magnificent oak tree surrounded by white bunnies and bell birds. She reminds me of someone.

This Charming Dilemma

'Good morning,' I greeted her after Brendan had a quick word with her about the camera crew and got her okay to be filmed. I moved to the back of my desk, aware Rick is watching me. Or it could be because of this camera crew.

I flicked a glance to the open page of my diary that Daniel so conveniently leaves open for me every time I have a client so I won't forget their name and what they are here for. He actually writes it in for me most the time too.

'Ellen,' I said, beaming at her, Ellen here to discuss wedding plans with… Rick.

Oh shit.

'Okay Ellen and Rick,' I said, inviting them to take a seat.

Oh my god this is going to be awkward.

'So you're here because…?' I stalled.

Oh god don't make me say it.

'We're getting married,' Ellen said, flicking a loving glance at Rick.

'Lovely,' I beamed, silently thanking her for saying what I would've choked on. I see Daniel has quickly exited the room. Bastard! Or maybe that's why he was trying to get hold of me, Daniel wouldn't be the type not to warn me about this.

I see Matt has gone back to his corner to drool over Marline.

139

'So what sort of wedding do you have in mind,' I asked, mustering the best smile I had.

'Well I have always wanted to get married in a rainforest,' Ellen smiled.

Snow White! That's who she reminds me of, Snow White, you know that scene where she is in a rainforest surrounded by bunnies and bell birds. Except she is a blond, Snow White was dark. Bit ironic for someone called Snow White really.

'Well I can recommend a lovely wedding celebrant,' I said, bringing myself back to the present, 'who would love to do a rainforest ceremony,' I smiled.

The same one that we were going to use to marry us, I felt like saying to Rick, I wonder if Ellen knows who I am?

Ohhh, it just dawned on me that I could be sitting opposite my child's uncle and aunt.

Maybe.

'That would be great!' she exclaimed, 'I haven't given much thought to any of it, I'm not very good at organising anything,' she smiled sweetly, lightly placing her hand on Rick's arm, 'that's why I was hoping you could.'

I was going to suggest that I also offer my celebrant services but cannot bring myself to suggest it. I don't think I could marry my ex fiancé.

This Charming Dilemma

Which means I'll have to bring old Rosie out of retirement for this one.

'Well let me run through some of our packages,' I said, rising from my seat to get her the information about bridal packages I painstakingly put together after I found my calling as an event planner. I notice Rick hasn't said anything yet.

Collecting my information, I glanced up at Daniel who has appeared in the room again whispering something in Brendan's ear while Brendan looks at me his expression mixed with amusement and revelation.

I gave them both a secret glare before sitting opposite my client with my game face on. It appears Ellen wants the full bridle package, which includes everything from me organising a wedding celebrant to me booking their honeymoon.

After negotiating and accepting a deposit, I handed over the forms for them to fill out as to what preferences they have and of course the wedding date etc etc. Rick doesn't appear to be that interested, he moves away to talk to Daniel, only coming back to his fiancée when she asks me a question.

I'm so concentrating on the situation right now I totally forgot the camera crew is here. While Ellen is filling out the paperwork I take the opportunity to study Rick, well I'm not actually studying Rick, I'm more like pretending that is Jake standing over there having serious conversations with Daniel in hushed tones. Which means I must miss Jake, therefore it must be his baby, yeah that's it, the baby is giving me a sign every time I look at Rick, after all it must be able to see from down there.

'I think that's it,' Ellen said, handing me back the forms and snapping me back to the present, again.

'Okay,' I said flicking through the paperwork, 'so… oh, the wedding date is set for the…?'

Shoot, same day as the Mardi Gras.

'Um,' I said, playing for time and scratching my head, 'I don't know if we'll be able …'

'Yes it's my Mum's birthday,' Ellen interrupted, 'she passed away when I was very young,' she said with sadness in her eyes.

'Okay, well I think we can do it,' I beamed, already playing out the whole explanation I am going to have to offer Betty for not being present for the CWA's biggest event of the century. It was like time stood still, they have been here for an hour and a half but honestly if feels like just minutes.

Thank god!

I saw them to the door with my business face on pretending that Rick is Jake and the woman is just a client and not engaged to my ex fiancé, and both of them aren't the future Aunt and Uncle of my unborn child which Brendan has no idea about yet, as he walks towards me.

This Charming Dilemma

'How did that make you feel?' he asked as I closed the shop door behind them.

'Fine,' I said, with all the effort I could muster as I made my way back to the desk.

'So that wasn't awkward for you?' he pressed.

'No, why would it be?' I asked, glancing at Daniel who was staring at me.

'Wasn't that your ex fiancé?' Brendan asked.

'Yeah Lisa was gonna marry him but then she chickened out,' said Matt from the sidelines.

'Shut up Matt, you chickened out of marrying Neroli.'

I am aware the camera crew have all eyes and lenses on me.

'Oh *him,*' I said to Brendan, pointing to the now closed shop door, 'well yes he was, but you know... distant memory now.'

'So you are okay with organising your ex fiancé's wedding?' Brendan pressed on, standing off to the side of the camera. I can see what he is trying to do. He is trying to get a reaction out of me for the camera. Well I am not about to go all Sylvania Waters on his production... well still not sure where I would like to take this production, but I refuse to be all dramatic like a Ricky Lake show.

Speaking of Rick, damn he is looking good.

'Lisa?'

'Hmmm?? Oh of course, sorry, um… no the answer to your question is no.' I beamed, shuffling the paperwork in front of me. I glanced down to catch her age 23! Ellen is 23?

'Well that's very professional of you Lisa,' said Brendan moving off towards Daniel.

'Yeah, yeah,' I waved my hand at him as I continue to look at her age in disgust. 23, like she is… almost 17 years younger than him!

No wonder she has flawless skin and looks like a blond Snow White.

Was Rick here to try and make me jealous??

Matt announced he was going to get coffee and left the shop, he would have been embarrassed by the comment I made in front of Marline. Serves him right.

But seriously what is up with Rick? Prancing around with a 23 year old woman who looks as pure as a fairy tale character with the body of a goddess in front of me, knowing full well that I would not say no to planning his wedding out of sheer pretence. There can only be one explanation for it.

Rick is still into me!

Shame I may be pregnant to his brother. Rick was looking really good.

A wave of depression hit me, maybe I am still into Rick and substituted Jake for Rick instead of the other way round.

This Charming Dilemma

And to think if I wasn't so stubborn back then it could have been me wanting to get married in the rainforest and have the reception at… oh my lord, at Abby'toir, they want the wedding dinner at my house!!

Could this day get any worse?

'Lisa dear,' exclaimed Betty as the shop door announced her arrival. 'I need to promote this,' she said handing over a clipboard supporting an A4 sheet of paper like her life depended on it.

It's a page of blank lines with the headings of Name, Address and Signature.

'What?'

'This…' she said, snatching the clipboard back from me and holding it up to the camera for a dramatic effect, 'is justice!' she exclaimed, tapping the clipboard. 'This open cut mine they want to do at the edge of town is going to destroy good farming land, not to mention the health concerns of all of us town folk. We will not stand for it. We here at the CWA, not to mention with the support of Lisa and her celebrity status, we will not be beaten.'

Oh good lord, celebrity status, I haven't even found my niche yet. Damn Betty!

'Our children's children do not deserve this, this is encouraged by a few families in this town who feel they can make decisions for all of us.'

'Well we have justice on our side,' Betty came around the side of my desk and grabbed my hand, 'and who is that voice of justice?' she asked, looking into the camera, 'it's Lisa!' she exclaimed, raising my hand in the air.

Huh!? What is happening?

Oh goody Daniel's coming. He will sort Betty out.

'Excuse me Betty, can I see that?' he said, smiling his charming smile that he knows damn well will get Betty to swoon.

'Of course my dear,' she beamed, going back to her sweet self, pulling off her reading glasses and popping them back into their case.

'So Lisa, care to elaborate?' said Brendan, still standing behind the camera.

'Hmm, nope,' I said, only because I have no clue on what Betty is on about, in fact, has anyone reminded her to have her medication? While Daniel is entertaining Betty's idea of changing the world, I notice the camera crew focus on the discussion Daniel is having with Betty so I take the time to stalk this new young fiancée of Rick's on social media.

I started by scrolling through Rick's online profile, but a search of his friends list came up with no Ellen, nor on his profile page, not that I am friends with Rick on any social media pages so it could be a settings he did to prevent me from stalking him.

This Charming Dilemma

But Rick is forgetting I am his wedding planner and I have Ellen's full name and date of birth right here in front of me.

Ellen Willow, her name is Ellen Willow.

Hmm, appropriate I suppose, goes with her fairytale looks. A quick search through the social networks reveals nothing, and according to the registration form she has filled out for me, she has put Rick's address in Wivial not her own, unless they are living together.

A Google search reveals there is not much out there in cyber space that entertains anyone by that name and nothing is coming up on any professional networking sites either. I mean what 23 year old warm blooded woman doesn't want to be stalked on social media!

'Lisa!' Betty called from across the room, 'are you going to come and sign this?'

Daniel is giving me a pained look as I reluctantly leave my work station and stroll over to Betty and the crew, without paying too much attention I put my signature on the blank piece of paper.

'Smile,' says Betty, as she snaps a picture on the CWA's iphone, 'there.'

She smiled proudly to herself at the photo she just took, 'you are now the official ambassador for our 'Ban the Mine' campaign.'

'I'm what?'

'Well I must be off,' she said, satisfied with the result of the morning, 'I'll upload this photo to our new facebook page Daniel has very kindly set up for me.'

Daniel doesn't really look happy that he set up a facebook page and I will definitely be asking later why he encouraged Betty to do anything with social media, I mean the last thing Betty needs is more encouragement to speak her mind!

Anyway not sure what being an ambassador for a Ban the Mine campaign entails but I bet it doesn't get far with Betty trying to navigate her way around a facebook page.

But if this day couldn't get any more well... interesting, I am now wanting some privacy to contemplate the possibility that I have it all wrong and it's actually Rick I crave and not Jake.

My god I'm about to cry.

I make my way back to my desk to start the process of putting together the wedding for Rick and the soon to be Mrs Crankshaw, Mrs Ellen Crankshaw, doesn't have the same kind of ring to it then Ellen Willow, or Lisa Crankshaw.

What the hell? Did I just *say* that? Phew, just thought it.

I am so preoccupied with starting the whole wedding thing I almost forgot the camera is rolling.

I logged on to my email and send off a message to the celebrant to see if she can do the service for Rick and this Ellen. I notice my hand is shaking as I navigate the computer

This Charming Dilemma

mouse, might be from lack of food as I am too afraid to eat anything in case I throw up in front of the camera.

'Lisa are you okay with doing Rick's wedding?' Daniel asked, with a look of concern, planting himself on the corner of my desk.

'Yes of course,' I scoffed, 'I'm a professional, I would do the same thing if it was you,' what the hell did I mean by *that.*

'And besides, I'm not going to perform the ceremony, I'm going to get old Rosie to do it.'

'Okay then,' Daniel said, satisfied, 'but if you need to talk it through.'

'Oh pfff, thanks, but honestly it's all good.'

'Lisa?' Brendan interrupted from the depths of his tablet. 'Just on that last statement, could you please elaborate on your feelings a bit more.'

'My feelings?'

'You know, just to give our viewers a bit more of an insight on how you feel about planning your ex boyfriends wedding.'

'Oh. Okay, well I feel like…'

I paused to ponder this, I feel like Rick had deliberately done this to make me jealous.

I mean seriously, isn't he batting above his average a bit with a 23 year old fairytale princess.

I mean okay yes we were engaged to be married so obviously Rick has high standards, it's just that, what would they have in common. Seriously Rick is like older than his age, he always acts older than 39 so what is the deal with dating someone so much younger!

'Lisa?'

'Hmm? Oh, well I guess if Rick is ready to take the next step in his life and marry someone who is much much younger than him to fill the empty egotistic void in his life then I am fully supportive of his choice,' I beamed. Not sure I said those exact words but something like that.

Brendan doesn't answer me but I can see he is pondering another question and I really don't want to go into the whole "am I jealous I am organising Rick's wedding" thing while there is a high chance I am in child with his niece or nephew, so I start to look busy and important again and go to my official wedding event check-list on my computer to see what I have to do next. Okay I have been doing this for a whole year now and I almost have it down pat but sometimes a girl needs a check-list so she doesn't forget the important things, like that time I was so caught up in organising Tara and Danny's wedding with a medieval theme (they were both into gothic stuff, well not really, they just mentioned to me that they liked Game of Thrones and didn't really have any ideas for a wedding so we went medieval) that I forgot to book the horse she was meant to ride in on. But thanks to Daniel's quick thinking while I frantically looked to hire a horse off the internet two hours before the wedding,

This Charming Dilemma

the whole day was saved. Can't say what exactly Daniel did as Matt won't let me mention it to anyone, but I now use a check-list to avoid any small things that could be overlooked.

So I have flicked an email off to the wedding celebrant, and put a star on that to remind me to chase that up.

Next is booking the reception and photographing venue. At Abby`toir.

God couldn't Rick have picked a different venue, I mean not only were we going to get married there after Matt and Neroli decided to go to McDonald's instead of getting married, but it's also where Rick and I met after he was hiding in the ceiling for all that time, which I may add has now been converted into a room which hosts many a honeymoon night, so I don't know what his game is but I'll go with it, I just don't have to like it.

'Lisa,' Daniel whispered, placing a piece of paper on my desk, 'you're frowning.'

'Frowning?'

'Yes, and squinting,' he whispered returning to his desk.

Oh that's right, I'm on camera.

Straightening my posture, and my face, I reach for the phone to call Millie to see if she can do the date for Rick's wedding.

I pick up the phone to call her in a poised and professional manner when Brendan interrupted.

'Lisa, could you please put that on speaker phone?'

'Um… why?'

'So we can hear how business is conducted here,' he said.

Oh shit.

'Oh right, sure.'

I dial the number and listen to the dial tone ring through the silent room, *please don't be there, please don't be there.*

Oh bugger.

'Abby'toir Bed and Breakfast,' Sid's dull and non inviting voice fills the silent room. Well thank god it's not Millie.

'Sid hi, it's Lisa… from Cannon and Collins Event Planning and Photography,' I added for professionalism, ignoring Brendan's "what the hell?" look.

'Yeah I know who you are,' said Sid sounding like he is not sure if it's a joke that he should be playing along with.

'I have a request for a wedding reception to be held on the 8th of October.'

'This year?' asked Sid puzzled.

'Well, yes.'

'Okay but isn't that the date of the knitted Mardi Gras?'

'What? How do you know that?'

This Charming Dilemma

'Cos Betty invited me to enter a float in the parade.'

Oh jeez.

'Well yes, yes it is, but we have to work around it somehow.'

'Can't your clients change their date?'

My god Sid is on fire today. Normally he agrees with everything.

Brendan is looking at me intently.

Actually what is up with him?

'That's a negative,' I said to Sid.

'Okay then,' he sighed like the Sid I know and love. 'Let me go and get the events book, Millie wants to talk to you.'

Noooo.

'What's happening?' asked Millie in her demanding voice.

'Oh Millie, hi,' I said in my upbeat voice, 'I'm just in my office with everyone,' I said with my hand waving gesturing around everyone in the room, 'and I have you on speaker phone,' I beamed.

Which I'm hoping Millie will take on board and therefore watch what she says.

'Well I was wondering, why is Fran insisting that the B&B enter a float in a parade. Did you suggest it?'

'No, no, not at all,' I rolled my eyes, 'it's just Betty's stupid... um I mean...' shit forgot cameras are on and this is going on TV. Must be diplomatic, 'I mean Betty's wonderful idea about maybe getting the local businesses on board.'

'Well you and Sid are on your own there, I don't have the time since this show has us running after this frikn...'

'Um... Millie,' I said, trying to stop her from going further, 'hang on I'll just adjust the speaker on this phone,' I said through gritted teeth.

Has Millie forgotten I have a camera crew following me? No, of course she hasn't, she was just about to bag them out on speaker phone. It's just Millie.

'Oh hang on Amy's just stuffing dog biscuits into her nappy again,' Millie said, 'here Sid wants to talk to you again.'

'Yes Sid, how did you get on?' I beamed, trying to get a little professionalism back into this phone call.

'Yeah I've written it in the diary,' he said, 'we having nothing else on that day apart from the knitted Mardi Gras so just get back to me on a time, and I need a name.'

'Ahem,' I cleared my throat, 'under Willow.'

'Oh that's a nice name,' said Sid, 'is that a first name?'

'Last. The first name is Ellen.'

'And the groom?'

This Charming Dilemma

'Do you need to know?' I asked, shooting a glance at Brendan who is still looking at me intently.

'No I s'pose not,' said Sid, 'I guess one name would be okay. Oh sorry, yes we do,' Sid said again, just as I went to breath out, 'I'll need both later anyway to have for the notice board.'

'I'll give it to you later, I mean we still have plenty of time.'

'Why don't you just give it to me now.'

'Cos umm, I have other stuff to do and can't really spell it anyway.'

Now Brendan is really looking at me with intense drama expectations. Is he waiting for me to have a meltdown over Rick? Of course he is, this is the kind of trashy soap opera direction he obviously wants to go in since he learned of my previous engagement to Rick, well I'm not going to give him the satisfaction.

'Okay well no problem,' said Sid's mopey voice through the speaker, 'you can tell me later, that's fine...'

'Rick.' I said, shooting a stern look towards Brendan.

'Pardon?' said Sid down the phone.

'Groom's name is Rick.'

'Rick,' said Sid, slowly repeating it as he jots it down in the event planner.

'Last name? Oh that's right you can't spell it, never mind I'll...'

'Crankshaw.' I said in another direct tone just to get my point across.

'Crankshaw?' asked Sid puzzled, 'as in Rick Crankshaw?'

'What!?' came the shrill voice of Millie.

Shit Sid must have also been on speaker phone.

'Rick Crankshaw, as in your ex Rick?'

'Ahem yes, that is correct but could you just confirm that date once more please.'

'Your Rick is getting married and having the reception here!' exclaimed Millie, 'oh my god that is hilarious, and who is the thing he is marrying?'

Oh god someone shoot me now.

'Oh she is lovely,' I beamed to the camera, 'and Rick and her are so happy and...'

'Ellen Willow,' sniggered Millie down the other end of the phone obviously looking at the name on the event planner, 'wow what a nerve Rick has.'

'Okay well thanks for that, better go now, will confirm, okay bye.' I disconnected the phone quickly before Millie starts spouting details off about Rick's and mine's former life together and how I met him in the ceiling of my house and I didn't think that was creepy at all.

This Charming Dilemma

'Think I'll go and get a cup of tea,' I said to the floor which will look on camera like I was talking to myself, but I had to say something after I disconnected from Millie, the whole room had fallen silent.

'Lisa, is this the same day as the Mardi Gras parade?' Daniel asked from the depths of his desk, looking at the conflicting dates in front of him.

'Oh yes,' I beamed, 'but it's all good, we will get around it somehow.'

'Yes, but you can't be in two places at once,' said Daniel.

'Agreed yes, but it's only the street parade, I'm sure Betty and the rest of the CWA crew will have it running smoothly,' I beamed, trying to get my point across.

'Yes I'm sure they will have,' Daniel chuckled, 'but aren't you meant to be their parade queen, not to mention the ambassador of Ban the Mine you just signed up for? I'm sure the focus is around that campaign.'

Yeah I was kinda hoping to avoid it.

'Well yes, but I'll work something out,' I pressed again, not knowing what the hell I am going to tell Betty but I'm sure some opportunity will present itself.

Daniel went to open his mouth again when my phone rang thank god, Brendan signals to me to put the speaker phone on again. I mean seriously.

'Good err, afternoon Cannon and Collins Event Planning and Photography...'

'Yeah it's just me again,' said Millie, 'I forgot to tell you the antenatal classes start this week...'

Arggh!!

'Oh look at that' I said red faced as the phone made a loud crashing noise as it hit the floor. 'I must have accidentally knocked it off the desk, silly me,' I tsked at myself, bending down to pick it up.

Bloody Millie, thank god for my quick thinking of swiping the phone off the desk.

I can feel four sets of eyes on me as I bend down to retrieve it, well three sets, Daniel knows so he is just probably looking for my reaction. Actually there is no dial tone coming from the phone so I hope I haven't stuffed it completely.

'Where was I? Oh yes, cup of tea,' I said to the room, replacing the phone back on the desk and carrying my burning face off towards the kettle.

I'm hoping no-one took notice of Millie's little reminder, and as I told her anyway I am not ready for antenatal classes yet, I mean I do have another four and a half months to worry about this type of thing so I don't know why she feels the need to sign me up now, and besides I am too busy. I have my ex fiancé's wedding to plan and a Mardi Gras parade all on the same day. But just in case Millie calls back I had better send her a text message.

This Charming Dilemma

I have just realised I haven't eaten anything and this baby is starting to remind me. I am starting to crave this cup of tea that seems to be taking forever to steep. Although I would rather not eat anything for a whole century right now it is best I have a biscuit with it. 'Want me to come with you?' asked Daniel, coming up behind me, as I reached for the jar of coffee biscuits we have for clients, 'to the antenatal classes?' he elaborated after I gave him a blank stare.

Which means everyone did take notice, or hopefully just Daniel, just play cool and no-one will suspect anything except Daniel cos he already knows. Okay over thinking now.

'Oh that, yes well I don't really think it's necessary just yet,' I scoffed, 'Millie is overreacting, as per normal,' I said, rolling my eyes to the heavens.

Tea has finally steeped, I am so looking forward to this moment.

'Lisa dear!' Betty's shrill voice calls out, followed by the shop's bell as I'm about to take a sip of glorious tea, 'where are you? We need you at the stall now!'

'She's in here,' Daniel called back to her as I look for possible places to hide. Damn that woman ruining a good cup of tea!

'Well we need her at the refreshment stand now!' Betty is panting like she just ran a marathon, 'we have the press there waiting for a photo and a story about our campaign, we need Lisa there.'

'Okay, well I'll just finish my tea,' I said through a mouthful of biscuit, and thinking about my next sip of tea and not about the fact that I don't want to be in a photo shoot or campaign and how the hell am I going to get out of this one.

'We haven't got time for tea,' Betty exclaimed, 'we need to be there now Lisa,' as she grabs me by the hand and steers me towards the door. 'Don't worry about that!' she said as I tried to grab my cup, 'plenty more tea after we finish. Come on Lisa, justice doesn't wait, I hope you have prepared a speech.'

I want to cry as Betty pulls me towards the shop door followed hastily by Brendan and the film crew, I come to the realisation that my life is still controlled by old people and I really must work on that!

But at least I got something into my stomach to hold me for half an hour.

The refreshment stall isn't far from the shop but it feels like I have walked the entire length of the Nile, especially when you have a camera crew in tow, everyone in town is staring, and you are still craving a cup of tea.

We arrive at the CWA refreshment stand and there are people everywhere! Including the local paper and some other official looking photographer.

Oh god and there is a small podium. I hope they are not seriously expecting me to make a speech.

Good god they are!

This Charming Dilemma

'Okay Lisa, you're up,' Betty said, shoving me in front of the podium while her, Fran, and Mary roll out what looks like a slogan on a piece of butchers paper.

I glanced at the paper to give me some clue as to what I am actually making the speech about and all it says is, *Ban the Mine!* Yep not really helping.

And there are a lot more people here than just a couple of newspaper photographers. Oh my god what has Betty organised?

Maggie and Gloria are also here but Maggie clearly doesn't want any part of it. Gloria is busy signing people up on the petition.

Actually I might go with team Maggie.

'Lisa!' Betty hissed, 'speech, now!' I look out into the faces in front of me and I have no clue why I am standing here, apart from the Ban the Mine campaign, but I don't know jack about that.

But Brendan is here with the camera crew and I have to say friken something.

'Good um… morning, sorry, afternoon,' I said as my eyes diverted to the town clock in the street so I am not looking at what seems to be half the town standing in front of me.

Oh shit, that's right, that clock stopped years ago.

'Argh I mean good… um… day, yes well thank you for all gathering here today to join us on our Ban the Mine campaign,' I started clapping, to drive my point.

Apart from Betty and Jono at the back who is always up for a ban anything campaign, I seem to be the only one clapping.

'Yes well, very bad thing this is for our um… area. Hope you all agree, thank you for coming,' I said, wrapping it up, I mean I'm sure the sign Betty is flapping behind me says it all.

'Lisa!' Betty hissed again as I tried to escape the podium, 'tell them why we are running this campaign,' she said, ushering me back.

I should just tell her I have no idea why.

Oh hang on, don't I have a brochure thing she gave me this morning? That may offer me some clue as to why they don't want a giant hole in ground.

I mean as long as no-one *falls* in the hole, then what is the issue?

Shit, left my bag back at the office.

'Lisa!' Betty hissed as the silent faces continue to stare me down with their expectations.

Which means I am going to have to wing it.

'Ahem, the reason we don't want a mine is because it, um, leaves a hole and if you happen to be walking along at night and happen to not see it, it could become a umm, safety issue.'

'Do you know if Council took into consideration the contamination that will run into the irrigation channels on the remaining farms?' came a woman's voice at the back of the crowd, someone who looked like they save trees in their spare time.

'Um, no, not personally, but I'm sure they have considered it being a Council and all. Okay, any other questions? Okay then well...'

'So why is such a small group of self righteous people like yourselves deciding for the rest of us that it's not welcome here? I bet none of you thought about the jobs it would create for this area,' said an aggressive male voice in the background, someone who looked like he would destroy trees in his spare time.

I can feel the wrath of Betty, she's seething behind me at the comment and I cannot blame her, I mean how rude, well yes okay, Betty can be stubborn and darn right impossible and yes self righteous is definitely in there somewhere, but no need to point it out to her. But I do have to agree with the scary man, if it is going to hand out jobs then seriously what is the issue?

'Good point!' came another voice from the background, 'what right have you lot got to boycott something that you obviously don't have all the facts about,' said the woman who looked like the she resented the trees and had been drinking since breakfast.

But again, I have to agree.

'And who had the authority to call this meeting anyway,' shouted another voice from the side, 'I don't see any of our local councillors here!'

'It's a public discussion,' Betty shouted back, 'we have a right to voice our disgust, no one has to authorise this.'

The crowd broke out into loud discussions amongst themselves and Betty, Fran, and Mary are pleading with me to do something. Maggie is standing there with "told you so" written on her face and Gloria has gone into hiding.

Matt appeared with his takeaway coffee in hand pretending to have a handle on the situation being a "bodyguard" and all, Damo is nowhere to be seen, so I guess the Men In Black duo don't really deliver when times call for it.

Betty continued to hiss at me to do something, but I mean the drunk lady is right, I don't have all the facts and I don't know why Betty is insisting that this proposed mine is evil, I mean it would mean more jobs so what is wrong with that. Just because Betty and the CWA ladies are retired and have time to knit doesn't mean that the next person doesn't want a job, well that's where I stand and I'm sure they will sort it out amongst themselves.

'Lisa!' Betty yelled, her face burning red, giving me a "get off your arse" look.

Oh god, okay fine, I mean it's not like I volunteered for this, Betty should be grateful I am here at all.

This Charming Dilemma

But unless I have all the facts here I'm going to have to make it up as I go along, and besides the drunk lady is right, what do we know, so I'll just start a calm discussion.

'Order, order!' I yelled to the crowd. The noise dimmed immediately, surprising me, I felt a surge of power at the fact that a hundred people are now hanging on my every word, shame I don't have any words to give.

Okay, make it up, at least it will get Betty off my back.

'Ahem, the reason we have put forward the idea of boycotting this mine and opening this discussion is, um, because…'

And then I saw an older gentleman in the crowd with one of those information brochures in his hand, yes that's it, I'll wave that around.

'It's because, well um…' I said, stalling for time as I strut into the crowd to grab the information from the gentleman's hands, who by the way seems reluctant to hand it over.

'… it is because of this,' I exclaimed, holding the brochure in the air, 'I mean come on community how much do we actually know about this mine?' I said, making my way back to my spot behind the podium, 'I mean is it a good thing, is it a bad thing, well we don't know because all we have is this!' I said, tapping violently on the brochure, 'so I say let's not judge, let's all join together for the best possible outcome, let's not ban the mine, let's just hear what they have to say first and then decide.'

Man I am on fire.

'Lisa!' Betty hissed, 'what are you doing? You are supposed to be our ambassador against this, I even posted your picture on facebook.'

'But Betty, they do have a good point, it might be a good thing.'

And besides that drunk lady is scary.

'Like contaminating water and cutting up good agricultural land! Coal is out, out I tell you,' Betty exclaimed, her voice getting louder and louder.

'Well we don't really know that,' I scoffed, realising that the aggressive man who started this debate is now standing next to the podium having an argument with Fran who is just shaking her head to everything the man says.

'Yeah, get ya facts straight first,' said the drunk scary lady.

'Did you want a go!?' said Betty, rising to her challenge.

Oh god there is about to be a punch up between old people and drunken aggressive people, I don't have a microphone or a gavel so I think I will just wrap this up by walking away.

To be honest a mine is a mine, don't know why people are getting so worked up about it, clearly they have nothing better to think about.

This Charming Dilemma

'Okay well discuss amongst yourselves, thank you for your time,' I said, about to depart while Betty, Fran, and the two instigators continue to verbally abuse each other.

'Um Lisa,' Daniel said, sidling up beside me. I didn't realise Daniel was here, I wonder what side of the fence he sits on? About the mine I mean, not about equal rights for same sex relationships, I mean we all know where Daniel stands on that one.

'You do realise that this mine is going to sit right on the boundary of your place.'

~

~~~~~~~~~
~~~~~~~~~

7

I'm finally back in the shop and as much as I dreamt about this cup of tea in the last half an hour, I cannot bring myself to drink it as I suddenly don't feel so good.

I mean a mine, sitting at the boundary of Abby'toir B&B. I can't imagine Sid will be too happy about it, Millie probably won't care as long as it doesn't interrupt what she is doing but really, can you imagine the noise? Not to mention the view of our surrounds.

Betty and Fran ended up having to be coaxed away from the scene by Daniel and Brendan after Betty threatened the drunk woman with her knitting needles. There had been a few heated discussions amongst the crowd, some good, some not so good. And Gloria, who was trying to hide, was suddenly overwhelmed by people wanting to sign her petition to ban the mine.

While the other half of the crowd decided to start their own petition to ban the Ban the Mine campaign, the rest of them wanted to put money on who would win a fight between Betty and the drunk lady, who I know now as Elaine.

This Charming Dilemma

Didn't help that Matt was egging Betty on by chanting "fight, fight" over and over, tainting the upstanding bodyguard image he was trying to project for the cameras.

But we have all gathered back in the shop for a nice cup of tea to figure out the finer details of what just happened and how on earth did Betty get so many people there so quickly. Apart from Fran who remained down at the lemonade stand.

'Facebook,' Betty said proudly after I, well, asked her directly how the hell she got so many people there in such a short time. 'I did a facebook event, it's the facebook revolution, see,' she said proudly, bringing the event up on her phone tagging everyone she is friends with on facebook, and yes there I am, the face of the Ban the Mine campaign.

'And it was a disaster,' said Maggie, scorning at us, 'I think we shouldn't be dragging the CWA into this political debate,' she said, her face stone cold, 'I mean look how that turned out, now the whole town is divided.'

'Well I for one thought that it went well,' said Betty, her face looking very smug.

Now I have read all the facts and saw the map of the proposed mine, I cannot believe no one told me sooner.

I mean aren't we supposed to be notified about these things?

Oh wait, I was.

'I think we should pull back,' said Maggie not letting her disapproval go unnoticed.

'Nonsense!' said Betty, sipping her tea, 'we need to protect this town, we are an agricultural area, not a coal producing area, you can't eat coal.'

'It's not up to the CWA,' continued Maggie, 'we are a scone producing, cake making organisation. We help in crisis's and support the community, not divide it over some political issue.'

Matt has arrived back in the shop and is now getting his phone out ready to record another round of fight club with Betty. Mary is watching the exchange between them like a tennis match, while I'm still thinking of ways to make this reality show a bit more exciting as John the cameraman zones in on Betty, I mean honestly isn't he falling asleep by now at the old people debate going on.

'Well I feel it's a good thing,' said Betty, continuing to take her stand, 'and besides tell Maggie here how many signatures of support we have Gloria.'

Gloria looks like she wants to hide.

'Oh never mind, pass it here,' scorned Betty when Gloria continued to stand there not knowing what side of the fence she should be sitting on.

'Fifty two!' Betty exclaimed, tapping on Gloria's clipboard in defiance at Maggie's wilting look, 'Fifty two and that's only from this morning! '

'And at Bingo last night,' squeaked Gloria.

This Charming Dilemma

'Look it doesn't matter how many signatures we collect!' Maggie carried on in frustration, 'the point is, we shouldn't be the organisation that is collecting them!'

'Ladies, ladies,' said Daniel stepping in as Betty looks like she is about to rise out of her seat and lunge towards Maggie. 'Can I suggest you all put it to a vote whether you want to continue this campaign,' Daniel said, his tone suggesting getting this resolved so he can have his office space back.

'Yes good idea!' Betty exclaimed, 'let's have a vote on it since all members are here, well except for Fran, she is at the lemonade stand but I can facetime her,' she said getting out her phone.

'You could always take this meeting down there,' mumbled Daniel who is now tapping away on his computer behind his desk.

Maggie rolls her eyes as she threw her hands in the air in defeat, 'well someone better take minutes,' she said, getting the last say in.

I am tuned into the conversation around me and I am a bit concerned about this mine but I am really still focused on my direction in this reality show as I still haven't found my niche or my fabulous, I mean these old people certainly are killing it.

'Lisa?'

'Hmmm?' I asked as I realised all eyes were on me.

'Are you going to lead a vote,' Maggie said with a stern look.

'Oh okay, is this a vote to see if we should…'

'Carry on with the campaign,' Maggie reminded me.

'Yes of course, well um, raise your hand if you are all for carrying on with Ban the Mine?'

'Okay Betty… and anyone else?'

I look at Mary who looks like she has a migraine coming on, while Gloria seems visibility shaken, but still no show of hands.

'Okay then, well that would be one so far.'

'Two!' snapped Betty, turning the phone around so I can see Fran on the phone screen vigorously waving her arm in the air.

Maggie rolls her eyes.

'Okay then, two,' oh god, I can see where this is going.

'All against,' I said casually as Maggie, Gloria and Mary raise their hands.

'Traitors,' grumbled Betty.

'Okay three, well then that must mean…'

And thank god no one asked me as it means I won't have to be the face of Ban the Mine campaign.

'It's not that I am for the mine going ahead Betty!' Maggie continued to argue interrupting my flow,

This Charming Dilemma

'it's just that I feel our organisation is not the right one to get involved in political matters.'

'How can you not get involved in this,' Betty continued, 'I mean after all, your husband's family and the Crankshaw's have been neighbours for two generations, which means it affects you more than us. And let's face it, we wouldn't be dealing with this if it wasn't for the Crankshaw's, you can't tell me it doesn't piss you off in the slightest that your neighbours betrayed you and forced you into this, so I cannot see why you wouldn't want to fight it.'

I can see this is going to be a long day and Daniel has already given up on trying to concentrate on his work as he goes to fetch another cup of tea in his fancy china cup while Maggie and Betty continue to argue, and as much as I quickly want to hurry this vote along, I feel like I have had a slight knock to the head, I mean I did ask for a sign and here it is.

A picture of Julia Roberts jumps out at me from a copy of a woman's magazine in front of me, oh my god, that's it! I could be the next Erin Brockovich.

I mean Betty did say something about this may affect the water or something.

Oh my god, why didn't I think of this before, Lisa Collins, fighting for environmental justice while planning her ex fiancé's wedding.

We'll just skip the part about me possibly expecting his twin brothers' baby.

And speaking of Jake and Rick for that matter, why the hell did they agree to this, I mean Rick was always spouting off about how important farming was to the family and how he despised Jake when Jake decided to sell some land off to developers for a housing estate. Hang on, but it wasn't a housing estate, oh my god!!

I remember that day. The day I broke into Jake's house - okay not "broke" into Jake's house per se, the door was open and we were seeing each other at the time so it was only a little break and enter to see if I could find anything out of the ordinary - but I do remember he had plans sitting on his kitchen table of the farm and some development going on, I thought it was for a housing estate, maybe it wasn't, maybe it was a proposed mine!

No wonder Jake came back, it wasn't to mend bridges with his family, it was to collect money, and what about Rick, is he in on it as well?

And oh my god, Mr and Mrs Crankshaw! They must have known, which means the house fire wasn't accidental, they were playing the whole town all along. The town that supported them through everything, the town they claim is their extended family, the town that their children's children grew up in and their nephews, and oh my god did Pamela know what was happening? Is that why her and Jake were secret lovers before he ditched her, it was all about money! Did they not care about the people left behind!

Well someone has to reveal the truth around here and that person is me.

This Charming Dilemma

Shit better do something before Maggie and Betty get even more out of control.

'We have all been hoodwinked!' I stated, rising from my chair, waving the mining information brochure around as the room suddenly went dead quiet at my outburst.

'A scam has been secretly operating right under our noses and we didn't even know it,' I said, waving my finger around now for effect. 'Not only have they sent us a little colourful booklet trying to fool us into thinking that this is for our benefit, they have been playing us for years!' I paused to take in the response from the room.

Betty looks around the room with an "I told you so" smirk on her face, while there are stony blank stares coming from the rest of them, but John seems to have the camera rolling pointing at me which is the plan.

But I don't seem to be having a shocking effect on them so I better step it up if I need team Ban the Mine while revealing the truth about the Crankshaws and Pamela Horton (only cos I don't like her and neither do the CWA members so it could give them a little nudge if they know she is indirectly involved) while making Lisa the Erin Brockovich of the reality television show world!

Daniel has reappeared from making his cup of tea and has the most astonished look on his face as I kick off my shoes and climb onto the coffee table for effect.

'Your community has been invaded!' I said, causing Maggie to roll her eyes, 'invaded by corporate um… greed.'

I really must work on my wording.

'And who sold out your community, it wasn't just the companies and the fact there is coal in these parts and they will um… contaminate our water, use up good umm… milk producing land, and pump fumes into the atmosphere with their big heavy machinery, oh no, it was your friends, your neighbours, people you have trusted to look after your grandchildren, it was… the Crankshaws,' I said in a dramatic loud whisper for effect.

Maggie rolls her eyes again, 'yes Lisa I get it, but again I must drive home the point that it's not up to the CWA to get involved with political matters for or against.'

'Oh that is rubbish,' Betty said, 'the CWA can get involved with whatever their blimmin well community gets involved in, I mean for god sake, we're not the gardening club.'

'Betty the CWA is incorporated, I think you will find it's written in the constitution that we cannot get involved with this,' Maggie pressed on.

'Constitution,' Betty scoffed, 'do you happen to have a copy of this *Constitution* Maggie, because I for one haven't seen a copy for years, let alone would bore myself with what it actually says.'

'We should have a copy somewhere,' Maggie insisted, looking at Gloria for confirmation,

This Charming Dilemma

'we are an incorporated organisation, and part of that is following the model rules of the constitution set out by our governing body in 1931.'

'Yes we do have a copy in our records, but I didn't bring it with me,' Gloria squawked, hastily going though the folder she had in front of her that she knew darn well didn't hold a copy of anything, but didn't want to get on Maggie's bad side either.

'That's okay,' Maggie smiled sweetly at Gloria, 'Betty should have read it when she was secretary.'

'That was years ago,' Betty scolded, 'how the hell am I meant to know what is written on a piece of paper, it probably got filed with the other useless information, it's like terms and conditions, no one ever reads those.'

'My point is again Betty that we cannot get involved.'

'Okay Maggie, if it is not written in the constitution that the CWA cannot get involved with political matters, would you?' pressed Betty raising one eyebrow.

Maggie rubbed her brow in frustration.

'No,' she said, 'no I wouldn't.'

Maggie goes to speak again when Daniel steps in, I am still standing on the coffee table but not really feeling like I have my leadership mojo going on, and John still has the camera rolling.

'Ladies, again, can I suggest that you vote or carry the vote that you just had,' Daniel said, his patience wearing thin, not helped by the fact he has a 3pm photo shoot he is trying to get ready for.

'Well as I recall, it was two for and three against,' said Maggie 'and the only person who didn't vote is Lisa, now is that right Gloria?'

Gloria quickly checks her notes she is holding in her hands, 'yes, that's right,' she nods.

Now all eyes are on me and I can see where this is going. Doesn't matter which way I decide, no one is going to be happy, even though Betty is looking at me with big expectations that I will swing towards team Betty and Fran, I need to take them on a new direction.

I need them to feel the burning desire to save their community, I need them to be on Team Lisa, environmental activist and revealer of truths!

And I better say something quick as all is silent and the camera is pointed at me.

'This is not about the vote!' I started, holding the brochure up again for effect, 'this is about our community!' Betty goes to open her mouth but I silenced her with my hand, 'this is about our land!' I said, pointing to the ground, 'this is about a small group of people selling us out!' I said pointing to nothing at all,

This Charming Dilemma

'this is not about whether or not the CWA needs to be involved, this is about us as a group of concerned citizens!' I said raising my voice a notch.

I notice Daniel has turned his attention to me so I must be moving in the right direction cos normally he doesn't react to my spiels he just lets me get on with it, it's like background noise to him.   Running with my newfound passion I stepped down from the coffee table to pace the room. 'I say stuff the vote and go with our hearts, as individuals, not the CWA!' I said shooting a glance at Maggie who raised one eyebrow at my statement. 'This community doesn't need a great big hole in the ground or um... horrible ground water,' I continued, 'or people like the Crankshaws and their good-looking nephews to sell us out to corporate companies leaving us dealing with the possibility of ruining our land and causing um... cancer...'

'Actually an open cast mine doesn't really cause cancer,' said Mary boldly before bowing her head at the wrath of Betty's glare.

'This community deserves to remain intact for our children and our children's children,' I said addressing all of them who have now formed an unofficial circle around me blocking the camera, grrr. I move back and climb on top of the coffee table for exposure to John who has now refocused the camera back on me and not the back of the old people. But now I have their attention, it's time to deliver the bottom line. 'Betty you have been here for two generations, does this town need a mine.'

'Hell no!' said Betty, fist pumping the air.

'Gloria, you're always supporting environmental issues, would you like to see the landscape ruined.'

'Um… no,' Gloria squawked behind her clipboard, not daring to look at Maggie.

'Fran,' I said yelling toward the phone Betty has now held up, 'you have been friends with the Crankshaws for 50 years, did you ever think you would see the day where they would sell our own back yard to development?'

'Bastards!' stated Fran through the phone.

'So I say, forget the CWA and its constitution, I say forget about offending people that we have known for generations, I say if you don't want a mine in our town then stand up for it as individuals all together for our town, I say let's Ban the Mine and take ownership of our community,' I said, pausing for effect, 'I say, let's take this corporation down, let's start banning the mine, so who is with me?' I said, raising my hand in the air in solidarity as I look around the room after delivering the first of many speeches I intend to deliver on my newfound reality TV path as I waited in anticipation for the chimes of a "hell yes" to fill the room.

Silent blank faces stare back at me and I know John still has the camera rolling. Oh for god's sake, now Betty decides to stop ranting as she starts cleaning her glasses. Have they all turned down their hearing aids, has no one heard what I just said. I'm sorry,' shouted Fran through the phone, 'are we still having a vote or what?'

8

Millie is rolling her eyes at me again.

It's early morning and after a very restless night of putting my plan together I decided to call a breakfast meeting and catch everyone while they are refreshed and enthused, I mean really I am about to launch something huge so I felt I need to capture the moment here. I knew Sid would be easy to convince to get on board with the whole Ban the Mine campaign but I knew Millie would be asking questions so I dragged out Amy's ABC environmentally safe, politically correct, toxic free blackboard and proceeded to draw them a picture of the potential devastation.

I wasn't feeling the enthusiasm I was hoping for from the CWA ladies back in the shop yesterday, especially in front of the cameras. I have to say it was a little disappointing considering Betty friken started it. You would think she would at least have fist pumped the air a little with my amazing speech.

But after much discussion about whether or not the vote was significant, we have decided not to use the CWA as the front banner for the Ban the Mine campaign. Betty got upset because she now has to redo the facebook page and Maggie was still adamant we shouldn't get involved at all, even as individuals. So it was finally decided to have another vote to quash the previous vote and a new motion was put forward to vote having an individual choice to get involved in the campaign to which Betty and I agreed.

Maggie and Mary disagreed, Gloria was still undecided due to offending people and Fran couldn't vote due to the phone battery dying which took more time as Betty fluffed around trying to find the charger. It was around that time Daniel gave up, postponed his 3 o'clock and went home to find peace.

So the result was:

Lisa Collins; face and president of the community Ban the Mine campaign.

Betty; vice president and social media expert (according to Betty).

And Fran.

And hopefully Sid and Millie once I convince them this is for the good of the community and not the fact I want them to help me build my environmental hero type image for my television career.

'Lisa what is that supposed to be?' asked Millie, pointing to my drawing of a big mining truck pumping emissions into the air.

'I think it's meant to be a train,' said Sid.

'Nah, its two giant beach balls smoking a joint,' said Damo who has made an awkward appearance with Matt.

This Charming Dilemma

'Look you're not getting the bigger picture here,' I said, frustrated with the lack of caring.

'They are going to build a big hole right over there,' I said, pointing to the direction of… well over there. 'That's next door to us Millie,' I said using my hand gesture to point it out to her.

'I think you mean *dig* a big hole,' said Sid, all coy and quiet.

'Oh she always does that,' joked Daniel in a teasing way, who has also happened to make an appearance after missing the conclusion of yesterday's meeting and the fact I messaged him inviting him to my presentation this morning.

'Lisa I realise what they have proposed for the area but at this stage we don't have all the facts.'

'It's all here in the brochure Millie,' I said impatiently tapping the brochure I have pinned to Amy's blackboard.

'Yes Lisa but have *you* read it.'

'Of course,' I scoffed.

I'm not going to tell her I skimmed over it.

'The thing is,' said Daniel, 'from what I have read, submissions haven't even been requested, the company has to present to the community before submitting an application so at this stage it's a proposal, not a sure thing.'

'Yes that's the way I read it too and that's what I am saying, my concern is if we jump on the bandwagon too soon it could easily divide us from the community and therefore hurt our business,' Millie added.

Daniel nods in agreement.

Bloody hell I thought he was on my side, bloody Millie takes all the good people for her side.

'It won't hurt our business,' I scoffed, 'we are simply defending our way of life, and besides do you really want Amy growing up around errr emissions and greenhouse gases and stuff.'

Now Millie is looking at me suspiciously. 'Why do you care about this so much?' she asked, folding her arms.

All eyes are on me, including the camera, I mean I can't believe Millie asked me this, after all she knows I'm pregnant, has she considered that it may be because *I* don't want *my* child growing up next to a hole, I mean that is part of it, but seriously does she need to ask?

But I have to answer her because everyone is expecting me to answer, including my potential future television fans.

'Because Millie, I care about environment and stuff and...'

'Lisa I finished downloading Erin Brockovich for you,' said Matt throwing a USB stick at me.

'Ah ha!' said Millie, with a smug look on her face.

Shit! Bloody Matt.

This Charming Dilemma

'What? I haven't seen that movie,' I said in my defense.

Bloody Matt, I asked him to download it to get some bloody tips.

Millie raised one eyebrow at me. 'You know it's about a woman who fought a major company on an environmental issue right?' said Millie, full of sarcasm.

'Yes Millie and it so happens I'm into caring for our environment!' I hit back, my face burning.

'Then you are better off watching a documentary on the effects of modern living on the environment if you are that concerned,' Millie carried on in a sarcastic tone.

'For your information Millie...' I said, not knowing what I was going to say but knowing I had to hit back somehow.

Oh I know.

'I got approached to do this,' I said, triumphantly, 'remember, from the CWA.'

'Is this over wif,' said Matt suddenly coming out of his vow of silence around Marline, 'cos me and Damo got stuff to do and dis is boring and Lisa woke us up really early.'

I look around the room and I can see that my presentation is still not going to convince them.

I cannot see why not, it's a killer picture of what we are dealing with here. And I can feel my face still burning red, it's like Millie has blown my cover plan to launch myself into celebrity stardom in front of the very camera that was going to make it happen.

But with Millie's constant suspicion and Daniel's logical insights and Matt's… well dumb-arse attitude about anything, I can see that I'm not going to convince them. Even if I covered myself in coal and went on a hunger strike they still wouldn't see it my way.

Daniel and Millie are still locked into a serious discussion about the division it will bring in the community. God this is so unfair, why can't they just see things my way and do as I want them to.

'Well sorry to waste your time,' I said in a huff, 'I'll just take this,' I said picking up Amy's blackboard and tucking it under my arm, 'enjoy the big hole next door,' I said before passing John and the camera as I hastily exited the kitchen. Couldn't hear what was said when I did but I am sure they will come round.

'Lisa wait,' called Millie.

I spun around and re-entered the kitchen to hear her apology.

'Did you want your phone?' she asked, 'cos it's ringing.'

This Charming Dilemma

Later in the day, and still not really talking to Millie.

Betty rang with the good news that she has enough funds available to help out with the campaign. When I reminded her that we cannot use the CWA funds due to the CWA not wanting to get involved, Betty assures me these "funds" are coming from another source. I got the feeling I shouldn't ask any more questions, so I didn't. The less I know about that the better. Fran's probably sold some crochet blankets or something. Anyway I spent the rest of the morning in my room, watching the movie Erin Brockovich on my laptop. I really should be at the shop with Daniel but I am really tired and, well quite frankly, annoyed with Millie, so hiding away. She has tried to come in to talk to me but I am trying to give her the silent treatment, not because I want to, but because Millie has to learn she can't just go around squashing people's dreams in front of reality TV cameras and exposing plans like that, okay yes Daniel sided with her but Daniel doesn't say it like Millie does.

And after watching only half of the movie I am already convinced this is the path I need to take to showcase myself to the television world, an environmental hero. Okay so it's not riveting TV because most people are into well drama and stuff, not really sure, but people like the environment and trees and stuff, and look how more people are getting into it these days, like banning plastic, I mean how cool would it be if I can lead a trend here.

I mean there is always stuff on TV about ice burgs melting an stuff.

And Julie Roberts makes it look so sassy.

But where to begin. Unlike the film I don't work in a lawyers' office or have the boobs for this thing and this brochure tells me nothing.

Jake suddenly enters my head and I start to fiddle with the bedsheets in my trance. I would like to think Jake knew nothing about this proposed mine, but I know this isn't true, after all it is going right across their family property, and how convenient that it burnt down. Yep the writing is on the wall, and what about Rick, does he know what is going on? My mind wanders to thoughts of Rick and my past relationship with him but my thoughts seem to flick back to Jake, in fact Jake is making me angry with the possibility of what he has done to everyone, I mean really, what a bastard! Coming back into town after having an affair with Pamela, one of the local older women (and Matt's mum), while she siphons funds from the CWA so her and Jake can run away together after Jake sold of his portion of the family farm to developers. That was before he came back all apologetic and sexy and then there was the whole "accident" of the remaining part of the family farm burning down after which his Aunty and Uncle brought a brand new caravan and left town leaving everyone shocked and suspicious.

And now what has he gone and done, left me with his unborn child!

This Charming Dilemma

Okay to be fair Jake doesn't know he has an unborn child and I'm not really 100% sure it's his, but really, what the hell.

'Are you talking to me yet?' yelled Millie as she banged on the door.

I had planned on not talking to Millie a bit longer but my thoughts about Jake and the fact that Millie is banging on the door prompted me to come up with a plan.

The only way I can convince people that the mine is a bad thing is to get the facts, the real facts.

Like why did Jake all a sudden leave me, I mean, leave the area, to go work in a "mine".

And why did Jake suddenly become withdrawn from me after his Aunty and Uncle's family farm burnt down and all of a sudden a "mine" is going in.

And why did Jake insist on starting something with me only to dump me again, I mean it's all connected to the mine somehow.

But the bottom line is, I need the facts and who likes snooping so much that she is in the process of making a career out it. Why Millie of course.

Slapping a sweet smile on my face I call back to her that of course I am talking to her. Millie abruptly opens the door supporting a bowl of chocolate ice cream in her hands. Better tread carefully, Millie is premenstrual.

'So that text message you sent me earlier stating you will never speak to me again because I am the destroyer of all your dreams is not valid now?' she said, shoveling another spoonful of ice cream into her mouth.

'Pfft, water under the bridge,' I scoffed, 'so how are things with you?' I asked, getting all settled in for a heart to heart.

'Fine,' she said shrugging her shoulders.

'So tell me about this new career path you're taking,' I said in a caring and interested way, patting the side of the bed inviting her to sit down, 'how are you finding it?'

Millie stares back at me for a moment. 'You sound very cheesy.'

'No, this is my normal voice when I am interested in what my friend is interested in,' I said in a now irritated voice.

'What do you want?' she asks.

'Okay, okay,' I said, defeated, 'I need a big favour, huge.'

Millie rolls her eyes as she sits on the edge of the bed still shoveling ice cream into her mouth. 'Go on,' she says.

'I need you to do some investigating... on the mine,' I added bravely.

'Oh god Lisa, are you still banging on about that,' Millie said, 'let it go, you should be concentrating on other things, like this baby for instance.'

This Charming Dilemma

'Um Millie, this is about the baby.'

'Really… how so?' she said, about to jump on the bully train.

'Well the mine might affect my baby's health.'

'And…' Millie said.

'And it might affect our business, ever thought about that!' I added.

'And…'

Oh for god's sake, Millie is just too good at sniffing things out. 'Okay it's also about Jake,' I add, defeated.

'Bingo!' said Millie triumphant. 'Okay then,' she shrugged, 'what do you want me to do?'

What? I can't believe it, Millie isn't arguing, she's actually going to do this. Okay this hasn't happened before so need to calm down, my insides are jumping.

Unless it's the baby kicking.

'I need you to stalk… I mean, acquire, information about Jake and the farm burning down thing.'

'Because?' probed Millie some more.

'Because it's a public service,' I said, trying not to make it all about me, 'you know, the facts and all. The community has a right to know what goes on in their town Millie.'

'Then, nah!' she said, about to get off the bed.

'What do you mean no!' I cried, 'you said you would!'

'Oh I will,' she said, 'but unless you are going to tell me the real reason why, I won't.'

Bloody Millie, damn her for being good at this shit.

'Okay, okay, well it's not just about the community, it's also a tiny bit about me,' I said.

'Really,' Millie said in a droll voice, 'I would never have guessed.'

'You see I want to look into Jake's involvement into this mine,' I said, 'and I need a professional.'

'And what does this have to do with your unborn child?' Millie probed some more.

'Um… because he is the father,' I stated in my factual voice.

'Is he?' Millie threw in, just to remind me of that mistake. 'So is that the only reason?'

'Well no.'

Okay Millie has just thrown me a curve ball of doubt so I am going to have to step up and convince her.

'I just felt that maybe errr, if Jake is the father then I um… need to know if err, he is, you know, pure and not an arsonist and that.'

'And?'

This Charming Dilemma

'And well, that he is good for child support.'

'And?' said Millie in her stern voice.

'Okay, okay, and because I want to get the facts so I can expose people and become an environmental hero.'

'And,' Millie repeated herself.

'So I can have celebrity status like Erin Brockovich,' I said defeated.

'Okay sure, why not, sounds like fun,' said Millie, gathering her empty bowl.

'Really?' I asked in a state of shock, 'I mean, you will do it?'

Millie shrugged, 'well it's not Watergate but it would be good practice I suppose, talk about it tomorrow anyway. If you want any ice-cream I suggest you get it now,' she said before exiting the room obviously on her way to get more ice-cream.

I take a moment to process what just happened, Millie is on board with the whole environmental/dig the dirt up on Jake thing and I didn't even have to make stuff up, even with the whole celebrity stardom thing!

I'm so excited I think I *will* celebrate with some ice-cream. I have my new-found life force energy and with Millie on my side it will mean I will never have to explain anything to her.

Well for a while anyway.

Now I have Millie on the trail I will get to the bottom of this in no time. Leaping out of bed I make my way to the kitchen to fetch much deserved ice cream, John the cameraman catches me coming out of my room and sets the camera rolling as I make my way to the kitchen and start spooning ice-cream in to my bowl. He starts asking me questions in the background about the earlier presentation I made with Amy's blackboard and how I am feeling about it all and blah, blah, but since Millie agreed to snoop on Jake… I mean, find out facts, I have automatically become like a celebrity and started to talk to the camera like one.

I mean how easy is this.

I explain to the cameraman that environmental matters have always been a passion of mine and even mentioned my vision to move to the country and be self sufficient, well I didn't really, that was an ex boyfriends dream before I moved here, I just got stuck with this stupid house but they don't know that.

I must have been talking for a while as John signaled to me that he has to renew the battery or something. I finished off my second bowl of ice-cream I had managed to scoff down in-between giving the passionate environmental speech to John.

John left the room as if he was more dying to use the toilet than change a battery on a film camera. I notice Daniel sitting there on the chair near the big kitchen window.

Huh? How long was he sitting there for?

This Charming Dilemma

'Nice spiel,' he said in his Daniel voice that I always appreciate. 'So you're really going to do this campaign?'

'Absolutely,' I said, stuffing a chocolate filled pastry into my mouth that I happened to find in the fridge after my brain had a temporary meltdown and went to put the ice-cream in the fridge rather than the freezer.

Daniel didn't say anything but just looked at me for a moment as if he was contemplating saying something.

'What you doing here still?' I asked through another mouthful.

'Actually come to see you,' he said, 'I want to ask you about your appointment, when is it?'

'You should know that,' I said, 'you write them down in my diary.'

'No not work,' he said, his eyes shooting to my belly, 'your ultrasound.'

'Ohhhh that,' I said forgetting for a moment I'm pregnant as I hunt the fridge for something else to eat. 'Ummm... not sure, haven't made an appointment.'

'What about the doctor or midwife?' Daniel pushed, 'have they given you a referral?'

Oh shit I think I was meant to have another appointment last week. God you would think they would ring you and remind you.

'Ummm, not sure.'

'Lisa when was the last time you went for a doctor's appointment?' Daniel asked, curious.

'Oh not that long ago,' I said trying to think of a subject to change to.

'Well when? Last week? Last month?' he pressed.

God I think with Millie being on board with my plans all of a sudden, Daniel has jumped off board. Maybe they have swapped roles.

'Lisa?'

'Hmmm?' I asked stalling for time.

'Doctors?'

'Oh um… I think it was back in February.'

'Four and a half months ago? So when you found out you were pregnant?' Daniel said in a Millie voice.

Hmmm I think they must have consulted on this.

'Yeah something like that,' I scoffed.

'Okay,' said Daniel pulling out his phone, 'you really need to have an ultrasound.'

As much as I silently objected to this, I watched Daniel as his professional phone manner kicked in arranging an appointment,

This Charming Dilemma

I didn't want to argue with him, there is no need to argue with Daniel you just know he has your best interests at heart.

He gets off the phone. '9am tomorrow morning,' he said.

I can't do tomorrow, I have a mine to ban and a camera to be in front of, what if John insists on following me. Shit I haven't thought this through.

'Um… no I think I have a client at 9,' I said to Daniel.

'Lisa I know your appointment book, I am the one that reminds you remember, you are free at 9am, so 9 it is.'

I so want to protest and I need to come up with a plan to divert John's attention away from me for half an hour. See I was afraid of this, being pregnant while trying to be a celebrity, I mean doctor's appointments are so going to interfere with my quest.

'Lisa,' Daniel asks, rubbing his chin as if he was going to contemplate asking me something serious, 'um, I know you probably want Millie to go with you but, would you mind if I went as well?' he asks after a slight pause.

Daniel wants to go to a pregnancy appointment with me? Well I suppose its better him than Millie, at least with Daniel he won't be suspicions if I, you know… go to the toilet and sneak out the back door or something, he'll understand. Actually it's better if Millie doesn't go, especially as she is still on her "tell the show producers" rant.

'Well Millie's probably not going to want to go anyway,' I scoffed, 'you know with the appointment being short notice and all, so yes if you um… want to tag along.'

'Not going to want to do what?' asked Millie, appearing out of nowhere and making another beeline for the freezer, honestly she must have it bad this month.

'Oh you know… things,' I said.

'I've just made Lisa an ultrasound appointment for tomorrow morning,' said Daniel.

'You haven't done that yet!?' asked Millie in horror, 'you told me you were going to do that last month!'

'Oh well you know… life. Must have slipped my mind,' I said.

Millie is staring at me in disbelief. 'Then how did you get in so quick through the public system? Usually you have to make that booking weeks in advance!'

I stared back at her dumbfounded, really? Weeks waiting lists? For a baby?

'Actually I made it through the private hospital,' Daniel piped up, 'I thought Lisa can have the option of going private for her checkups, and of course birth and postnatal.'

Now Millie and I are staring at Daniel dumbfounded.

Does Daniel mean he is offering to pay for my care? Maybe it's a tax write off, I shouldn't question, just agree.

This Charming Dilemma

No better ask in case he means for me to pay for it. Pfft, I'm not a rich celebrity, yet. Better make it sound like it's a business deal.

'Can I claim it though the business?' I asked like a professional.

Now Millie is looking at me dumbfounded.

'No,' Daniel chuckled, 'I have private health insurance, I don't use it, so the offer is there,' he said getting up to leave, 'anyway, think about it but I'll pay for your appointment tomorrow anyway.'

Shame Daniel is gay, he is so noble.

'Can you make it tomorrow Millie?' Daniel asks on his way out.

'Oh it's fine,' I quickly interjected, 'Millie's got heaps to do especially with her new um… project, eh Millie,' I said hoping to send a message to Millie that I'm okay with her not going and would probably prefer that she didn't.

'Meh,' she pondered, 'I'll see how I go.'

'Well Daniel has offered to go,' I said casually, 'so you know, if you're busy.'

'No I should be ok,' said Millie.

God dammit.

'Well then I'll catch up with you later,' said Daniel, ignoring my silent plea to uninvite Millie, 'don't forget to confirm that celebrant for Rick's wedding,' he reminded me as he left the room. I turned around to meet Millie's gaze.

'What?' I asked her as she gazed at me.

'Why does Daniel want to go to your ultrasound?' she asked, puzzled, 'and more to the point, why is he happy to pay for it?' she pondered.

I stared at her blankly because to be honest I have no clue as to why, other than maybe the fact Daniel is gay and may not easily experience the whole child bearing thing. But Daniel is Daniel and not Millie and I would much prefer if Daniel was there not asking questions like Millie would, so I need to convince Millie she is much better off looking at the grey ultrasound picture on the refrigerator and not the screen monitor at the clinic.

Well maybe not on the refrigerator, maybe behind closed doors away from everyone who doesn't know I'm pregnant.

And besides Millie has done this before, Daniel hasn't.

'Weird,' she pondered as she exited the room without even expecting my answer, this is cool it means Millie is in her detective mode and with a bit of luck, inspired to get started on digging up the Jake stuff. I know Daniel's suggestion about booking the celebrant for Rick's wedding was his subtle hint about me going into work today and I have been really good not thinking about Rick's wedding, although I should,

This Charming Dilemma

I'm the one organising it, but the fact that it's Rick's wedding seems to have dulled my senses a bit because I don't even care anymore that he is marrying another person at the same venue we almost got married at. I gazed out the window to see John and Marline following Sid around as he points out various things around the property. Matt is also out pretending to case the yard but really he is staring at Marline through his dark glasses.

I'm starting to feel flutters in my belly and even though I have had some ice-cream and a couple of other things I am really hungry still, but it is nearly lunch time so I should just eat something.

Actually looking at the time it's nearly 2pm, no wonder I'm hungry. I know Daniel is wanting me to put in an appearance today but I'm sure he will agree food is important, especially in my condition. I can hear the quiet clacking of the computer keyboard in the office which means Millie is in the middle of stalking… I mean investigating, Jake, I'm getting goosebumps thinking about it.

I have been staring into the open freezer for a few moments now, actually I have forgotten why I am looking in the freezer.

'How's it going?' The sweet but strong voice of Marline said, entering the room, which means Matt is lurking behind the door. 'I've been meaning to ask,' she said, moving past me to get into the fridge to grab a bottle of sports drink from the fridge door, 'is there a gym in town? Might go down and do some weights since I have the afternoon off.'

I stopped to ponder this, I've never seen one but I'm sure there must be something.

'It's okay,' she smiled, taking my blank facial expression as a sign I really don't know, 'I'll Google it.'

As she whipped out her phone to search, it dawned on me that I haven't really gotten to know these people who have been following us around for the past couple of days, and Marline is always just lingering in the background. I do know that she always seems to be moving, like she cannot sit still for a moment and she smiles all the time. I mean I'm sure Matt knows her every move by now but I haven't really talked to her.

'So you like working out?' I asked her as she tapped away at her phone.

'Yes I train three times a week,' she said, 'I have missed a couple of days being here but I did go for a run to the old burnt down farm up the road yesterday,' she beamed, 'you're so lucky to have all these quiet country roads to jog on, so peaceful.'

'Um… yes very lucky,' I said, remembering the only time I ever walked down that road was walking home from my shameful night playing scrabble at Jake's, and shameful because I had to sneak out of my own house to secretly see Jake, only to end up just playing scrabble. Although the last time might have gone beyond scrabble…'

This Charming Dilemma

'Uh, yes there is a gym,' she said triumphantly, pulling me away from my thoughts of my lovely night with Jake, when I didn't play scrabble with him and conception may have happened, 'at the old tennis court building, according to this,' she said waving her phone at me before popping it back into her pocket, 'did you want to come?' she asked, as her eyes diverted to the stack of cheese slices I held in my hands.

'Oh, no it's all good,' I said, 'I'm heading to work soon.'

She smiled sweetly at me before bouncing out of the room. Well that was a short glimpse into her life.

'You should have gone,' said Matt coming out of his hiding place and gazing out the window to catch a glimpse of Marline hoping into the 4WD in her active wear.

'I'm not going to do your stalking for you,' I said to Matt as I slapped the cheese between two slices of bread.

'Na I don't mean that, I mean you're getting podgy, I mean look,' he said, pointing to my tummy.

'It's not fat,' I said, immediately defending myself at Matt's judgment and slightly shocked that my stomach has popped out quite suddenly.

Shit, damn, where did that bump come from, oh my god it's started! I'm showing.

'It's not fat,' I scoffed, 'it's um... bloating.'

'Yeah from all the food you've been eating,' stated Matt, opening the fridge door, 'and who stole my éclair!' he exclaimed, 'I was saving dat.'

'Oh was that yours?'

'Goddam Lisa, you're eating everything.'

'I am not!' I argued at his absurdness.

'You are! I mean you ate all of Damo's Maltesers the other night, you and Millie did, Millie can, she could be preggo but you're just being greedy.'

'Matt where is all this coming from?' I said, irritable at his outburst.

'I'm just saying that you should like go to the gym and stuff.' he said, 'get into health and fitness and stuff.'

'Which I'm all for,' I said, shoveling bits of my cheese sandwich into my mouth.

'Then go to da gym then,' he pressed on.

'And I told you I'm not doing any stalking,' I sighed. 'If you like Marline so much then why don't you ask her out,' I said, regretting even talking to Matt let alone bringing up the subject.

'It's not dat simple Lisa, and it's not about dat, it's about being healthy and shit.'

This Charming Dilemma

Frustrated to hell with Matt I left the room to go get ready to drag my sorry arse into the office, I really don't want to, especially now that John and Marline have taken the afternoon off so John and Brendan can do some editing. I mean what is the point going into the office to showcase yourself as an environmental hero if you don't have a camera following you. Well actually I have to go in and start these wedding arrangements but I'm sure I could have thrown in the environmental stuff as well.

'Lisa?' Millie called out as I walked past the office, 'did you say that the Crankshaw's had insurance on their farm when it burnt down?'

'Apparently,' I said walking into the office to see Millie reading a document on the computer screen, 'well according to Daniel they did, he got that information from Rick.'

'Well the strange thing is...' said Millie, bringing up yet another document on another window, 'I can't see a policy on the farm even existed and there was no insurance on the plant or buildings but there was a payment made of 4.5 million to the Crankshaw Family Trust.'

'Woah!' I examined, 'then they must have had insurance.'

'It wasn't worth that,' said Millie in a bland voice, 'those buildings were old and unmaintained, 4.5 million is a bit over the top.'

'Maybe they had income protection insurance or something,' I said, trying to be helpful.

'Not sure so I thought maybe it was the mining company that brought the land so I googled the depositor.'

'And?' I asked, getting all excited at the prospect that Jake might be a rich man and my child may do well if Jake is the father.

'Well not much luck there, but did find it's not the mining company that is proposing the development of the land,' said Millie, 'in fact there is not much information coming up, just a reference of 'BFPC'.'

'Millie, how are you getting this information about who has insurance policies and who hasn't?' I asked, suddenly thinking that Millie being a detective is maybe not a good thing.

'Industry secret,' she said with a slight "don't you dare ask" tone to her voice.

'Woah!' she exclaimed as she turned around and caught a glance at my protruding belly, 'well didn't that just pop out there.'

'I'm not that obvious,' I scoffed, now wondering how the hell I'm going to hide this from the cameras.

'So is Brendan aware you are starting to show?' asked Millie, focusing her attention back on the screen in front of her.

Shit, I can't remember if I did tell Millie I told Brendan or I was *going* to tell Millie I intended to tell Brendan. Doesn't matter I suppose, as Millie obviously thinks I told Brendan and really,

This Charming Dilemma

I haven't told Brendan, but if Millie still thinks I did, well she hasn't brought it up for a while so...

'Shoot I'm late,' I explained, looking at my pretend watch and exiting the office to avoid questions. I went back into my room feeling a bit jaded. I was meant to be doing something but can't remember what.

It will come back to me.

So now I need a new wardrobe of clothes that still shows off my figure but hides the obvious, this is so unfair but I'm actually thinking the universe is maybe working in my favour as popping out of baby belly has happened on a day John and Brendan are holed up in Brendan's caravan editing what they have done so far, which means no camera around to catch the evidence, therefore I have time to hide said belly.

Although my clothes are all tight fitting ones, why universe, why.

Oh this might do. It's a top my mother gave me which I have never worn due to the fact... well I just don't like it, but it swings out a bit and would look okay over jeans so I guess that will do for tomorrow.

I can hear Matt's ute pull up outside which is weird cos I didn't hear him leave, maybe he took my advice and asked Marline out. Poor lady.

But after going through the contents of my wardrobe my choices at this stage are a spotted dress that wraps around me, making my bum look big but hiding my belly.

A tie dyed top that my mother also brought me from some hippie market in Queensland, or my drawstring pants and a tee-shirt. Hmm not looking good, need to go shopping but don't want to spend too much money on stuff I'll never wear again. Maybe I need to raid Millie's wardrobe.

'Ready to go?' asked Matt, bursting into my bedroom wearing active wear and jogging on the spot.

'Ready for what?'

'Fitness and stuff, you said you would.'

'I did not.'

'You did and I'm here to help,' said Matt, stopping to stretch his legs.

'Help with what Matt?' I said impatiently.

'Your waist-line Lisa, you're getting fat.'

'Matt! That's not a very nice thing to say to someone.'

'I'm only being honest, that's what friends do Lisa, they be honest wif each other, you would tell me if I was getting fat.'

'No I wouldn't,' I scoffed, well actually that is a lie I would so tell him. 'And besides you're not doing this for me, you're doing it because Marline is a gym junkie.'

'Am not.'

This Charming Dilemma

'You are too Matt, since when have you ever run anywhere. Apart from away from the cops when they busted stoner Damo that time for having a marijuana pipe.'

'I'm a bodyguard now Lisa, I have to keep toned and buff, are you coming or not, we only going down as far as your old tosser boyfriends farm.'

'Matt why are you doing this to me?' I groaned, pushing my slim clothes aside and sorting through my limited fat clothes.

'Do I have to repeat myself, look you even can't fit your clothes anymore,' he said looking at the hippie oversize top Mum got me. 'You need to lose weight, anyone would fink you're the one preggo, not Millie.'

Jeez my hearts just skipped a beat, and Matt obviously still thinks Millie may be pregnant after finding her pregnancy book. But it just occurred to me that Matt could be right in one way, if I am seen running and attempting to get fit, it might throw people off the scent and then if they did notice I am big, they will think I am trying to lose weight and improve myself.

'Okay fine!' I protested just to keep the game up, 'but not fast.'

Can't believe Matt talked me into this.

My lungs feel like they are going to explode and we are only fast walking. Matt is jogging along with hand weights, he looks like an idiot especially with his skinny white legs poking out.

After he convinced me to warm up by doing star jumps, my insides feel like they are going to fall out. God I hope I didn't rattle the baby's brain.

Thank god I'm going for an ultrasound tomorrow, make sure he/she is okay.

Oh my god, sudden realisation I am going to have a real baby that might be a boy or girl.

'Lisa!' Matt said, pulling me from my thoughts,' whose dat over there?'

Oh we're at the Crankshaw farm already. That didn't take long. Thank god, as need to catch my breath.

Standing at the edge of the old fence-line, memories came flooding back of the night of the fire that burnt down the main house and the old milking shed. Jake's Aunty and Uncle owned that farm for generations and Jake had only just came back to the farm after leaving me the first time for Matt's mum Pamela. They had been having a fling and Pamela had embezzled money from the CWA funds to help them move. It all came back to bite her as Jake ended up leaving her and she eventually went in to a mental health unit after having a breakdown. Matt doesn't like to talk about it, the thought of his mum "doing it wif a tosser like Jake" sickens him (his words) but all was forgiven when Jake came back to help his Aunty and Uncle around the farm and it looked like things with Jake and I were getting back on track, until the fire happened.

This Charming Dilemma

I remember that night, I borrowed Betty's scooter to go down to Jake to tell him that I wanted to marry him and have babies, when I arrived to see the place engulfed in flames. Now Jake is gone and I am having his baby. Well, I think.

'Must be da mining people,' Matt said, still jogging on the spot. I squinted into the distance at the official looking flash white ute parked amongst the charred remains of the old house. There seems to be four people standing around, there is one wearing a wide brim hat but very official looking in what appears to be dress pants, looking across the old farm land. They all look like woman… wait a minute.

No, surely not! Is that Betty?

I squinted some more, it was hard to make out for sure from this distance but I swear that is Betty and the other old lady next to her looks like Fran. Don't know who the other two are but I am sure it's Fran and Betty. I wonder if they are meeting up with official mining people.

And without me!

I mean who is the environmental hero here, not to mention the face of Ban the Mine campaign.

What is going on? Unless Betty tried to call me? But no, because if she wanted me there she would have come around home and annoyed me like Matt did.

Hastily making my way to the entrance so I can surprise them with my sudden appearance and of course to ask them what the hell is going on, I started to slightly jog to catch them.

It seems like they are wrapping up their little meeting as they are all making their way back to the vehicle and if I don't hurry I'm going to miss them.

'That's da spirit Lisa,' says Matt coming up behind me still sporting his hand weights, 'see, just a bit of motivation.'

'Shut up Matt,' I puffed, 'can't you see what is going on, they are having a meeting without me.'

 'Who are?'

'The mining people!' I yelled at him, my god does he have to question everything. I mean this is huge. If it is the mining people, then I have a chance to confront them in person and not just through emails. My god that really does look like Betty. Wait till I catch up with her. I mean I am the CWA president for god sake, why are they keeping me in the dark!

'Betty!' I yelled at the top of my lungs, hoping to catch them before they leave. I try to move faster but my lungs are already pounding out of my chest. I yelled out to Betty once again but they can't seem to hear me.

No point yelling out Fran's name as she is a deaf as a doorknob.

Come to think of it, so is Betty sort-of.

Maybe I should whistle instead, studies show that whistling is 10 times more likely to...

Oh shit they are leaving.

This Charming Dilemma

'Matt quick, whistle!' I instructed, remembering I can't.

'Why?' asked Matt, then withdrew his question after seeing the wrath of my glare for questioning me, through my attempt to put air back into my lungs.

Matt let out a whistle loud enough that I'm sure the cows next door will be deaf.

'Bloody hell Matt,' I said, rubbing my ear.

'God Lisa you wanted me to whistle, you're never happy, why do you have to be so angry all the time?'

But it worked as four faces look in our direction.

'Heyyyy!' I waved frantically as I started to jog up the driveway towards them.

Oh my god they look startled. Actually, are they making a beeline for the vehicle?

They are!

'Shit they're leaving,' I exclaim, 'Matt run after them.'

'Probably cos you're angry and bossy!' whined Matt, 'no-one wants to talk to an angry person, no wonder they didn't invite you.'

Oh for god's sake, I'll do it myself.

'Hey!' I yelled louder, trying to go faster but pain is appearing in my sides as the stitch takes over.

The four bodies scrambled into the ute before making a hasty u-turn and heading down the driveway towards us a high speed. Shit are they going to slow down!

'Better get out da way,' Matt said.

Expecting them to stop I moved off to the side, but they don't seem to be slowing down at all. In fact they are speeding up. Are they trying to run?

'Hey,' I yelled as the ute approached, waving my arms at them to stop. The ute just raced past, but I couldn't make out if it was Betty and Fran in the back seat as they had their heads down and covered over with what looks like yellow raincoats! The driver I also couldn't make out as she had her hand over the side of her face and with her wide brim hat on I couldn't see. Dust and gravel spray in our direction as it passed us at high speed. 'Oi!' I yelled at the rear taillight that was getting more and more distant.

'Quick Matt!' I said, 'go after them!'

Matt sprinted off after the vehicle still with his hand weights. But it was too fast and Matt gave up when it exited the driveway and sped off towards town. What the hell!

'See Lisa you shouldn't be so angry, you scared them off!'

I quickly whip out my phone to see if I can get a quick photo of the brand of ute when a message from Daniel pops up on the locked screen.

'Lisa are you coming to work at all today?'

9

I did not have a very good sleep due to a million things going through my head.

Okay not a million, but it was pretty full on up there.

Luckily Daniel was understanding after I totally forgot to go to work the day before and when I messaged him back to say that I have cramping muscles and didn't want to go into work because I was feeling exhausted, he messaged back to tell me to take it easy. Didn't want to tell him it was due to Matt's exercise routine resulting in chasing a mystery vehicle down a country road.

I didn't have the energy to make it back home after that fiasco so I made Matt run back and get a vehicle while I lay down in the soft grass on the side of the road and waited until I could feel my body again.

But I am still puzzled as to what went on yesterday. Naturally I rang Betty when I got home, and after listening to her lengthy discussion about what is going on with her medication for the fluid retention on her knees and not being able to get a word in edgeways,

I finally asked her if she was at the Crankshaw's farm today with official mining people to which she insisted that she couldn't have been due to going to the doctor to get her medication corrected for the fluid retention in her knees, which she then said she's been telling me for the past fifteen minutes and why wasn't I listening.

I also rang Fran to see if she had an alibi, she thought I was being a bit ridiculous as why would she be out at that time in the afternoon when she hasn't missed an episode of the Bold and the Beautiful in 27 years and she would be getting the dinner on.

But after I told them both that I was almost run down by people in a white utility whilst I was out running with Matt, they were a bit shocked and stunned that I *was* actually out running with Matt and told me that maybe I needed to get a high-vis vest so cars will be able to see me and then I won't feel like they are trying to run me down.

So according to Fran and Betty, it wasn't them at the Crankshaw's farm with two unknown people, and even though I swear on my grandmothers grave it certainly looked like Fran and Betty, I am going to have to take their word for it.

And maybe install cameras to watch their every move.

Oh my god yes, that's what I can do.

This Charming Dilemma

'Lisa can I have a quick word,' asked Brendan, plonking himself in the empty chair beside me at the kitchen table, ipad in one hand.

'Sure,' I said as I watched with envy as Matt devoured a bowl of coco pops while I am stuck here drinking a glass of water since Daniel had messaged me this morning to remind me about drinking heaps of water and eating nothing.

'Now I need John to be on you the whole day today,' said Brendan. 'We edited a bit of film last night but we really need to push a bit with your daily stuff, it's just the way we make it. So comments about your day and this whole mine thing that you are getting involved with, and your general work,' said Brendan, 'and tomorrow we will focus on Daniel and then the others the following day.'

Oh crap.

'Um… today's probably not good, you see, as I'm um… sick,' I quickly said, followed by a slight fake cough for effect.

'You better not have the spew bug again,' exclaimed Matt, covering up his bowl of coco pops.

'Are you going into work?' asked Brendan.

'Not sure,' I said in a weak voice, 'might, you know, have to go back to bed.'

'Okay, that's no problem,' said Brendan, upbeat,

'what I might do is get them to focus on Daniel today instead and see how you feel tomorrow, but then again it is a reality show, people get sick.'

Shit!

'I can't come with you this morning after all,' said Millie, bowling into the kitchen with great life force, 'I have to take Sid's stupid laptop to the repair guy in town, it seized up on me last night just as I was about to download some stuff, stupid thing!'

Oh phew thank god!

'So I will have to meet you there after I drop it into the shop and Amy into daycare, what time did you say it was, 9am?'

Shit!

'Is where you are going worth John coming along with the camera for?' asked Brendan, not wanting to pry but wanting to pry for TV sake.

'Oh very worth it!' chuckled Millie at Brendan's question before exiting the room on her mornings mission.

Bitch!

'Oh no,' I scoffed, 'you know, just a doctor's appointment, making sure I haven't got the flu,' I said, faking another cough, 'you know, boring, boring.'

This Charming Dilemma

'Okay well I'll give Daniel a call, make sure he is good for today,' said Brendan moving off before I got a chance to say anything.

'Why don't you just take some cold tablets if you got da flu,' said Matt from the depths of his breakfast bowl, 'only sooks go to da doctor for a cold, you're not even properly sick. If you started being more healthy Lisa you wouldn't be sick all the time.'

'You know coco pops are not that healthy,' piped up Marline, coming in for her morning protein shake.

Matt sunk to the depths of his bowl as Marline set about getting her ingredients ready for the blender.

Ignoring him, I am starting to panic about how I am going to divert nosey people from following me to my ultrasound appointment, Matt should be easy, I'll just tell him Marline is at the gym again and that should have him running around the block twice, and hopefully Daniel will divert John for an hour because Daniel will be noble enough to think about it, so that will only leave Millie.

Hmmm Millie is going to be tricky, maybe some skill required on my part.

Oh speak of the devil.

'So is John going to tag along this morning?' Millie asked, catching up on the conversation she missed.

Aware that both Marline and Matt are in the room, even though I am pretty sure Matt's ears will be ringing from the mere presence of Marline, I cannot start this conversation with her in this room, as this may lead to more questions.

Oh actually, on second thought I *can* divert conversation.

'No, change of plan, John's following Daniel today,' I said, making a beeline for the door.

'But isn't Daniel coming with us?' Millie asked.

Shit.

Thank god Marline at that point proceeded to put her earbuds in and Matt appears to be gazing at her and ignoring everything else, I am pretty sure the universe is working in my favour and did that on purpose.

'Well yes Millie but you know… it's personal, you'll never know what they are going to find so…'

'Hopefully a baby,' she chuckled, grabbing Amy's bottle bag and bolting out the door again. I quickly glanced at Matt but yes it looks like he is definitely on another planet, drooling into his coco pops bowl and didn't take in Millie's comment.

Better get out of here before Millie broadcasts something on a loud speaker.

Glancing at my phone back in the bedroom I notice I got a missed call from Betty. She has also left a message to call her back as soon as I got her message, but not going to do it at the moment. I think I should talk to Daniel first and make sure he is not going to have John following him to the clinic.

And I'm pretty sure I am meeting Daniel there so that is just perfect.

Betty is trying to call again, I can see the number appear on call waiting as I am waiting for Daniel to answer his phone. I haven't given much more thought as to what I saw at the old farm site yesterday, I've been too preoccupied with pulling this appointment off in top secret. First of all, I wondered if these people were from the company that paid the Crankshaw's all that money, I mean the vehicle they were in certainly didn't look like a mining car, normally they have flashing lights and sign writing. These looked like a bunch of older people out for a Sunday drive and a sticky-beak, well apart from the driver, she had dress pants on and a dress scarf and looked official from the distance. After filling Millie in on my findings last night and after she finished laughing over the fact I was out on an exercise regime with Matt, she suggested it could have been representatives from the company that are financing the deal, after all they want to see how their investment is going, but she did think it was a little strange they don't want to be known.

I love it how Millie is almost thinking like me and not raining on my parade like she normally does.

Daniel finally answered his phone and after my "if he brings John and the camera to my appointment my life is ruined" spiel, he confirmed that he will meet me there and not to worry as they were going to have a quick interview with Betty this morning anyway. Thank god, I knew Daniel would sort it.

And speaking of Betty, she has tried to call me again.

But I don't have the time to call her back as Millie has just called out that she is leaving which means I better get moving as must be near 9am. Even though I am feeling a little more relaxed that I won't have any cameras there, I still feel nervous about the whole thing. I mean what if it doesn't turn out to be a healthy baby, or doesn't turn out to be a baby at all, just one big air bubble waiting to explode. Actually that would be a relief if I found out I wasn't really pregnant. Or would it? Feeling a bit confused about the whole thing.

Oh I should see what fat clothes Millie has, she looked so stylish when she was pregnant with Amy, not that Millie is like that all the time but when she was pregnant she made such an effort with her appearance cos she didn't want to feel like a big oompa loompa wearing a sack all the time.

I called out to her through the window as she was putting Amy in her car seat, didn't hear exactly what she said but it didn't sound negative. Arriving at Millie's wardrobe and flicking through her stacks of clothes hanging, I see a few A-line dresses that would be perfect as they hide all sorts of stomachs. Millie never throws any clothes away so it's like an opportunity store in here, you'll never know what you will find. I whip off my current clothes to try this summer A-line dress on,

This Charming Dilemma

wait a minute I probably need to be wearing something two-piece today since they need to access my belly. Finding such, I proceeded to try on Millie's over size Barbie-doll top and pants.

'Oh!' exclaimed Sid coming into the room and catching me with my arms stuck through the sleeves.

'Oh!' he exclaimed even louder as his eyes focused on my protruding belly popping out from the band of my pants. We seemed to be locked in a stare like a possum caught in headlights and I really do not know what to say. Luckily Sid proceeded to pick up his jaw from the floor and run out of the room.

'Nice outfit,' Millie said as I approached her in the carpark at the clinic.

'Didn't you tell Sid?' I asked, mortified that Sid had even caught me in my underwear trying on Millie's clothes let alone saw my naked protruding belly.

'No, you told me not to,' she said in a way like she was offended I had to even ask. I don't get Millie, happy to tell the world everything about you but ask her to say nothing and well... she says nothing. 'I did warn you he was around,' she chuckled. Obviously Sid had texted Millie and told her about our little run-in. So I guess that cat is out of the bag.

No sign of Matt thank god so have no idea where he went to, probably still frozen to his cereal bowl. Some bodyguard he is.

Daniel was waiting to the entrance to the clinic when we arrived. Alone thank god.

'Drunk enough water?' he asked as he observed the water bottle in my hand. I'm so hungry and really need to go to the toilet and I feel like a waddling duck so hopefully I can get to pee soon.

Stepping inside the clinic, Daniel went to the front counter to let them know of our arrival as Millie and I took a seat. I noticed a very pregnant woman sitting opposite us. I gazed at her swollen belly with a bit of shock at the realisation I am nowhere near that stage, I mean seriously, how the hell am I going to hide that!

'Lisa dear!' Betty's shrill and annoying voice rattled in my ear.

I turned around to see John standing there, with Marline and a camera pointing in my direction.

'Fancy meeting you here, I have been trying to contact you all morning!'

I can feel the colour draining out of my face I look around for Daniel to send him a silent SOS as Millie is hopeless, and not helping by having her head stuck in a magazine, but Daniel still had his back to me at the front desk.

'Honestly, three messages I left you,' she said, plonking herself in the seat next to me, 'Brendan and John here want to talk to us both about the mining campaign.'

This Charming Dilemma

John's red light on his camera has switched off. I have worked out that when it does that it means he has stopped recording because the person in front of the camera is well... conversing with the crew on a personal level or something. Also means if I can work stuff out like that it means I'm destined for the television world.

'Lisa?'

'Hmmm?'

'What are you doing here?' Betty asks me, leaning past me to acknowledge Millie with a warm smile. 'I see you have Daniel with you.'

'Oh um... yes.'

'Hello Betty,' Daniel greeted, appearing and giving me a pained and sympathetic look over the cameras being here.

'Oh hello Daniel dear,' Betty blushed, 'I was just saying to Lisa, fancy bumping into you lot here. Especially since I left Lisa three messages this morning,'

'Yes, small world,' Daniel said politely.

'Is everything okay?' she asked, fishing for information.

I glanced up at the camera and notice the red light has switched on, which means he's recording again.

'Um... yes, just fine, we are here for um... Daniel.'

'Daniel?' Betty asked in alarm, looking at Daniel.

'Yes Daniel, he has an um… hernia,' I said, the only thing that popped into my head since Daniel's crotch is in my line of vision. I didn't dare look at Daniel's face.

'Oh,' exclaimed Betty, also glancing at Daniel's crotch, 'and both you and Millie are here?'

'Yes you know… for support.'

'Lisa Collins,' the lady technician appeared with a clipboard in her hand, calling my name.

Shit.

I looked at Millie. 'Don't look at me,' she mumbled, looking slightly amused with her head still in the magazine.

'Lisa I thought you said it was for Daniel,' asked Betty, puzzled.

'Oh it is,' I scoffed in a loud voice, 'must be a mistake,' I said, getting up to make a run for it.

'Oh' exclaimed the receptionist puzzled, overhearing my comment, 'I'm sure the appointment was for Lisa, I'll check.'

Daniel signaled to the receptionist that everything is fine.

'I have a Lisa Collins here,' said the technician, addressing the receptionist.

'Okay well while you sort that out I'll just go to the toilet,' I said, trying to run to another room.

This Charming Dilemma

'Excuse me Miss Collins you can't go to the toilet if this appointment is for you,' the technician reminded me as I attempted to waddle off.

'No it's fine,' I scoffed, 'just maybe a mix up with names.'

'Oh for god's sake,' said an exasperated Millie, dropping her magazine beside her and getting out of her chair, 'we'll sort out who's getting what in the clinic room,' grabbing both Daniel and I by the arms and walking off.

Daniel still looks bewildered, as I climb up on the bed.

Millie hasn't said anything yet, and after confirming with the technician that it is indeed me and not Daniel that has an appointment everyone has calmed down and now I guess I am about to see what is inside this protruding lump.

Daniel and Millie gathered around the bed as the black and white image appears on screen. The lady moves her cold magical device around my stomach.

'Oh wow,' whispered Millie, looking at the screen misty eyed. I look at the screen and all I can see are black shadows. Daniel starts asking the technician questions like does that measure the baby's length and blah, blah.

'Can you see the arm?' she asks, pointing to the grainy image on the screen.

'Oh so it is,' said Millie.

'Amazing,' said Daniel.

Nope still can't see anything.

'Okay so now we will listen to the heart beat,' she said, turning up the volume on the screen.

And there it was, a faint rhythmic thumping coming out of the monitor. I can feel tears welling up and a lump has started to form at the back of my throat, doesn't help that Millie has just squeezed my hand and Daniel had just done a heartfelt rub on the arm.

I mean it's a human in there, a real live human. And I created it.

Shit I'm going to be a mother!

And I'm not ready for it. I should just tell this lady that I have to go, I mean I have stuff to do like this mining campaign and becoming a TV celebrity.

'Hang on…' the technician said looking puzzled, turning a knob on the machine, and moving her stick around my stomach, 'I think there is…'

What!?

She listens intently to the monitor before making notes. 'I just want to check something,' she said as she switches off the sound and moves the stick around like she is looking for something.

'Everything okay?' Millie asks, looking concerned.

This Charming Dilemma

'Yes it's fine,' the technician assures her, 'I just want to double check something,' she said scanning the screen a bit more.

The rooms falls silent as we watch the screen, I can't make out anything. Oh hang on, did that look like a head.

'Is that a head?' I asked, looking at the little round image on the screen.

'Yes it is,' she smiled, 'good spotting, I'll take a picture of that.'

'Oh look, it looks like you in the morning,' joked Millie at the messy blob on screen. Well I hope she was joking.

Okay, shit just got real.

'And is that another head?' Daniel said, pointing at another image.

God I really hope *he* is joking.

The technician said nothing as I looked to see what Daniel was looking at. And he is right, another little skull like head shape has appeared.

Oh my god, maybe my baby has two heads.

Shit maybe it is Damo's!

'Did you want to know the sex,' she asked, glancing at both Daniel and I. Daniel looks a bit awkward at the question and quickly tells her it's my decision.

'Sorry,' she said at the realisation she had made an error in judgment about Daniel and I being a couple.

'It's fine,' said Daniel as I didn't know what to say so said nothing. Millie let out a small grin at our awkwardness.

'So the sex?' she asked me.

Hmm, haven't thought about it. But wouldn't it be cool to know if I am having a boy or a girl. I seem to be getting all excited about this baby all of a sudden. I mean, me, a mother, I can paint the room blue or pink and then I can start buying stuff for him or her. I can make all sorts of grown up decisions about him… or her.

'Okay,' I said, wiggling with excitement.

'You sure?' asked Millie, 'you don't want it to be a surprise?'

I looked at Millie, I mean honestly she should know by now that I wait for nothing and I mean come on, the technician just asked me if I wanted to know, not knowing would just kill me more.

'The not knowing would kill her Millie,' Daniel mused.

'Yeah true,' agreed Millie.

See Daniel knows me.

'Okay,' said the technician, running her device around again, 'well see that,' she pointed to a small grainy part on the screen, 'that looks like a boy to me.'

This Charming Dilemma

A boy, a little boy, wow, which means Millie and I between us will have a pigeon pair. Just having images of a little boy playing with Monty Dog and kicking a ball around teaching Matt how to play catch. I notice Daniel has a slight grin of pride on his face, hmm that's funny.

'Oh, and a girl,' the technician smiled as she takes a still picture, 'well that confirms that,' she added.

'And a girl?' I spat looking at Millie's puzzled face, 'you mean to tell me my baby is intersex?'

'Does twins run in your family?' the technician asks.

The colour just drained from Daniel's face as Millie lets out a small gasp. 'Um, no I'm an only child,' I said, slightly panicked. 'Are you sure?' Millie asked the technician.

'Yep 99%,' she said, 'I just wanted to confirm a couple of things, but I picked up two heart beats before, healthy ones,' she added.

Daniel is the colour of an albino.

I can't be having twins. I've never heard mum mention any twins on either side of her or dad's family.

Which reminds me, I'd better call my parents and break the news... hang on a cotton picking minute, Jake is a twin. Jake and Rick are twins. I should know, I have dated them both.Which means its likely to be Jake's baby. I mean babies.

Jake is the father of my babies.

10

Daniel hasn't said a lot since we came back from my appointment, he is acting weird and still has no colour in his face. Millie is still in a bit of shock I think and I'm sure she has gone home to tell Sid we are going to be busy. I'm having images of Sid having to deal with triple lots of washing and hiding under the bed.

I was going to go straight home but Daniel reminded me that I have Ellen, Rick's new fiancée at 11am to discuss, well her wedding, which I had totally forgotten about and really don't care about at the minute.

Because I am having Jake's baby.

I mean babies. I have not only created one human, but two.

The technician was 99.9% sure after Millie grilled her to the bone about her qualifications, I don't blame Millie, I mean all of a sudden she could see a house full of nappies, two babies and a toddler. But she also couldn't contain her excitement as she fished in her bag for her phone to call Sid and tell him.

Daniel is acting weird though, maybe it's just him having sentimental moments about not being able to go down the baby road due to him being gay and not in a relationship with anyone (to my knowledge) and I feel pretty guilty as I am having two babies. He did thank me for letting him come along and share but he hasn't said a lot since.

There was no sign of Betty or the cameras when we all staggered out of the clinic room in a daze. And thank god. I'm still dreading the interrogation from Betty about the mix up with Daniel's "hernia".

I know I'm meant to be talking to the wedding celebrant and confirming a booking for Rick and his fiancée's wedding and I guess knowing what I know now it's going to be even more awkward with Rick, not only being my ex fiancé but now the uncle of my babies. Rick knew I dated Jake before we went out together so it's not like it's going to be a shocker, and the fact that I have just eaten something that has made me feel really lethargic hasn't helped my tired brain go into overdrive.

I mean what if Jake doesn't want these babies. Really feeling emotionally confused right now.

But I have the biggest opportunity of my life to get a spot of stardom as an environmental hero and what am I doing, staring at a computer screen.

In fact, where are these cameras.

'Lisa?' Daniel finally spoke from the depths of his computer as he edits some photos from his last photo shoot, 'have you thought about having a word to the show producers about your expected arrivals?' he suggested.

Obviously it's playing on his mind. 'They need to know you are expecting and you're not going to be able to hide it forever.'

You see I was afraid of this, he spends just a little time in Millie's company and suddenly he is turning into Millie.

I assured him that I will when the time is right and even though I didn't look at Daniel, I can feel his disapproval at my response. I still feel I need to establish myself as a TV personality first before revealing I'm with child, whoops I mean children. I mean these babies are just sitting in there, I can't have them holding up my life, they're not even here yet!

Right, from now on Lisa Collins will have a camera in her face at all times fighting for environmental rights! And where is Betty, she is off gallivanting somewhere stealing all my limelight. Better track her down.

Picking up the phone after my little motivational speech to myself, I glanced at Daniel, he looks a million miles away, normally it's me gazing into space, while he is the one that is focused, so hope everything is okay.

'Yes Lisa dear?' Betty's voice appeared down the line.

'Betty where are my camera crew?' I demanded, taking back ownership of my show.

'Oh well we were just up at the clinic as you know, getting my knees looked at, and now we are just popping down to the lemonade stand for a quick cuppa. Then I think we are going to pop in and see you dear, hang on I'll ask John.'

This Charming Dilemma

Betty is so going to ruin this show if she kills John with boredom.

I hung up not waiting for her reply as I'm pretty sure the local Councilor has just walked past the shop. I have to seize this moment, if I want to become a face for a campaign and launch myself into stardom, it starts now by getting facts! He's with the local Council, which means he has information.

I cannot remember his name but I remember seeing his face everywhere during a recent campaign. Lucky there has been an election recently and it's not the same man that I saved from landing on a hot BBQ plate after he tripped over Monty Dog and I was snapped by the local paper pushing him out the way of the searing hot BBQ before landing on top of him. But that's another story.

'Excuse me?' I called out to him as I stepped out of the shop, Daniel put his head up from the depths of space to see what I was doing. I can see Betty down the road slightly, getting out of her parked car followed by John and Marline. The Councilor turns his head at my call but seems to keep walking, obviously didn't hear me. God I wish I could remember his name, I called out again as he is gaining some distance and has picked up his pace. He turns again to the sound of my voice. His eyes widen as I pick up my pace and run towards him. Actually he is moving again. Is he?

Oh my god he is, he's trying to get away from me.

Why are people running from me lately?

Unless he recognises me from the Ban the Mine campaign and wants to avoid questions. Yep that must be it, he knows something and is not going to reveal it.

'Betty, stop him,' I yelled out to her as the crosses the road with John and Marline in tow. Betty can see what is happening and starts to move faster towards him, the Council man panics slightly and starts to move faster himself.

'I'll stop him,' Fran appears out of nowhere on her electric scooter she has just purchased off Ebay, blocking his path. Betty catches up and prevents him from going any further by stretching out her arms so he doesn't move around her.

I stop to catch my breath before introducing myself. John hasn't got the camera up and I am guessing he has noticed the official name badge and realises he needs permission to film. Owen! That's his name, Owen!

'Just wondering if I can have a quick word,' I gasped.

He looked surprised when he saw the camera but seems to be more concerned about what was behind John.

'Yes, why were you running?' said Betty in a threatening manner, almost grabbing him by his shirt and interrogating him.

'Who are you people?' he said, mainly directing the question at John.

This Charming Dilemma

'I'm Lisa Collins from Ban the Mine campaign,' I said, introducing myself in a professional manner as Fran gives him a look that could strip paint.

I wish John would start filming this.

'So who are they?' he asks as Damo and Matt caught up to us in what I could only describe as cage fighting gear, bare chested with no shirt on.

What the hell?

'It's called Ju-Jitsu Lisa,' said Matt, after I asked him why he was running down the street looking like a caveman.

'It's a sport, it's about taking on another dude and making them submit on the ground.'

'And you were running down the street with paint on your faces because...'

'Because me and Damo were at the gym training and we left to get a sandwich and saw you running after that guy and us being your bodyguards and all...'

'Scared the living bejezzers out of me!' piped up Owen as Betty is now fussing over him and handing him a cup of tea.

'I thought I was about to become a victim of a random street riot,' he said, sipping his tea.

Daniel is just wondering why we are all in the office and not elsewhere.

'It's actually a sport about skills and outwitting,' Marline said, setting up a better sound for our interview, 'it's the fitness that drives you. I've been competing for 10 years,' she smiled.

Ahhh so that's why Matt is suddenly looking like an idiot in gym gear.

'Maybe I'll give you some pointers,' she suggested to Matt, unaware Matt has probably just messed in his pants.

'Um… yeah I think I'll go change,' he mumbled as him and Damo left the shop.

So after all the confusion was cleared and Owen from the local Council was assured he wasn't going to be beaten to death by two old ladies and two youths looking like caveman in front of a camera, he agreed to sit with us and discuss our concerns about the mine, which was all fine until he realised it was Betty who organised the rally in the park and Fran is the admin of the Ban the Mine campaign Facebook page so now it's not really like an interview, more like a Mexican standoff. We haven't even started yet and he looks uncomfortable. Maybe that's because Betty's hostess skills have expired now we are getting down to business and she is glaring at him like a cat ready to pounce.

But this is my chance to set the ball rolling and even better cos John is finally here with the camera.

'So Councilor Owen,' I started in my polite voice leaning against my desk with my arms folded for effect, until I remembered that I don't have anything prepared.

This Charming Dilemma

I mean apart from this flyer from the company explaining the proposal, I've got nothing.

Oh and Millie's findings. And the fact people were at the site the other day, undisclosed people. Okay, Lisa start off light and work your way to the hard facts.

'Ahem, as I was saying Councilor Owen, when do they propose a start date for the mine?'

'Oh, well there has been no start date, it's only a permit application by a company called Acrabobe Mining at the moment Miss Collins.'

'But it is being considered?'

'By our council yes, only in initial stages, this has just popped up out of nowhere since the site became available,' he said clearing his throat.

'Which means?' I said, raising one eyebrow, gee I'm getting good at this interrogation stuff.

'It's still on the table as a possible application, I can't tell you much more than that at this stage.'

'And why is that?' I asked, glaring at him.

'Because I don't know much more than that,' he said.

'Oh okay, well that's fair enough.'

'Liar!' snaps Betty as Fran swings her leg in frustration.

'The council supports the choking of our precious farmland? You companies are all in bed together, how much money are you going to receive Councilor?' Betty ranted while Fran continues to shoot daggers from her eyes.

'Let me assure you, the Council will not support a mine if it would have a negative effect on the community,' he said, getting flustered, 'we know as much as what you do at the moment ladies, all we have is a proposed development application in its very, very early stages and a brochure explaining their intentions that we did not authorise or know anything about.'

'How much more do we have to pay in our rates if they're going to be hard on our roads?' Fran started.

'It's nowhere near that stage,' he nervously chuckled, 'those types of details are a while away yet.'

'But it is going ahead?' Betty pushed him again.

'No, I didn't say that, I said its early stages.'

I'm standing there listening to Fran and Betty throwing question after question, John is capturing it all and I seem to be drifting off into my own thoughts. Twins, I'm having twins, hmm maybe it is a good idea to get hold of Jake, I mean facts are facts, conception date on point, twins run in his family...

'Did you have any involvement with the fire at the Crankshaw's farm to get your way?' Fran seethed.

This Charming Dilemma

I glanced at Daniel who is now raising both eyebrows and has a slight amused look on his face at that last question.

'Is this going to affect the waterways?' Fran ranted.

'Okay I think we can wrap this up,' Councilor Owen said, pulling off his microphone with the help of Marline.

Shit he's leaving and once again I have let old people take the focus off me. I better reel him back in.

'Before you go,' I said, making sure John is now focused on me, and knowing I have insider information thanks to Millie.

'A company called BFPC has been a big player in financing Acrabobe mine, can you shed some light?'

Oh my god that sounded sooo good.

He looked puzzled, 'who is BFPC?' he asks.

Betty and Fran start to shift uncomfortably in their seats. And I can feel the tension from both of them start to rise. Hope they don't start up again. They have had their turn.

'The people who seem to be financing this mine,' I said.

'I'm sorry I haven't heard of such a company,' he said, sounding genuine, 'but our interest does lie more in the impact it will have in our community, good and bad,' he added when I went to open my mouth. 'But as long as everything ticks our boxes we don't get involved with company workings,' he said, delivering me a wink with his last statement.

'So no one from the council attended the on-site meeting yesterday?' I asked getting bolder as I go, thank god for Matt and his absurd idea about exercising.

'I was not aware there was a meeting?' he said puzzled, 'nothing has been scheduled from Council. As we said, we know as much as what you do Miss Collins,' he said.

Okay so Matt and I may have stumbled on to a private meeting yesterday. Betty and Fran remained quiet and glued to their seats. Weird, before they couldn't stop tearing strips off the poor man. Maybe they are aware that I need to have the limelight for a change and it's not all about them.

'Let me assure you, if there was any information moving forward the Council will hold a public meeting to inform the community about what is going on, we are all in his together you know,' he said getting up to leave, 'ladies, and gents,' he added, addressing John and a bewildered looking Daniel, 'I thank you for your time, it's been a, err, pleasure,' he said, looking at Fran and Betty who seem to have lost all their fight and are sitting there pale as anything.

I thanked him also. My mind is ticking over as I don't know but for some reason I can't explain, something is not right.

'Fran, we didn't ask him what was happening with the footpath down Maple Street,' Betty reminded her as they came out of their silent protest and ran out the door after him.

This Charming Dilemma

Closing the shop door behind them I noticed John has stayed behind so now it's down to the real business of stardom.

'Well that went well,' I said, upbeat, returning to my desk. Daniel just stared at me for a few moments as I pretended to shuffle papers on my desk as his non-response is making me feel uncomfortable. I don't know what's got into Daniel, he's been acting even stranger in the last few minutes.

I'm actually feeling pretty chuffed with myself over the meeting with the Councilor. John asked me a few more behind the scene questions about how I felt about the outcome. It's a small start but it's a start. But in order to get the real facts I have just goggled surveillance cameras and am now looking online to buy one.

'Lisa your 11am is here,' Daniel said from the depths of his desk. My heart jumped in my mouth when I saw Ellen, Rick's fiancée walking through the door, I totally forgot she was coming. And thank god she doesn't have Rick with her. She also didn't have any white bunnies and bell-birds following her either but she still looked as radiant as ever.

I slapped on my smile as she made her way inside and after pleasantries were exchanged, she walked over to talk to Daniel while I frantically looked for her file and made her a cup of herbal tea.

She and Daniel seem to be at complete ease in each other's company considering they haven't known each other long, but I suppose Rick being Daniel's best friend they probably spend more time together than I am aware of.

Unlike when Daniel first met me when I was going out with Rick, he didn't like me at all, well it wasn't that he didn't like me, he just well... seemed to be mean to me, which is weird considering we are now business partners and close friends. But Daniel's pretty laid back really, apart from his OCD about cleanliness and space and organisation and god forbid if you don't put your pen back in its holder or spill tea in the saucer, but other than that type of stuff, he's pretty good.

But he doesn't appear to be giving Ellen a hard time like he gave me.

Wait did he just kiss her on the cheek.

'Lisa I'm off to do a location shoot,' Daniel said as I went forward to kiss him goodbye on the cheek but missed entirely and it just ended up me looking over his shoulder.

'Look after her,' he said, gathering up his man bag.

She gingerly sat down as I approached the desk. Shoot I forgot to confirm the booking with the celebrant. Okay fake it, I'm sure it will be fine

'So the date has been set,' I said, crossing my fingers as I quickly wrote myself a reminder to book the darn celebrant, 'and the venue is booked so I guess we should talk about the rest of the day.'

'So thoughts about colours or themes?' I continued.

'Well I know this is going to sound silly,' she said with a shy look on her face,

This Charming Dilemma

'but I was thinking about what you suggested about themes, and I guess well, since I was a little girl I thought it would be kinda cool to have, you know, a fairy tale themed wedding. Like Snow White or something.'

Bahahahaha

'Oh that's a fabulous idea,' I said with a straight face.

But seriously I swear I am psychic, I mean didn't I say she reminds me of a blond Snow White.

'I'm no good with colour schemes,' she said, seeming embarrassed, 'so do you have any books or something I can look at to give me some ideas, Rick said you would be good at this sort of stuff.'

He did?

'Yes of course,' I said, flicking through my books. I have a lot of elegant and traditional bridal magazines but nothing of a fairy tale theme. I do have a Lord of the Rings subscription magazine I got from Sid after a previous client wanted a Game of Thrones themed wedding and Sid didn't have any magazines from his nerd comic online store just Lord of the Rings. But the theme was pretty much the same and we got some fabulous ideas from it. Trying to rack my brains to see what ideas we can look at for a fairy tale wedding.

Ah ha! I've got it, the universe so works in my favour sometimes.

'Here you go,' I beamed at her, handing a copy of Amy's Disney book Cinderella that she left here and I put on the coffee table for clients with little kids.

Ellen hesitates taking it from me as I beamed at her and moved back behind my desk. 'Take your time,' I smiled as I frantically composed a new email to send to the celebrant. I might just text her actually, she might read it faster.

'Ah Lisa, you're still here,' Fran said, making her way through the door after parking her new scooter right across the front entrance, 'I have finished your costume for the Mardi Gras.'

'I'm with a client at the moment Fran,' I said with forced politeness.

'Mardi Gras?' piped up Ellen with interest.

'Yes dear,' Fran smiled, 'we are going to have a Mardi Gras in October.'

'Here in Taromeo?' she asked her eyes sparkling. 'That sounds like fun.'

'Yes it will be, great fun,' I said, 'now if you would excuse us Fran...'

'I just need you to try this on,' Fran continued, handing me a hideous mustard yellow two-piece outfit,

This Charming Dilemma

'I have noticed you've put on a little bit of weight Lisa, so if it needs adjusting I can drop the stitches and make it a bit bigger across the waist, the wool does stretch but don't want it to stretch too much otherwise it will become see through, but I'm sure you're going to wear underwear underneath it anyway.'

'Oh it's nice,' Ellen said politely as I held up the hideous yellow two-piece. Seriously, even I can see she wants to burst out laughing.

'I'll try it on later,' I said, stashing it next to the rubbish bin.

'Lisa is going to be the parade queen on our float,' Fran continued to inform Ellen, 'so we thought the theme being erotic knitted wear, you know, being the CWA and the Mardi Gras.'

'Oh are you a member of the CWA Lisa?' Ellen piped up with interest.

'Yes, regrettably so,' I said, glaring at Fran.

'Yeah Lisa is our president and of course younger than all of us ladies so we thought it would be fitting for her to be our parade queen.'

'Of course,' Ellen beamed.

'So did you want to come along?'

'Well I was just about to ask that,' Ellen said, 'I would love to be involved.'

Oh no.

'Well, save the date dear, it's on the 8th of October, actually Lisa dear you should get this lovely young lady to come along to the next meeting.'

'Sorry did you say 8th of October?' Ellen quizzed.

'Yes dear.'

'And Lisa is your parade queen? But that's my wedding day,' said Ellen puzzled.

Shit.

'You're getting married? That's lovely dear, we are looking for volunteers for earlier that day if you could spare some time,' Fran went on, handing Ellen the new CWA business card.

Ellen is still looking at me puzzled and waiting for an explanation. I would offer her one if Fran would shut up! Oh she has, now they are both looking at me and probably for different reasons.

'I am one hundred percent committed to your big day,' I said to Ellen in my professional voice, delivering it across with a smile, 'I promise you are going to have the best day.'

Actually I shouldn't promise that because I can't be that sure things are going to happen if this darn celebrant doesn't text me back.

This Charming Dilemma

'Ohh is Lisa organising your wedding?' Fran piped up again, 'well it should be so much fun, Lisa here will make sure everything is well... running.'

'What time is your parade?' asked Ellen, totally not convinced I am committed.

'It's scheduled for 2pm, it's in the last CWA minutes so it's definitely that time,' Fran went on as I went to open my mouth to reassure Ellen it won't clash with her wedding, my god I wish Fran would shut her mouth.

'So you being in the parade isn't going to clash with our wedding time?' Ellen asked me.

You know, Ellen may look all Snow Whitey but she is really starting to show her pushy side.

'I hope not,' Fran piped up, again, 'with Lisa being the parade Queen, not to mention the face of Ban the Mine, we are going to need her for most of the day.'

Now Ellen looks freaked out. 'It's going to be fine,' I reassured them both as my phone chimed alerting me to a message.

'I don't see how Lisa, you can't be in two places at once you silly girl,' Fran scolded.

It's a text back from the Celebrant, 2pm on the 8th of October is the only time she is available that day, as well as the weekends either side, due to family commitments and holidays.

Of course she friken is! I mean, my god isn't that woman retired.

'Well ladies I'm sure it will work out on the day,' I said, rising from my seat to frantically see Fran to the door before she ruins my business and so I can convince Ellen on my lonesome that I am one hundred percent committed to her on the day.

Or…

'Actually Fran,' I said in a disappointed voice after having a sudden brain wave, as I looked at the hideous two-piece lying on the floor, 'I have just had word that the Celebrant can only do 2pm on that day for Ellen's wedding, the same time as the parade so it seems you are right Fran, I *can't* be in two places at once,' I said. 'Shame that, but maybe Gloria could be the parade queen, she's a better candidate anyway, being the second youngest and would look far better in your lovely outfit then me,' I said smoothing things over.

'That's absurd,' Fran scolded, 'Gloria's old and has varicose veins, we need a fresh young thing like yourself and besides Gloria will never get into the bloody outfit. The CWA is 100 years young Lisa, that's the theme we are going for remember?'

'Yes, yes, I know, such a shame,' I said, still trying to sound disappointed, 'but Ellen and Rick have chosen this day because it's special to them and well…' I said, hoping Fran will fill in the blank and realise this is my bread and butter, even though the real reason is this is my excuse to get out of wearing this hideous thing in public, especially now this belly is protruding even more.

Okay, feel like I want to throw up with that reality check.

'Aren't you a wedding celebrant?' Fran asked, 'can't you perform the ceremony?'"

'Lisa's a wedding celebrant as well?' Ellen said, her eyes widening.

Shit!

'I can't… due to um… organising two things at once.'

'You know Lisa was engaged to a Rick,' Fran said to Ellen, leaning around me and ignoring my last sentence.

Shit!

'Oh really,' chuckled Ellen.

'Yes, didn't last long though,' Fran rolled her eyes, 'in fact she was seeing his twin brother before that, couldn't decide our Lisa,' Fran tutted. Okay I have just lost my stomach, I'm sure it's in my mouth somewhere.

'Well what a coincidence,' Ellen smiled.

'Well dears, better be off,' Fran said as I was still trying to decide if Ellen was pretending not to know about Rick and I, or does know and is choosing not to say anything.

Oh and I have only just noticed John and Marline are still here with the camera rolling. This must just be all second nature to me now if they have been filming me in my natural environment and I didn't know they are even there, reality TV is agreeing with me.

'Wait!' Ellen said, looking at the copy of Cinderella in her hands and mulling it over.

'I really don't want to throw a spanner in your celebrations,' she said to Fran, 'I know you need Lisa and well so do I as I have never organised anything and do really need some help,' she said looking like she wanted to burst into tears with that statement. 'So I don't know… maybe we could get married on the parade float,' she said, going all shy again, 'and I don't know, but it would be kinda nice if it were you performing the ceremony'

What!?

'That way everyone wins,' she said, 'I would hate for you to miss out on that Lisa, seems just as important as our wedding.'

'Oh it is,' piped up Fran.

'No really it's fine,' I scoffed, 'there will be another errr 100 years coming up, you only get married once.' *I hope.*

'Nonsense!' exclaimed Fran, 'it's not fine! Ellen dear that is a lovely idea and very generous of you to share your special day,

This Charming Dilemma

maybe you should come along to the next CWA meeting and we can discuss details,' Fran said, writing down the next meeting on the business card.

'That would be great,' she beamed, her eyes lighting up at the invitation.

Hmmm Ellen seems too excited about a CWA meeting, think our Ellen doesn't get out much.

'But what about your fairy tale wedding?' I asked.

'Well it kinda will be,' she said, 'and well my brother is gay, so the whole Mardi Gras thing will be a hit,' she said, getting excited about the idea.

Grrr, once again I have let old people take over my life.

Fran takes her smug self out of the shop and jumps on her electric scooter. This is my chance to make sure once again that Ellen is okay with getting married on a float in the middle of a small town Mardi Gras parade surrounded by people wearing erotic knitwear. And besides someone getting married has nothing to do with 100 year celebrations so I shall be raising that point at the next meeting. I excused myself as I go and lock the shop door in case Betty comes in and suggests we have their reception at the lemonade stand. I'm not done with Ellen yet, lots to discuss about this wedding and I am the wedding planner,

I want to make sure very sure that Ellen is aware it's me she should be listening to and not a bunch of old ladies who have nothing better to do but to take over your life.

I also want to probe her a bit more to see if she does know about mine and Rick's past relationship.

Oh god now John is talking to her from behind the camera. Marline puts her hand up to let me know not to get in the frame while they are interviewing Ellen.

'So you're really going to get married on a parade float?' I heard John ask her.

I haven't had a chance to discuss this with Ellen and now not only old people are trying to take over my business but it seems camera people as well!

'I guess I am,' Ellen answered, all coy with a hint of excitement.

'And what would your fiancé think of this idea?' John continued.

Actually good point, Rick will hate the idea.

'I'm pretty sure he will think this is a fun way to do it,' she beamed, 'Rick is an adventurous guy and he would be thrilled to tell people in years to come he got married on a parade float, I'm sure he will love the idea,' she said with confidence.

Pfft, she really doesn't know him at all.

This Charming Dilemma

Oh god I just felt strong flutters of movement in my belly which seems to be protruding more than ever, it hasn't been that obvious before, I'd better suck it in.

Marline's head suddenly jerks in the direction of my belly and is looking at me puzzled.

Shit.

'Big lunch,' I mouthed to her, patting my stomach as her puzzled expression didn't change. Okay I may have to change the way I'm standing, minimize the bulge.

No still there.

Marline diverts her attention back to Ellen.

Phew.

'So how did you two meet?' John asks her.

Ohh this would be interesting.

'I grew up with Rick,' she beamed with loving eyes, 'although we were in different classes at school, he is best friends with my brother.'

Hmm I wasn't aware Rick had another best friend besides Daniel.

'So you grew up here?' John pressed on.

Oh god, may as well get a cup of tea, it looks like it's going to be all about Ellen for a while, but any more liquid and I will end up looking bloated. I'd better figure out a wardrobe that is going to hide this thing before Marline figures out I'm not overeating all the time.

I haven't seen Brendan since this morning. Normally he is here for this crap but we are just in the daily routine of filming so I guess he doesn't have to be present for everything.

As my thoughts drift off I keep thinking about Jake. I really should contact him and let him know. Being a twin and me having twins, surely there is no doubt who the father is, thank god, I knew it couldn't be Damien's, I didn't think he had it in him and being a virgin surely it isn't likely to work properly the first time, but really must stop thinking about that cringe-worthy moment.

But I really don't know where Jake is or where he is working. I had his number but the last time I rang it, it told me the number I have dialed is not available. And of course I didn't have a forwarding address. Hmm I wonder if I should get Millie onto it.

I can hear fingers clicking.

Oh it's Marline trying to get my attention, she frantically points to the door to see Daniel standing on the other side. He has his hands full and is trying to get in the shop, oh that's right, I locked the door.

Marline tells Daniel with a hand signal that they need background noise at a minimum as I unlocked the door and can see he was about to ask me why the door was locked.

This Charming Dilemma

He navigates the door carefully with his gear, I go to help him but he refuses, good thing about being pregnant is it seems to get me out of a lot of stuff around here at the office, even forgetting to come into work yesterday seems to be forgiven easy.

Daniel's eyes also quickly pass over my belly as he navigates past me, for some reason it's sticking out more than usual and even though I adjusted my top so it hides it, on the right angle it seems it's not hiding anything.

Oh my god there it goes again.

I let out an involuntary gasp as my stomach starts to move, Daniel eyes are as wide as saucers in amazement as my stomach wobbles a bit with the movement going on inside me, I know he is dying to put his hands on my stomach, thank god he has his hands full of equipment and if I wasn't in the middle of a reality TV show and trying to be quiet and not to mention trying to hide the fact that I am pregnant, it would be such a scrapbook moment.

Shit Marline is looking at me with suspicion again.

Ellen is still talking to John and I feel like clicking my fingers back at Marline to let her know to concentrate on her task and not my out of control stomach,

I'm not sure if she knows what she saw but just in case I will have to keep an eye on her, but all the same I better find a safe place to stand to hide this stomach until I get home and find another outfit.

Marline indicates in my direction again to be quiet and I was just about to inform her of already taking a vow of silence with a hand gesture of my own when I realised she was referring to Betty who had just walked through the door. I really must reinstate that bell on the door.

'Lisa dear,' Betty whispered, as I moved to a different position so she wouldn't notice my protruding stomach,

 'Fran wants to know if you have tried the outfit on yet, she did text but you're not replying? She is a bit worried since it seems you have put on a bit of weight since she last measured you, I told you too much of those almond finger biscuits you seem to be addicted to would catch up, moment on the lips… Lisa.'

Oh for the love of…

'No I haven't had a chance,' I whispered back in my snappy whisper voice, 'I have been with a client! Fran knows this.'

'Ohhh yes that's right, our little Ellen, I heard she wants to get married on our float, how exciting, and she might join the CWA, competition for you dear,' Betty teased, 'another young one on the team.'

I'm going to ignore that.

This Charming Dilemma

'Hello Daniel dear,' Betty whispered in an even louder voice 'how's the hernia?'

Marline is now glaring at the both of us, even though we are whispering, my god they don't need it this quiet when they talk to me, or Daniel, maybe our Ellen is the type of person who demands special treatment.

Not on a conscious level, on a subconscious level. Like some sort of vibe she is putting out there.

'I remember our young Ellen and Jake,' Betty continued to whisper, unaware of the wrath of Marline.

'Her and little Jake Crankshaw often caught behind the hay shed,' she chuckled, 'had quite a crush on him she did, always hung upside down on the bars of the milking shed with her knickers exposed,' she mused.

Grrrrr.

'And then later on it was Rick and her we had to keep an eye on,' Betty tutted fondly at the memory of it, 'couldn't decide on which brother she liked the most, bit like you dear,' Betty chuckled again.

Grrrrr.

Great, now Daniel has moved into the frame and is standing behind Ellen. Wait a cotton-picking minute here. Why is Daniel being interviewed with Ellen and why is she looking at him fondly.

I was right, Ellen does put out that vibe of needing special treatment. Sitting there looking all innocent like Snow White, I'm onto her.

Marline is glaring at the door again as I turn around to see Rick walk gingerly into the shop. Okay my insides just lurched and my face is burning red, for a moment there I thought it was Jake walking in. So yes we are all cozy in the shop and these babies seem to be moving again at the presence of Rick. Which is understandable, Rick is their uncle.

'How's it going?' he whispered to me as Marline looks like she is going to throw something at us, 'so we are being interviewed I see,' he says with a slight amusement.

'Hmmm,' I mumbled, not knowing how to answer as I'm starting to get slightly put out they are talking so long with Ellen, I mean this is my gig!

'I was just telling Lisa here about Ellen being chased by both you and Jake when you were kids,' Betty whispered, 'and she had such a crush on both of you.'

'Yeah but the best brother won in the end,' Rick joked, delivering a wink to Betty.

Grrrr.

He made his way over when John put the camera down for a second. Seems like the interview is over.

About time.

This Charming Dilemma

Ellen fondly puts her arm on Rick and delivers the news about the idea of getting married on the float, Betty is now joining in the conversation and while Rick looks a little surprised, he doesn't seem to be too put out over the idea.

I'm still glued to the spot, I found standing behind Daniel's big glazed pot an ideal spot to hide my belly. There used to be two glazed pots, a matching pair, but one ended up well... had to be thrown out after I didn't make it to the toilet the morning after the drunken night when I woke up in Daniel's bed, so Daniel being OCD couldn't just have one glazed pot at his house since everything in his house is coordinated, so he brought it into the office and put it by the entrance. I mean I'm pretty sure the universe works in my favour as if I didn't throw up in the pot at Daniel's house, resulting in discarding of that pot, then this pot probably wouldn't be here to hide my belly from the cameras.

Yep it's all connected.

'Was this your idea?' Rick asked me with amusement, 'sounds like a Lisa idea,' he chuckled.

'No actually it was mine,' Ellen said, all coy, stealing my limelight again, 'Lisa is meant to be parade queen on the day of the wedding so I thought we could combine it, saves her missing out, oh and did you know, Lisa is also a wedding celebrant.'

'Really!' Rick said, looking in my direction, 'that's awesome, maybe you could marry us.'

261

Grrrrr.

'You're so thoughtful,' Rick says, delivering Ellen a peck, 'that's why I love ya, I think it's a great idea.'

'Yes Fran and I thought so too,' Betty said, putting in her two cents worth.

'Do you mind if we add a few of your comments?' said John, getting the camera ready again, 'Lisa do you want to get in the frame?' John asked.

Shit.

'No, I'm good,' I said, still standing in the same spot.

'Are you sure?' John said, 'after all you are the wedding planner.'

'Yeah come on Lisa,' Rick encouraged, 'maybe you can tell us how crazy we are,' he chuckled, looking all gooey at Ellen again.

Hmm if he carries on like this then this glazed pot is going to end up with the same fate as the first. Actually I noticed Daniel hasn't said much about this change of wedding plans.

'No I'm good, I'll just stand here, err… cramps,' I said rubbing my thigh.

'You need to eat more bananas, must be lacking in magnesium,' Betty piped up.

This Charming Dilemma

Marline is looking at me with a slight knowing and smug look on her face.

'Okay well when you are ready Lisa just come and sit behind your desk.'

I look down at my belly and the top that is not hiding anything. I could just brave it and walk over hoping that no one would notice but I'm pretty sure Marline is onto me and Betty would sniff it out in a heartbeat, it's what old people tend to do.

'No I think it's better here,' I said, 'errr… more light,' I said pointing to the window behind me.

'More light?' said John, not sure what to say to that statement.

I send Daniel a silent message that my belly is the problem when he looked at me with a puzzled expression, his frown turned into a smile as he sent back a look of acknowledgment.

'Okay we'll just move over to Lisa,' Daniel said, taking charge of the room as John reluctantly agrees and Marline starts the task of making sure she shifts the wires so no one trips over them.

Love Daniel.

John starts the camera again and asks Rick how he feels about the whole idea about the wedding being carried out on the main parade float.

Rick starts talking and somehow Betty is adding snippets in there. God I don't even know why she is here or why John is allowing her to interfere. My thoughts are starting to drift off again as I half listen to Rick and Ellen, it would have been nice if it was me in that frame talking about my own wedding, not to Rick, I had that chance. But I can safely say now that I did make the right choice about not marring him. Or did I? I mean let's face it, bastard Jake is not the one here standing beside me being interviewed about a wedding as I am standing behind a tall glazed pot hiding a pregnant belly.

'And being Ellen's brother,' John went on focusing on Daniel, 'I guess your best friend is obviously the right one,' John joked.

Wait a moment, why did John say that and is now focusing on Daniel.

Daniel is Ellen's brother?

'Yeah he will do,' Daniel joked back as him and Rick exchange a bit of banter between themselves.

Ellen is Daniel's sister?

11

Back home and I have exactly one hour to find clothes suitable to hid protruding belly. Thank god John is going on a lunch break, and I have my suspicions that he is currently talking to Brendan about whether or not to edit the piece of film where after I discovered Ellen is actually Daniel's sister because instead of answering John's questions about the up and coming parade wedding, I stood there staring at them both in disbelief with my jaw on the floor unable to speak.

It wasn't easy waiting for everyone to leave the office before I could come out of my hiding space, luckily Daniel took the reins again after he also realised I was turning blue with wanting to go to the toilet, and suggested they all go out to the local tavern for lunch, including Betty who was waiting to see me to go over a brochure she had drafted about Ban the Mine campaign. Daniel has his suspicions she will be sucking up to *Cannon and Collins Event Planning and Photography* about sponsoring the printing of them all.

So that is where they have all gone, out for lunch, and I made an excuse that the reason I was standing behind the big glazed pot was because I had spilt something down the front of me, after Betty kept asking me why I am standing behind a big pot and Marline had a smug look on her face waiting for an answer.

I think Marline is going to be a problem, after all I am pretty sure she suspects something and I know it won't take much for her to tell John, then John will tell Brendan and then that will be the end of my career as a reality television celebrity! I suppose the only way to divert Marline is to get my useless bodyguard to watch her every move.

Actually where is Matt?

'I was wondering how long it was going to take before you started to really show,' Millie said as she stands in the door frame looking at the pile of clothes on my bed, 'I have some maternity pants and some bigger tops, did you find them?'

'No I didn't have time this morning after Sid burst into the room,' I said with a snappy tone, thinking back on the mornings events with a red face.

'Yeah he's probably still haunted by that,' Millie chuckled in a dry tone, 'Sid's a bit freaked out by the news but he is happy, he'll come out from wherever he is hiding soon enough,' she said like she doesn't care that her husband has ran off and is hiding somewhere over the thought of not only one baby but two in the house soon. It takes a while for Sid to adapt to change. 'Anyway cheer up, you're actually looking amazing,' she said in a cherry voice, 'have you told Brendan and the rest of the crew you're having twins?'

'Did you know Ellen and Daniel are brother and sister?' I said quickly, ignoring her question.

'Ellen who?' she asked.

This Charming Dilemma

'Ellen Willow, the lady that is getting married to Rick.'

'If they are brother and sister, why is her last name Willow and not Cannon? Has she been married before?'

'Ohhh, good point,' I said picking up the phone to send Daniel a text message to ask if Ellen is his sister then why does she have a different last name.

'He did say he has a twin sister,' said Millie, shrugging.

'Daniel has a twin sister? How do you know that Millie?'

'He told me once,' she said, about to leave the room.

'Well it's not her, she's only 23 years old,' I said, why do I not know these things.

'Well maybe he has more than one sister although he only mentioned the one. If you took a bit more interest in others Lisa you might just find out these things,' she said in a bitchy voice just as I was about to open my mouth to ask why don't I know about these things.

Millie amazes me about her ability to know exactly what I am thinking!

'Anyway I will go and get those clothes,' she said exiting the room.

I collapse on my bed, rolling over onto my back and start to think about Jake again and how I am going to present news about expecting children.

I could just hire a pilot to fly a light plane past with a banner informing him, if only I can find out his exact location. Or I can send him a letter, but again it depends on his exact location. I know it's as easy as asking around but I do have to have a valid reason as to why I need to track Jake down, and I haven't had that idea come to me yet. I could just get Daniel to ask Rick as I already suspect that Daniel knows Jake is definitely the father, but after the scan Daniel is acting a little strange and distant. I am actually feeling pretty tired and could sleep here for hours in this position but I know I have to keep going as I have this TV show to take back, especially after this mornings' little episode of hiding behind the ornamental pot.

But if I am going to own the environmental hero title I'd better get into gear and get something happening, organising a wedding on a parade float will not make me stand out on national television. I need action, I need to stand up and fight against the corporate giants. An interview with the local politician and an up and coming discussion with Betty over a newsletter draft is not going to excite anyone.

I'll start as soon as Millie gets back with my clothes.

'Here you go,' she said, throwing a heap of clothes at me, 'try these on.'

My phone chimed, alerting me of a message that will be Daniel's reply.

I strain myself up to sitting position and pick up my phone.

This Charming Dilemma

'Okay the reason Ellen has a different last name Millie, is because she changed it by deed pole after she had a stalker issue,' I said reading out Daniel's message to her, 'as well as her unofficial birth date, on the form she said she was 23, Daniel is 39, actually I'm going to text Daniel again and ask him why she said she is only 23.'

'Well that's fair enough,' shrugged Millie, 'oh speaking of stalking, as I drove past the Crankshaw's farm this morning I saw two more vehicles go in there. I didn't have time to see where from, so keep your eyes open and if you see one get a number plate or something so I can run a search on it,' she said exiting the room.

More vehicles! There must be something going on, I think it's about time we installed cameras, after all this is about collecting evidence. I jumped up and grabbed my laptop to log onto the site about surveillance cameras. Actually I wonder if Millie can get a discount, you know being a private investigator and all.

Millie doesn't really want to get involved in the campaign, and may not entirely approve of the cameras, but if she isn't that interested then why did she mention the vehicles and want to know their number plates.

I guess I'll just have to spit it out, if she can't get a discount then I'll just order them anyway.

Throwing on Millie's maternity pants I quickly surveyed myself in the mirror, yes I definitely need to wear a non conspicuous top over them. Flicking through the clothes I pick out something semi okay and make my way to Millie.

I have never liked loose pants but a loose top and loose pants makes me look, well like I am getting fat all over so I guess it's going to have to do because at least now I don't look pregnant.

Millie is clacking away at her computer keyboard when I enter the office, she's frantically trying to get as much done before she has to pick Amy up from daycare again shortly.

'They look better,' she commented on my choice of outfit, 'now you look like you just love food,' she mused.

'Can you get a discount on surveillance cameras?' I asked getting straight into the point before I lose my nerve.

'No need, I have some,' she said wheeling her chair over to the other side of the room, 'came with the job, Sid wants to put them on the front gate for extra security, I mean we have a notice up but well, you know what Sid is like, feels like he is lying to the world by having the sign and no cameras. He has trouble sleeping at night over it. Where were you thinking of putting them?'

'The front entrance to the Crankshaw's old farm,' I said quickly, waiting for Millie to tell me it's a dumb idea.

'Ohh excellent idea,' she said, her face lighting up, 'especially with all the activity coming out of there.'

This Charming Dilemma

Millie looks like I have just told her Christmas is coming early.

'I thought you didn't want to get involved?' I asked, not being able to help myself.

'Well as long as you don't drag my name into it and no one finds out I have any involvement, then, yeah, whatever. So you want them?'

Well that was easy, after 35 years of friendship I finally know how to make Millie tick. Underhand, seedy stalking and snooping activities.

Millie handed over the box containing the two cameras and we both squealed, unable to contain the excitement.

'So when do you want to do this?' she said, rubbing the excited goosebumps on her arms.

'Tonight,' I said, also getting excited at Millie getting excited, 'that way we can sneak out without John or Brendan knowing where we have gone.'

'And Amy,' Millie added.

Ahh yes, of course Amy, she is going through a phase at the moment of not letting Millie leave the house without her.

I left the room, cameras in hand, before Millie and I start doing back flips, but it did occur to me in my excitement dance with Millie that I should have John down there with the camera. After all this is about me and my daily activities.

But after a quick conversation with Millie she hastily pointed out that she really doesn't want a trespassing prosecution and the whole idea of installing cameras is to catch people out so the less people that know, the better. So on that harsh Millie note, operation "Mine" will discretely commence around 8pm.

Well, it all depends on whether Amy settles by then. We can't make it too late, Millie gets cranky if she has a late night.

But I really must get back to the office as I'm sure Daniel and the rest of the crew would have finished lunch by now. Oh speaking of, Daniel has replied. *She picked her age, to make sure the stalker can't find her, by choosing her favourite number.* Weird.

'Afternoon Lisa,' Brendan greeted, entering the kitchen as I was fetching my car keys.

'You didn't join the others for lunch?' he asked.

'Um, no, slight... wardrobe incident,' I said, tutting at myself. He half smiled as he proceeded to make his coffee. It occurred to me I haven't actually asked Brendan how things are going with the filming, I mean Brendan hasn't really said a lot and let's face it, it's been nearly... two weeks?

It's been two weeks!

'Everything alright Lisa?' he asks as I stand there wondering where the hell two weeks went to.

This Charming Dilemma

'Oh… yes fine, I was just wondering how things were going? You know with the filming?'

'So far it's okay,' he said, not wanting to give me the answer I was seeking, 'but it's early days yet,' he smiled as he finished making his coffee and wished me a great rest of the day and left.

What did he mean by that?

Driving back to the office Brendan's words are swirling around in my head. What did he mean by "it's early days", does he think we are boring and not really entertainment enough to warrant a show? As I drove past the Crankshaw's old farm, I couldn't help but think if Brendan does think that we aren't giving the show the cutting edge it needs, then maybe I should invite John to come along to operation Mine so he can see we do have an exciting time here, I'll be risking life and limb to expose environmental issues.

But I know Millie will cut off a limb if I invite John there with his camera so I think I will just have to film it myself, in secret, without putting Millie in the frame.

Yes that is it, I can record it on my phone, not having Millie in there and show it to Brendan later and he can add it in after the campaign is over! That way, people can see the behind the scenes effort I have put in to expose the company and its wrong doings to the land!

But knowing Millie she would want a hand to put these cameras up and blah, blah, so I am going to need backup.

I pick up my phone to text Matt to inform him to keep tonight free, he is needed. If Matt wants any involvement in this film he will have to put himself to good use and help Millie install these cameras while I secretly film the whole operation. The screen on my phone is swamped with messages from Betty once again. God what could she possible want now! I press the call back button but as per usual, the line is busy. What is it with both Betty and Fran, the only ones on the CWA committee that have the phones and yet every time I call them they are busy, surely they can't be talking all that time.

Who am I kidding, it's not so much talking to people as it is annoying people.

My phone rings again, but this time its Matt's wheezing voice that comes through the blue-tooth.

'Yo, what's happening?' he puffed as I can hear the Eye of the Tiger song belting out in the background.

'Be at my place around 8pm,' I said getting straight to the point, 'we have a mission to complete…'

'What's da mission?'

'Never you mind, I'll tell you when you get here.'

Knowing Matt he will tell everyone before we get there.

'Okay sweet, can I bring Damo?'

'Yeah whatever,' I said, not wanting to get into a discussion on it.

This Charming Dilemma

'Sweet,' he says again but this time with a painful groan.

Shall I ask?

'Matt, what are you doing?' I caved. Dreading the fact I *did* ask.

'Me and Damo are at his place practicing our Ju-Jitsu,' he said, 'then we are going for a run and going to do some weights, you should come and work out wif us.'

'Um no, don't think so, but thanks.'

'You should, even Damo finks you're getting fat, and Damo doesn't say that stuff about anyone.'

'Don't forget about tonight,' I said, disconnecting the call as I pull up at the office, ignoring Matt's last statement before he starts his "not looking after myself" rant he has suddenly adopted since he found out Marline is a fitness freak. Glancing across at the office window I can see John and Marline through the glass, they are obviously filming Daniel so it's good they are still here and not following Betty again, honestly no wonder Brendan is finding us boring.

'Lisa dear,' Betty appears at the side of my car window, scaring the bejezzers out of me. Gathering my bladder before it spills everywhere, I hit the window button.

'I've been trying to call you,' she scowled, 'we have changed the meeting till tonight,' she said, 'Ellen can't make the next meeting and Gloria has some figures she wants to go over for the parade.'

'But I thought that would be discussed next week?' I said through gritted teeth, wondering why the sudden change.

'Well yes, but that means Ellen won't be able to attend so we discussed it over lunch and it's been moved till tonight, everyone thinks it's better tonight anyway,' she said.

'Who is everyone?' I said with a sigh, feeling a headache coming on.

'Well everyone from the CWA,' she scoffed, 'honestly Lisa if you weren't such a clutz and didn't mess up your clothes you could have came to lunch with us and we would have told you ourselves.'

I let out a calming breath through my nose, then it hit me, it can't be tonight, operation Mine is happening.

Shit.

'Well tonight is not good for me,' I said gathering my bag and opening the car door slowly as Betty navigated her frame around my open car door, 'I have errr… stuff to do.'

'What sort of stuff?' Betty asked, obviously unsatisfied with my pre-apology for not attending the meeting.

'Err I have to work late,' I said, glancing at the office as I lock the car door.

'Well that's okay dear, we can move the meeting to you, so I'll tell everyone to be here around 7pm.'

Shit!

This Charming Dilemma

'Um, no because um… Daniel is also working and we might disturb him,' I said, wishing she should just leave.

'Daniel's not working dear, he is going out with Rick tonight, it was discussed at lunch.'

Shit.

'Okay well um… I have changed my mind, I'm not working here, I think I'll just um… take some work home with me,' I said.

'Well did you want us to come there?' Betty asked, clearly not getting the point.

'Betty I have work to do,' I said impatiently.

'I realise that dear, but this is part of work and we cannot pass certain items on the agenda without you.'

'Can't you just email it to me,' I mumbled, not expecting an answer.

'Don't be ridiculous dear it would take too long.'

Like this conversation.

'Okay, okay, fine, but only for an hour, and to be held at the hall,' I said, realising that if I move the meeting along it should be over with by the time operation Mine commences. Yes we could move the time, and date but Millie is feral if she stays up too late and Sid has his conspiracy theory meetings in the city for the next two nights.

Since Trump was elected president of the US the agenda items of the Conspiracy theory club have been filling up so he doesn't want to miss that.

'Of course dear,' Betty said, patting me on the arm with a triumphant look on her face, actually I wonder if Sid's conspiracy theory buddies have any theory on spaceships, I might go along to find out where they are so they can take me.

Entering the office and John immediately focuses the camera on me, luckily I have been conditioned to put my game face on whenever John is present.

I moved over to my desk to begin the ever-daunting task of wedding preparations, but to be honest everything I had in mind for Rick and Ellen's wedding now must be condensed to a parade float. As I dialed the celebrant to ask if she has any objections about performing on a parade float, I spied the knitted garment still lying on the floor next to the bin and let out an involuntary groan.

'What's up?' Daniel asked, clanking away on his computer, I pick up the knitted garment to show him, he smiles at my facial expression as Marline lets out a snigger.

After speaking with the celebrant and explaining to her about the change, and her conditions, she informs me she won't be able to do the ceremony after all, which means Ellen will get her wish of Rick's ex fiancée performing the ceremony. The universe is really trying to put the past in my face. I look around the somber energy of the working office.

This Charming Dilemma

I can see what Brendan was referring to. Not a lot is happening here and for John and Marline it must be like watching paint dry. I really think they should come out with us tonight, I really want to scream this at them so they have at least something to look forward to. Poor buggers just standing there watching us work away in silence on a computer. Well Daniel is, I'm typing Jake's name into Google.

Actually out the corner of my eye, I can see Daniel looking at me. Like he is pondering something. He's been doing that a lot lately.

Okay so nothing new is coming up on Google about a Jake Crankshaw.

I messaged Millie again about letting John come down tonight but the response I got was my cue that the answer is definitely no! Millie just doesn't get how my career could be over before it's begun if I don't provide some action soon! Unless they just happen to show up...

'Lisa do you have dinner plans tonight?' Daniel asks, his head back in his computer.

'No, apart from a CWA meeting,' I said, lifting the ugly knitted two-piece up again and rolling my eyes.

'Aah yes, the "garment"', Daniel laughed, 'what about after that?' he asked.

You see this is why I love Daniel, he has the ability to tune into what I want, this is my opportunity in front of the cameras to raise John's suspicions that there is something going down.

'No can't after that,' I said in a clear voice, 'Millie and I are on a mission,' I said in a casual but secretive voice.

'What mission is that?' Daniel chuckled.

Shit haven't thought the answer through.

'Ah, never you mind,' I said tapping my nose, 'it just involves night time activity,' I said, glancing at my computer with a straight face.

Ha! Hope John captured every moment of that.

My mobile phone chimes and I instinctively fish it out of my bag. Nope not me, must be Daniel.

Daniel glances at his phone but doesn't pick it up. Silence falls in the office again and my eyes flick to John to try and read his expression to see if he is pondering what I just said.

Hmmm maybe I need to get Matt's indiscreet arse in here, John would have the details within 30 seconds of him entering the building. Actually on second thought, no, Marline is present, Matt wouldn't be able to talk.

The phone chimes again, causing everyone in the office to jump.

'Lisa that must be you,' Daniel says from the depths of his computer.

'Not not me,' I said, looking towards the camera at John, Marline indicates in silence that it's not them either as they have their phones switched off when filming.

This Charming Dilemma

My eyes diverted to the direction of the phone noise, it looks like it's coming from the coffee table. I walked over to find a phone underneath one of the magazines. Oh a client must have left it here. Actually this is a CWA phone, it's even labeled "Property of CWA" on the cover, it must be Fran's as Betty has the other phone.

'Hello,' I answered, expecting to hear Betty's voice.

'Um hello,' a male voice appeared at the end of the line, 'I was just calling about your service,' he said, sounding coy.

Oh joy it's a telemarketer, Fran wouldn't have thought to add the number on the no-call resister.

'We are happy with our service,' I said, about to disconnect.

'This is my first time,' he quickly said, sounding nervous.

Oh god he is new to the job, well I shall let him do his spiel, poor guy, his supervisor is probably standing beside him.

'What did you want to know?' I said, sitting back behind my desk showing to Daniel the label that reads CWA on the back of the phone on my way past.

'Oh,' he stuttered, 'um, well I'm not sure how this works,' he said all nervous again.

Okay I can see this is going to be a hard one, I mean if I have to tell the guy how to do his job then he really shouldn't be doing this.

However I can just picture a dopey eyed, vacant youth on the other end of the line so I better guide him through.

'Well if you are calling about the service then I am telling you I am happy with the phone service unless you can convince me of a better deal,' I said.

'So you want me to sweeten the deal?' he asked, confused.

'Yes yes, like, ask me some questions,' I said, typing in "all mines in Australia" hoping that it might give me some clue as to where Jake went.

'I'm really hot right now,' he said, in a squeaky quiet voice.

'Hot for what?' I asked, scrolling down the search results, there does seem to be a coal mine just west of here, actually it's not that far when I have a quick look on Google maps, it's only like a five hour drive.

'Um... hot for you?' the telemarketer said again, all nervous.

God this guy is not going to make it in sales, he can't even string a proper marketing sentence together.

'What is hot for me?' I asked impatiently, I'm willing to help the kid out by not being rude but he hasn't even told me about the product yet.

'You know?' he said, all coy.

'No I don't know, because you haven't even described the goods?' I said in a slight amused, slight hurry this up voice.

This Charming Dilemma

'Well it's hard,' he said in a voice that's just above a slight whisper.

'Of course it's hard,' I said, 'it's meant to be hard for your first time,' hmm maybe this guy needs to have a conversation first, break the ice. The things I do.

'Is it raining where you are?' I asked, looking at the slight drizzle that has started to fall outside and remembering that Jake said he was flying out so it wouldn't be that mine otherwise he would have just drove out.

'Why, are you wet?' he purred down the phone.

Okay this is too much hard work.

'Have a nice day,' I said down the line, pressing the disconnect button. Jeez I don't want to be mean but I don't have the time to play phone charades of guess the product.

'Who was that?' Daniel asked from the depths of his computer again.

'Oh just a telemarketer,' I dismissed, my thoughts intently trying to think back to the very brief conversation with Jake at the door that day he said he was going away to work, trying to find any clue. He did say up north so that means he must be in Queensland, I never was any good at finding Wally.

'Did he try and sell you your thoughts back?' Daniel mused, catching my deep intense stare at the floor in front of me.

Actually, I should just ask Daniel, I mean after all I'm sure he has figured out by now these are Jake babies. And Daniel is not Millie, he won't lecture me like her.

'Do you know where um… Rick's brother went to work?' I asked, flicking my eyes to the camera so Daniel can get the hint not to mention any names in front of John and Marline.

'Oh!' Daniel said, caught by surprise, as he flicks a discreet glance to my belly, 'I believe he is up near the cape, do you need to get in touch with him?'

'Yes for um… business purposes,' I said, typing "Cape Mines" into Google search.

'Do you have his phone number?' asked Daniel.

'No, I thought I did, well I did have it, but he must have changed numbers or something.'

'Are you sure you want him in your line of business?' Daniel asked, with a slight sharp tone to his voice. I stared in disbelief for a second as it doesn't sound like something Daniel would say, normally Daniel is handing me over the phone number by now, not questioning my motives.

'Well I feel he has a right to have knowledge of my business,' I said, shooting a quick glance at John behind the camera.

'And are you positive he is the one that proposed this business idea with you in the first place?' Daniel asked, with one eye raised, 'didn't you say you had another offer on that business deal.'

This Charming Dilemma

What?

'Well yes, but he seemed to be the one with the double offer,' I said, hoping Daniel will realise that Jake is a twin and so are these things inside me.

'That doesn't always guarantee the right businessman,' Daniel said again.

Okay this code thing is really frustrating, I am about to drop the pretense and asked Daniel what the hell his problem is all of a sudden.

Maybe I should start texting him. Nah takes too long and John will have his suspicions if he sees both of us playing with our phones.

'Well considering the other business proposal is inexperienced and not part of a double deal I would say my chances are pretty high,' I said, trying not to lose my discretion, 'so if Ja... this person, is notified of my proposal, then he can decided whether he is willing to conduct any business with me.'

'I doubt he would be interested in your business proposal,' Daniel said, rolling his chair back from his desk and grabbing his empty cup from the corner of the desk.

'Why do you feel that?' I asked, not really wanting to know the answer.'Because he doesn't seem the type to be interested in the type of business you are proposing,' Daniel said getting up off his chair and heading towards the kitchen area.

I got up to follow Daniel into the kitchen ready to give him a serve but as soon as I get up to follow, so does John and Marline, so I pretend I was fishing something off the floor and sit back down again.

That was a bit unfair, I mean it's not like Daniel doesn't like Jake, I mean they are not the best of mates like Rick and Daniel are, but they seem to get along and Daniel has never said a bad word about Jake.

Fran's phone chimed again and the call screen came up with a private number.

'But if you do wish to proceed with him,' Daniel said, coming out of the kitchen, 'I'll ask his brother if he has a contact number,' he said, grabbing his coat and announcing he is stepping out for a short while and will be back to lock up. Actually Daniel seems pissed about something.

Fran's phone is still chiming, and clearly she hasn't got her voice mail switched on. Private number, it must be one of the CWA ladies, because they all have private numbers after the great bust when they were accidentally selling eye pillows filled with marijuana to the local youth. Well I will answer it and tell whoever it is down the line to tell Fran to come and pick her bloody phone up.

'Hello,' I said irritably as I still feel put out about Daniel's comments. Daniel of all people, is the last one I expected to put his judgment on me about wanting to inform Jake that I am pregnant with his children.

This Charming Dilemma

'Hello there,' another male voice appeared on the other end of the line, 'are you ready to get down to business?' he purred.

Oh god sounds like another telemarketer, well at least this one sounds a lot more confident than the last one. But I'm not in the mood for this.

'Listen,' I said down the phone, 'I have had a really frustrating day, so I'm not really interested in whatever business you have to offer.'

'Are you sure?' he purred again, 'I will offer you something that would really take that frustration away.'

Oh good lord! I really don't have time for this, I pressed the end call button and threw Fran's phone into my bag, at least I'll catch her at the meeting to give her bloody phone back. A wave of excitement came over me as I remembered the mission Millie and I are going on tonight, okay yes it's only installing cameras at the site of the old Crankshaw farm, but it feels like it's the start of something really big.

But first I have to get through this CWA meeting, the thought of it is already making me yawn, I wonder if I will have time for a nap before the meeting. Well I will if I go home now. It's been a big day and with everything that has happened this morning, I still really haven't had a lot to time to process the fact that there is more than one baby in there.

I really should tell mum and dad but I know they will be down here as fast as you can say overbearing parents and if that happens then I might as well kiss my chances being a television celebrity goodbye so best I leave that until the opportunity presents itself. Daniel comes back into the shop just as I was packing up the last of my things on my desk.

'I'm off,' I informed him as John shuts down the camera and Marline starts packing up her end, I bet after the day's events, those two would probably have had a few naps behind the camera.

'Yeah I'm going to call it an early day too,' Daniel said, making his way to his desk and turning off his computer, he seems to be a lot calmer now. 'Lisa just following our discussion, can I ask that you hold off getting in contact with the person until you consider another proposal,' he said, gathering his man-bag and flinging it over his shoulder.

What the hell does he mean by that?

 I left the shop quickly not stopping to quiz Daniel some more as he locks up. I want to get home before my body shuts down completely. All of a sudden I feel super tired and want to just lie down. Fran's phone chimes again with another private number displaying on the screen, I swipe the decline button and climb into the car, my eyes are so tired. I don't even have the energy to start the car, think I'll just sit here for a few minutes before heading home.

12

I can hear chiming in my ears, it starts, then it stops, then it starts again, but my neck seems to be sore and it's awful hot all of a sudden.

Great, now I can hear knocking, chiming and knocking, can't a girl get any peace?

Actually that's better, it's like someone has turned on a fan, there's a breath of fresh air just breezed in.

'Lisa?' John's voice appeared as I felt a hand on my arm. I jerk in fright and focus on where the hell I am. It's just on dark outside and I seem to be sitting in my car... outside the office.

'Sorry,' John said as I squinted towards him trying to wake my brain up, 'you were sleeping.'

'I was?' I asked, noticing John has the camera in hand as I wipe a pool of dribble from the corner of my mouth.

Marline lets out a slight snigger.

'Yes sorry, I thought I should wake you up, we were just coming back from getting a burger and noticed your car still here,' John said.

'No that's fine,' I said, locating my keys and trying to sound normal, 'I um, must have dozed off, better get going, have a meeting tonight.'

The chiming started up again and I noticed Fran's phone still sitting on top of my bag. I picked it up to swipe the decline button again. 17 missed calls, Fran has 17 missed calls?

Does Fran even know 17 people?

Shit and I'm late for the meeting! Nearly 40 minutes late.

Great now my phone is ringing. Yep and it's Betty calling, and I bet you all the CWA scones under the sun she is wanting to know where I am. I'd better go straight there.

'You okay to drive?' John asks.

'Oh yes, sure!' I said, 'must have just had a big day, thanks for um… waking me up, well better go, late for a meeting.'

I quickly shut the car door in haste and gather my thoughts, I hope John didn't film me asleep in my car, and come to think of it, I don't remember falling asleep, I remember leaving the office and getting to my car. Shit I better start drinking coffee again, all this herbal tea that Millie is shoving down me is making me a bit dozy.

Pulling out of the car park towards the meeting hall I glanced at my bag to see the surveillance camera box sitting inside my bag. Thank god, as at this stage I might just have to go straight from the meeting to the site, I quickly message Millie and ask her and Matt to meet me at the Crankshaw's, explaining I have a meeting. Betty and now Gloria are still trying to call me, but I am almost there. I can't believe I nodded off, feel a bit better for having a sleep but I must have been there for a good two hours, I mean who else saw me?

I glanced at the headlights in my rear-view mirror as I pulled into the hall car park, John and Marline pull up beside me so they must have stayed in town waiting for this meeting.

Or maybe they followed me when I left the office and decided to get a burger while they were waiting for me to wake up.

Well I'm sure people fall asleep in their cars all the time so what of it. Thank god I wasn't driving.

'Well about time you're here!' Betty scolded as I apologised to everyone as soon as I entered the hall with John in tow, 'we couldn't wait any longer, we started without you.'

I ignored the wrath of Betty's scolding but thank god they have already started so I can get out of here on time to set up these cameras.

I notice Ellen's sitting up the front next to Betty as I reach in to my bag to hand Fran back her phone. The damn thing chimes again, with another private number on the call screen.

'Where did you find that?' Fran asks, looking all wide eyed in horror at the phone as she looked at the call screen.

'You left it at the shop,' I said, 'it's been ringing all afternoon.'

'You didn't answer it?' asked Fran, exchanging a glance with Betty.

'Only to a couple of telemarketers,' I said taking my seat, 'honestly Fran get off the call register,' I said, getting my own back and taking a seat at the front desk tucking my bag beside me.

Betty and Fran exchange another glance of horror with each other.

Hmmm wonder what that's about?

Gloria hands me a copy of the agenda and quickly briefs me about where they are up to.

'Okay so you're up to... item two,' I said slowly, my god doesn't seem like I have missed much, they have barely made it through the apologies.

Great, just flipping great.

'Well we couldn't do much until we knew you were coming,' Betty scolded again, 'honestly Lisa, a phone call would have been nice.'

'Yeah um... battery went dead on my phone,' I mumbled, noticing Marline raising an eyebrow at me from the back of the room.

'Well then why didn't you use Fran's phone?' Betty scolded again.

This Charming Dilemma

I rub my brow in frustration, I should know by now I will never win anything with Betty around so I better just get on to item two.

'Okay item two,' I said, clearing my throat and wishing I had eaten something, my stomach is starting to rumble.

I wonder if I can ask John to nip out and get me a burger as it's all I am thinking about now. A beef burger followed by chocolate mousse, topped with gravy.

What the hell?

I spied a granola bar in my bag underneath the camera, that is going to have to do until I can get to more food.

'So item two, the financial report.'

'Before we do,' Betty said rising from her seat, 'I would like everyone to meet Ellen, for those who don't know her which is only really you Gloria,' said Betty.

Oh my god, why couldn't she have done this while she was waiting for me.

'Ellen here is Rick Crankshaw's new fiancée,' Betty said, after which smiles and greetings are exchanged for surprised looks, 'she is here because she has wants to get involved in a special way with our parade float,' Betty said with pride.

'Ohh that would be nice,' Mary said to Maggie who was sitting next to her.

'Hi,' Ellen greeted, slightly shy, waving to the room, 'um… yes I was chatting with Lisa and Fran today,' Ellen said, addressing the room carefully which I have to say I don't blame her, it can get pretty ruthless in here at times, 'and well, if you all don't mind, I would like to get married on the parade float during the celebrations.'

Ellen looks all coy again as the room exploded with gasps and cheers, great, just bloody great, item two is officially stuffed.

'What a fabulous idea,' Mary said, 'that would tie in nicely with the 100 year celebrations.'

Um… how so?

'A real live wedding on a parade float, we'll be the talk of the district,' said Maggie.

'The talk of the nation,' Mary said again, elbowing Maggie and pointing at John.

'Ohhh yes,' Mary said all wide eyed.

Looking at the agenda, Ellen's flippin wedding isn't even on the flippin agenda. I pick my bag up from the floor as the excited chatters continues, I better get this granola bar into me because it looks like it's going to be a long time until we get to item two.

I am trying to be discreet as I fish in my bag for the bar I had spotted.

This Charming Dilemma

I lift the camera box out of my bag, trying to locate it. Why is it you see things in your bag then all of a sudden they become invisible when you want them.

Ohh my gavel is in here, I must have thrown it in my bag this morning, thank god because the way this meeting is going, I'm going to need it. Fishing out my gavel and locating my snack bar I glance up to notice Betty's eyes focus on the camera box with a suspicious look, better put it away before it becomes item three on the agenda for discussion.

I take a bite of my snack bar and bang the gavel on the table to get this meeting back on track, we have five items to get though and have already wasted twenty minutes on discussing... well nothing really.

'Okay ladies, yes well we are all very excited about Ellen's wedding, can we make an agenda item please,' I said to Gloria who has given up taking minutes so she can get in on the wedding plans.

'Are you organising Ellen's wedding?' Maggie asked, looking surprised.

'Yes, yes I am,' I said, trying to move things along so the room doesn't burst into another discussion.

'Well isn't that a bit awkward given your history with Rick?' Mary said, almost causing me to choke on my mouthful of nutty goodness as Ellen turn to Mary with a puzzled look on her face.

Honestly old people need a filter.

'No, no, it's all good,' I said through my mouthful, spilling some of the contents on the page below me.

'I think our Lisa here is very professional,' continued Fran.

'Item two!' I exclaimed, banging my gavel on the table before the details of Rick and my past relationship are discussed. 'The financial report Gloria if you please.'

I can see Ellen looking at me with a bit of confusion on her face, so maybe she doesn't know about Rick and I. Funny you would have thought she would have at least asked me especially after Fran mentioned it to her at the shop, or maybe Rick told her a completely different story. But then again, I didn't know she was Daniel's twin. Maybe they are just the type of family that avoid issues.

Gloria passes around the paper with figures on it and starts her spiel about the budget. I glance in Betty's direction and notice her and Fran suspiciously looking at the camera box that is poking out of the top of my bag.

I discreetly pop it in my bag out of sight and zip it up, I'm sure both Betty and Fran saw that, but as long as they don't interrupt the meeting to ask questions about it they can continue to look at me with suspicion all they want.

Gloria runs down the expenses throughout the month as I stare blankly at the budget sheet in front of me.

I don't dare look at Ellen as I feel she still has a look of confusion on her face, but seriously, has Rick not told her at all.

This Charming Dilemma

Hang on a cotton-pickin minute.

I grabbed the budget sheet in front of me and almost fell off my chair. *Thirty thousand dollars.* The lemonade stand has brought in thirty thousand dollars this quarter!

'Okay so I would like to move that the financial report be accepted,' said Gloria.

'Hang on, hang on!' I said, still staring in disbelief at the figure in front of me. 'Thirty thousand dollars in income, is this a typo?' I exclaimed as Fran jumps and shoots a glance in John's direction.

'Lisa!' Betty scowled, 'we can't discuss financial business in front of, you know,' she said, her head jerking towards John.

Oh for god's sake, but happy to spill my relationship history out there.

'I'm just surprised that the stand is doing that well!' I exclaimed.

'Yes well it is an icon now dear,' Betty reminded me as Fran's phone chimed again.

I glance at the faces in the room but I seem to be the only one that has even raised an eyebrow at this, I mean after all we sell soft drinks, light refreshments and ugly creations, it's not the Eiffel flippin Tower. But everyone seems to be at a hush because John and his camera are in the room.

'Fran needs to take this call,' Betty said as everyone shuffles to assist Fran in leaving her chair to take the call outside.

Honestly when someone leaves the room it has to be announced, followed by the entire room having to reshuffle themselves to suit. But I better hurry this along because I have now 43 minutes to get through three more items and get down to the Crankshaw's gate. While everyone gets resettled from Fran's temporary exit, I quickly text Matt to let his know I'm at a meeting and to meet me at Crankshaw's gate, and be discreet about it.

These figures in front of me on the financial sheet are jumping out at me and something doesn't seem right, I mean it's all itemised and it all seems to match, but seriously, the rate the CWA is going we would have enough to open a small mine ourselves.

And Betty did say something about having the funds available for the campaign, but she also mentioned they are not coming from the CWA.

'Lisa?'

'Hmmm?' I said, looking up to find many sets of eyes and one camera staring at me.

'We're waiting,' Mary tutted.

'Honestly, short attention span this one,' scoffed Betty.

'Oh right um, item three.' *Oh good lord.*

'Yes about our costumes,' Betty said, again standing in for Fran, 'now Fran, god bless her, has done such hard work and they are looking fabulous,' she said as many knitted ugly

This Charming Dilemma

erotic items are being passed around and I want to bang my head against this desk in front of me as the room breaks out in discussion again. Ellen also seems to be getting involved with the discussion. I may as well give up now.

'Now if you can all pick your costumes and try them on,' Betty said as the murmurs of chatter fill the room, Marline is standing behind John looking like she is about to wet herself with laughter as Maggie holds up a pair of knitted stockings while Mary is trying on one of Fran's g-string knickers over her brown slacks. The room is filled with hooting and laughing as most of Fran's ugly erotic knitwear is now making its way to unmentionable places. I better rein it in, John is starting to look uncomfortable and Ellen looks like she might be wondering if she stepped into a board meeting for a funny farm.

'Okay order!' I yelled, banging my gavel on the desk as the hooting and laughing gets even louder.

'Have you tried yours on yet dear?' Betty asks me, over the raucous noise, 'Fran might have to let a couple of stitches out,' she said, glancing at my waist line.

'Yes you have put on a bit of weight dear,' Gloria says, adding to Betty's observation.

My phone beeps and Millie's message appears on the front of my screen, shit she is already down there waiting on me, I better wrap this up. 'Okay well if there is nothing else,' I said as the noise starts to die down, 'then I declare the meeting closed at 8.02 pm, thank you everyone, next meeting will be err… next week,' I hastily picked up my bag.

'But we haven't got through the next item,' Betty scolded, 'honestly Lisa it's the parade schedule, Ellen here has come along for this, we need your approval on some items.'

Oh for god's sake, then why didn't she make it item one.

'As your president I solemnly approve anything that is about to be discussed,' I said, hastily leaving my seat.

'You don't even know what it's about,' Betty argued, 'honestly what could be so important that it's got you rushing everywhere.'

'I bet you it's dinner,' Mary said, 'have you eaten dear? I was just staying to Maggie you are looking awfully pale.'

'No it's not dinner, it's just um… work stuff,' I said, backing away.

'But this is work stuff,' Betty argued again, 'Daniel has done up an itemised cost of the parade advertising, it needs your expertise.'

'Yes well I have already had a quick glance at it earlier and it seems to be fine,' I said, slowly making my way to the exit, Honestly it's like trying to escape prison.

'How could you have seen it dear, he's only just emailed it to me!' Betty snapped, holding up her iphone.

This Charming Dilemma

'Sup?' Matt greeted, coming up behind me causing everyone's attention to divert to him.

Oh my god.

'You ready?' he asked, causing Betty to raise an eyebrow and Marline to let out another slight snigger.

'Matt what the hell are you wearing?' I mumbled through gritted teeth.

'You said be discreet,' he whined as he stood there in camo gear with his face painted in war colours.

'Oh and I fink someone is doing it behind da hall,' he said, unaware how ridiculous he looks right now, 'there's a lot of moaning and stuff.'

'Okay, well better go,' I said, taking Matt by the arm as four sets of eyes are looking bewildered while the other two sets of eyes, Marline and Betty, are looking suspicious. "

'Um… better get him cleaned up, tch, youth of today,' I scoffed as I hastily left the hall to the safety of the cool air outside. I really want to belt the shit out of Matt for turning up but I can't keep Millie waiting, she could change her mind in a heartbeat.

'Hurry up and get in the car!' I hissed as Matt tried to take a glance around the side of the hall.

'Seriously I fink someone is doing it,' he droned on as I impatiently waited for him to shut the car door before moving off.

'Doing what?' I asked, reversing out of my parking spot.

'Doing it!' Matt pressed, 'you know, sumfung you haven't done since poor Damo.'

'No one is doing it Matt!' I snapped, 'it's the CWA, no one does it.'

I can see Betty and Mary in the car park followed by John in the rear-view mirror as I exited the car park.

'God Matt you could have waited outside,' I hissed.

'Well I didn't know, and we left Damo back there,' he said, 'god Lisa what is so important.'

'We'll just leave Damo there, we haven't got time,' I said, 'and it is important Matt because well… Millie is on board with it and it's our future that we are dealing with here.'

'Yeah but what is da future shit,' Matt pressed on, 'better not be killing another rooster Lisa, remember what happened when you forced me to do that last time, you chickened out.'

'I did not chicken out Matt the thing died of fright before the deed could be done. No this is about the mine.'

'So what are we doing?' Matt asked, pulling out his phone from his camouflage pants pocket.

This Charming Dilemma

'We are putting up cameras up at the front entrance to the Crankshaw's farm.'

'Is dat it?' said Matt in a flat voice, 'I fought you said it was important!'

'Putting cameras up at the Crankshaw's is important,' I pressed, 'we need to see who is coming and going so I can get facts, if there are no facts, there is no campaign,' I said as the fire of justice stirred in me.

Oh hang on, I think that's just indigestion.

'Like da other day with dem utes?' Matt asked.

'Yes like the other day Matt,' I confirmed. Honestly it's like talking to a three year old.

'Yeah but dats not exciting,' Matt continued to complain as I looked in the rear-view mirror and noticed two sets of headlights behind me. My phone beeps and I know its Millie wanting to know where I am. The Crankshaw's farm is approaching so I speed up a bit more and so does the car behind me.

'Matt, I think someone is following us,' I said.

'It's probably Damo, I told him to follow us. Man is he going to be pissed as well when he finds out we are putting boring old cameras up. He had to borrow army gear for dis you know.'

'Matt, I didn't ask you to bring Damo along, you just did it. I just want you to help Millie while I film it on my phone,' I said, 'Damo can hold the torch.'

'Boring,' Matt mumbled.

Approaching the Crankshaw's gate, one set of headlights has dropped off so I guess it's just Damo behind us now. I couldn't see Millie's car until I pulled up at the gate.

'Where have you been?' Millie asked impatiently as I got out of the car, 'and who is that?' she asked.

'It's me,' Matt said, 'you probably can't see me cos I'm in camouflage.'

'No, not you, you idiot, who is driving your car?'

'Oh dats Damo,' Matt said as Damo also gets out of the car wearing camouflage gear.

'Okay well whatever, the more the friken merrier,' Millie said shaking her head, 'let's get this over with.'

She pulled out another set of cameras from her car, 'I got these from Sid, he's had them for a while, he was going to set them up in the clearing in the bush behind the house to see if there is any intelligent life visiting but he never got around to it. So since Dumb and Dumber are here we may as well put a set up at the old milking shed as well.'

Loving Millie at the moment.

This Charming Dilemma

'So you two may as well head up there,' she said to Damo and Matt, taking charge and handing them the box of cameras.

'But we don't have a torch,' whined Matt, 'how are we supposed to see.'

'You don't have anything in your car?' asked Millie as she removes the cameras from the box.

'Well it's not like we had notice,' Matt complained, 'if we had known we would have to be camera technicians we would have brought some tools.'

'You would think a third year apprentice mechanic would carry some tools with him?' Millie quizzed.

'I'm on holiday being Lisa's bodyguard,' Matt carried on, 'it's not like I need tools for dat.'

'Yeah okay whatever, just hold this,' Millie sighed, handing Matt her torch as I got my phone out to start secretly recording so I can show it to John later. Millie tied the camera to a fence post with a strap and started to position it to the right spot. I was meant to do a quick narrative while I was driving out here to explain what we are doing but Matt turning up threw out those plans so I will have to do it later.

'Lisa do something useful and stand over there,' Millie said, pointing to the spot she wanted the cameras to focus on as she positioned it right, and then blue-toothed her smart phone up to it to see if she had the right spot.

'Perfect,' she said, pulling out a small tool and beginning to fasten it to the post, 'now just stay there,' she said as she picked up a step ladder from the grass and opened it up. 'We'll put one on the opposite side of the gate a bit higher.'

Millie is such a professional at this, I'm so happy she's chosen to be a private investigator, it's sometimes just like digging up lost funds etc, but still I think she has found her calling at last.

'Think there's a car coming,' Damo said, the first thing he has said since arriving.

'It's probably John and Marline,' said Matt still holding the torch as Millie finally fastens the last of the camera to the pole, 'he was at da old peoples meeting Lisa was at.'

'And you didn't think to divert or let him go first so he wouldn't drive past?' Millie said in a dry tone getting off the ladder.

'Errr,' I said, not knowing what to say. I know it's dark and we are only working with a bit of torch light and the glow of Damo's mobile phone as he checks his social media notifications but I'm sure Millie is rolling her eyes at us as she gets down off the ladder.

'Okay, you and Damo get in the car and quickly drive it up to the old milking shed,' she said, handing Matt the box containing the other set of cameras, 'just get started on this. Lisa quickly go pop the boot on my car and grab the tyre jack, we are going to pretend we just fixed a flat tyre. We will meet you boys up there after they go.'

This Charming Dilemma

Millie's so brilliant.

'And don't turn your headlights on,' she said to Matt as he ran back to the car like a sniper.

'Den how we meant to see?' he asked as he got to the car door.

'Stick your head out the window!' Millie snared, throwing him the torch.

Matt and Damo slowly negotiate the driveway as the headlights get closer then stop as John and Marline pull up, sporting a concerned look as Millie quickly throws the camera box in the front seat of her car.

'You guys okay?' John asks.

'Yes fine,' Millie said, 'I was just on my way into town when I got a flat, all good now,' she said, picking up the jack for effect and placing it back in the boot and closing the lid.

'Yes that is why I had to err... rush off,' I said, following on from Millie.

'Is that why Matt and Damo needed to follow you looking like they have just stepped out from barrack training?' John mused.

I didn't know what to say to that so I just looked back at him.

'Anyway, you should have told old Betty that,' John continued, 'her and Fran seemed to be a bit put out that you didn't explain what you were doing.'

'Well I was just changing a tyre,' I said, pointing to Millie's tyre, 'tch, old people huh.'

And yes I'm sure Millie is rolling her eyes in the depths of the darkness again.

'Yeah,' John agreed, 'so where did Commander Matt and his Lieutenant go?'

'Oh I think they went to a um… costume party,' I said.

Yes Millie is probably eye rolling again. But I couldn't think of anything else.

Loud screams ring out from the Crankshaw's shed echoing through the night air causing everyone to jump.

What the hell!?

"What was that?!' exclaimed John, opening his car door and climbing out.

Millie appears at my side exchanging looks of concern. Surely it couldn't be Matt, that scream sounded more like a girl. But then again…

'Probably a feral pig,' Millie said, willing me to not say anything else.

'Oh that's right, forget you get them around these parts,' said John, getting out of his city roots for a second.

Loud screams ring out again, this time it was followed by gunshots.

This Charming Dilemma

'Yeah we also get hunters,' Millie said, hastily making her way to the safety of her car.

John reached in and grabbed the film camera, as Marline jumped from the passenger side and made her way beside John.

Honestly what part of hunter with a gun didn't they understand. More gunshots followed by screaming echoed as John aims his camera towards the source. It seems to be getting louder. If fact it seems to be coming this way. John shoots the camera up the Crankshaw's driveway, the illumination captures a glimpse of figure running toward him.

'Quick, drive, drive,' Matt yells, running down the driveway like Forrest Gump, followed by Damo, 'we're under attack!'

Another gunshot rings out as all of us run to the safety of our vehicles. John and Marline are the first to speed off as I wait until Damo and Matt dive head first into the backseat of my car as Millie drives off in the opposite direction.

13

'So did you get to put the cameras up?' Millie asked Matt after they are parked up on the sofa back at the safety of the house, with Matt holding a cold cloth to his head, I don't know if he injured himself or is just being melodramatic.

'No we dropped them. God is that all you care about, Damo and I were nearly killed!' Matt whinged as Damo sits and stares at the floor with a bit of cobweb dangling from his head.

'Let's see if we can see anything,' John said, coming back into the room with some device attached to the camera that allows him to play back footage and zoom in on any background.

'It's definitely hunters,' Millie said, sounding skeptical at Matt's theory that there was someone stalking them at the shed and shooting at them when they started to assemble the cameras. According to Matt they didn't even get to go anywhere near the shed when someone from the darkness started to fire shots. In the haste to get away they dropped the box containing the cameras.

'I'm telling ya now, it wasn't hunters, hunters don't hunt in sheds Millie!' Matt exclaimed.

Sid has also entered the room but looks a bit bewildered at the sight of Matt and Damo in their camouflage gear.

This Charming Dilemma

'Well can't see anything in the background,' John said looking into the device off the side of the camera as the sound of Matt's muffles screaming come from the camera, 'just you running and screaming,' John said, turning the device around so Matt can see. Sid pokes his head over Matt's shoulder to have a look.

'Did you say you were shot at?' Sid asked, watching the screen.

'Yeah me and Damo were almost killed, you can hear the shots,' Matt said in his whinging voice.

'Yes I can hear it, but I would have thought you could see some sort of gun flash,' Sid observed, looking at the screen sideways.

'Yeah that's true,' John said.

'So no one believes us, well dat's just great, some friends you are,' Matt said suddenly coming back to life and trying to remove himself from the sofa in a hurry to drive the point home that he is not happy, but looking more like an earthworm trying to wriggle its way out of a cocoon. 'Well Damo and I don't need dis shit, the only reason we were there was cos you asked us to be.'

'Calm down Rambo,' Millie said, 'we didn't say we don't believe you, we're just saying if someone did shoot we then we have to make sure our facts are right.'

'What were you doing there anyway?' John asked with a sudden suspicious look on his face, 'I thought you were at a costume party?'

'Nah, me and Damo got conned by Lisa to come and help install stupid cameras.'

'So there was no flat tyre?' John said, looking at Millie with one eyebrow raised.

Millie answered by throwing her hands in the air in defeat.

'You got a flat tyre?' asked Sid.

'So you were there putting cameras up?' John probed again.

'Yeah and why did we have to do dat in da dark,' whined Matt again.

So many questions are being thrown around the room I think I'll just sit this one out. Marline has come back in the room but Matt so far hasn't realised, so until he does there's going to be no shutting him up.

'Okay,' said Millie with an impatient sigh, 'we were putting cameras up at the old farm, which as you all know, will become the new mine sight. Lisa needs to find out what company is coming and going from the site so she can put a campaign together.'

'Isn't that trespassing?' John asked, sounding amused.

Millie shrugged. 'There are no signs up to tell you otherwise,' she said.

This Charming Dilemma

'Yeah true,' observed Sid, 'if they have bought the site then why haven't they put some form of sign up?'

'Or cameras,' mumbled Damo, the second thing he has said all night.

We all pondered this for a moment, well they did, I was thinking about Jake and how to go about telling him about the babies again.

'Did you take my box of cameras?' Sid asked Millie, breaking the silence.

Millie ignored Sid's question, 'well we are going to have to go back and get retrieve the cameras that team commando here dropped,' said Millie, 'because it's got "property of Sid" written on it.'

'I'm not going back there!' Matt exclaimed with a hint of terror in his eyes, 'Damo and I aren't your targets Millie.'

'Well you dropped them,' she said in her mothering voice, 'and Sid can't, he didn't drop them in the first place, and besides it's his name on the camera box.'

'What about Lisa?' Matt questioned, looking like he is about to throw a toddler tantrum, 'she needs the exercise!'

'Lisa can't do it,' Millie scoffed, 'she's...'

'Tired!' I exclaimed loudly, stifling a yawn, I'm errrr... really tired.' Marline looks at me with one eyebrow raised.

Bloody Millie, she needs a filter.

'Well don't look at me,' John said amused, 'I'm bound by contract,' he said, holding up the camera, 'I can't participate in anything illegal.'

'Yes but you do have to follow us,' Millie said in a bit of a cheeky voice, 'even if we are doing something illegal, aren't you bound by your contract to film under any circumstances?'

'Yes, but stalking is not my thing,' he smiled.

Okay Millie is flirting, which means she is trying to get John to do it.

'It's too risky,' John continued, 'especially tonight. They may be waiting for you to come back so I don't want anyone going near there and getting hurt knowing the risks are there, why don't you wait till morning, I'll go with you then,' John smiled at Millie.

Hmm is John flirting back?

'Well you sort dat out,' Matt said getting off the sofa, 'Damo and I are going to da pub, yous coming?' he said, addressing John and Sid and only just realising Marline is standing next to John as he looks like his voice-box suddenly dropped out from underneath him.

'Are girls allowed?' Marline said with a hint of amused sarcasm. Matt didn't answer her and continued to look like someone had just frozen him to the spot.

Sid looks at Millie, unsure what to do as John also extends the invite to Sid.

This Charming Dilemma

'Yeah off you go,' Millie said to Sid.

The room emptied quickly including Marline, leaving me feeling a little left out that no-one invited me.

'Well you did say you were "tired",' Millie said, using air inverted commas and crashing on the sofa when I complained that I didn't specifically get invited. 'Honestly, just admit to everyone you are pregnant and get it over with, it's not like you're not showing now,' she sighed, looking at my slight protruding belly.

Which by the way, had better get food into it fast before I starve my children.

'It's not that I won't Millie, it's just that I don't want too many people knowing until I talk to Jake, I mean it's not like he's not coming back to town, I'll see him at Rick's wedding, what am I going to say, "Hi Jake meet my twin babies". I mean I'm sure it won't take long for him to do the math and...'

Shit Jake is going to be at Rick's wedding!

Okay now I feel sick.

'Speaking of the potential father, I found out where Jake is,' said Millie, fishing in her jeans pocket.

'Here,' she said handing me a piece of paper, 'it's the phone number of the company he is working for.'

I can't believe that I hold Jake's contact details in my hand, it's like holding the code to a lost city, I mean how brilliant is Millie.

'It must have taken some digging,' I said, opening the paper to reveal the company name and phone number, oh and email address.

'Nah not really, I asked Sid to ask Matt,' Millie said, stifling a yawn, 'I don't know why you just didn't ask Daniel.'

'I did and... well... he kinda went all funny about it,' I said, thinking back to the conversation at the office when Daniel suggested Jake would not show any interest in the babies, in fact the thought of contacting him is making nauseous, I mean what if he rejects us, then what?

'We really do have to retrieve that box,' Millie said, with a hint of worry, 'that camera box has Sid's name on it. And I didn't want to tell you earlier especially in front of John, but the proposal that the mining company has put through to the public, well they *had* put in a planning application to the council yes, but it's only a permit to take samples to see if there is coal there. Acrabobe Mining Company, which by the way is only small fry compared to the bigger companies out there, was approached by the land owners.'

'By who... the Crankshaw's?' I said, trying to process the whole well... process.

'No, by this company called BFPC. The thing is...' said Millie adjusting herself on the sofa,

This Charming Dilemma

'the brochure informing the public of a proposed mine, which your councilor friend doesn't know anything about, which is a typical story yes, but he really *doesn't* know anything. The first he heard of this was when brochures starting appearing in letter boxes around town. The company is denying that they even put the brochures out, which isn't unusual, they want to rally support in the community before applications are put in so they are very much like the politicians and spin anything to get the off siders on side, but when enquiring about who financed the brochures, well it really wasn't Acrabobe Mining, nor was it this other company, BFPC, but an anonymous third party.'

'So another company?' I said, getting over my Jake nerves and now starting to feel really hungry.

'No, a private entity,' she said baffled, 'so that is why we need to get that camera box back, I don't have a good feeling about this, I need to erase any links back to us until I find out more.'

'Okay,' I said, stifling a yawn, 'we'll do that tomorrow on my way to work,' I said as the thought of food and bed are so appealing. Millie didn't answer as I left the room and made my way to the kitchen still clutching the bit of paper containing Jake's contact details. I have decided to call tomorrow from the office phone. Daniel won't be in the office till mid morning so it's perfect timing to ring Jake and tell him.

But how to tell him...

'I think we need to go back now,' Millie said, coming back into the kitchen.

'Back where?' I said through a mouthful of left over curry.

'Back to get the camera box,' Millie said, looking worried again.

'Um… people shot at Matt and Damo,' I said, wondering where Millie's common sense went to, it's normally Millie lecturing me on my absurd ideas.

'And that would be perfect because whoever that is wouldn't expect us back tonight.'

'Um… what about Amy?' I said, trying to reason with Millie without being blunt.

'Well Brendan is here… but I really can't ask him to watch Amy, I'll call Sid and get him to come back,' she pondered, 'or I'll wait until Sid gets back.'

'I like the last option,' I said, gathering my food plate and heading for my bedroom, Millie can't hassle me if I'm asleep.

And besides I shouldn't really be doing this in my condition like she had almost pointed out.

I have to say I am feeling rather pleased with myself that finally I have some action going on with the whole reality show, I mean yes it's dreadful that Matt and Damo got the bejezzers scared out of them but at least John was there to witness it, and it proves things do go on around here if well… you wait long enough. The pilot episode of the show is meant to be aired soon and despite me trying to convince Brendan to make a whole new pilot episode due to the fact that the

This Charming Dilemma

first pilot episode is filled with moments I would rather forget, Brendan just reminded me it's the episode that won over the investors so I just have to get over myself and blah, blah. It's good to finally have some action over the mine so I can go into damage control after the nation thinks I am some mad country woman.

Brendan has a meeting with Daryl Loft tomorrow. He didn't sound positive when he informed us earlier in the day he wasn't going to be around tomorrow so I hope they don't decide to cut it before it begins.

Anyway better get some sleep.

Bloody hell, there goes my phone. It's okay, it's just Matt, I'll let it go to voice mail.

I can feel flutters in my stomach and every time I do, I also feel nerves kick in about contacting Jake.

Shit my phone is beeping again, and it's Matt, he's probably still ranting on about being shot at. Honestly he really needs to find an outlet here and stop being so melodramatic. I switch the phone onto silent and snuggle down under the covers. Now where was I?

Oh that's right contacting Jake.

And there go the flutters again.

'Lisa!' Millie exclaims, bursting into my room.

God can't a girl be left alone for five minutes to think about telling the father of her babies that he is going to be a father.

'It's Matt, he's been trying to call you,' Millie said, 'he reckons he is being followed.'

'Probably someone he's picked up at the pub,' I mumbled from the depths of my covers.

'Noooo, him and Damo didn't make it to the pub they got run off the road by someone who has been following them since they left here, Sid's on his way home to sit with Amy.'

'It's Matt, he probably ran off the road by swerving around a bunny rabbit.'

'Well it doesn't matter what he did, we gotta get those cameras.'

'No, I'll just stay here,' I said, pulling the covers back over my head, 'and besides why can't Sid go and I'll stay here with Amy?'

'No Sid refuses to go, now quick, I really want to retrieve those cameras including the ones on the gate.'

Oh my god Millie has turned into danger mouse.

'If someone has run Matt's arse off the road deliberately and he was truly shot at, then don't you think we need to call the police? You're not being a thoughtful mother, putting yourself out there Millie.' I said, being brave from under the safety of the covers.

This Charming Dilemma

'And that is why I want to go and get the incriminating cameras,' she hissed, 'because Matt is heading to the police station. So come-on!' she demanded, pulling off the covers.

I seriously don't know why Millie is insisting on taking a tired, pregnant woman stalking but begrudgingly I find myself getting in the car.

Maybe Millie can do the cameras while I sit in the car and have a little snooze.

'Lisa I think someone is following us now,' Millie said, pulling me from my trance.

'You sure you haven't picked up Matt's paranoia,' I said, wiping drool from the side of my mouth and looking behind me to see lights in the rear-view mirror.

'In fact, where are we?'

'No, I'm not paranoid, because I have gone up Carnivorous Road, down Watts Road and now we are driving on the old forest road towards Crankshaw's farm and they are still behind us.'

Shit have I been asleep the whole time!

'So now I'm approaching the intersection I think we might just head towards town,' Millie said, putting her indicator on with her eyes locked on her rear-view mirror. 'And boom,' she smiled, picking up her phone and punching in a number.

'You!' Matt's voice rang out from the blue-tooth speaker.

'Matt you need to go and get those cameras… all of them,' Millie demanded, 'Lisa and I have our stalker following us into town.'

'What? After me and Damo were nearly killed you want us to go back and get shot at again, that's really nice Millie, I wouldn't want *you* to get killed or nufing.'

'No, now would be the perfect time because the people that followed you are now following us,' Millie said with gritted teeth, 'so you better hurry up because I can't hold them off forever.'

'Well me and Damo have just pulled up at the police station and are waiting for him to get back. He's got a sign saying he'll be back soon.'

'So you have time then,' Millie said.

Silence from the other end.

'And another thing, your finger prints are on those cameras, they could charge you with trespassing.'

'God that's so unfair, you don't care if we get into trouble, god Millie…'

'Matt!' Millie interrupted him in her dangerously stern voice.

'Yeah okay, we'll do it, you better remember us in your Will Millie.'

'Yep, you can have Sid's stamp collection. Lisa and I will meet you there as soon as we shake this person, just hurry alright.'

This Charming Dilemma

Millie quickly disconnected from Matt before he started ranting again. She looks in her rear-view mirror to make sure we are still being followed. I'm still thinking about what I'm going to say to Jake tomorrow.

'What kind of headlights do you think they are?' Millie asked me, pulling me from my thoughts again.

'Um… bright ones?' I answered.

'No plonker, I mean like Camry, Honda?'

'Oh… I don't know,' I said turning around, my thoughts back on Jake. You know it's funny because right now all of this seems surreal, I know I should be excited that we're being stalked and it's all over a mine that I am meant to be boycotting to present myself as an environmental hero to the nation on public TV but all I want to do is go to bed and eat tons of cookies with BBQ sauce.

The dim lights of town approach and the car is still following us, Millie makes a comment mainly to herself, willing them to follow us into the lights of the town. But just as the first street lamp approaches, the car turns off down a side road.

'Goddammit!' Millie exclaimed, 'well goes to show it was definitely following is, now hang on, I'm going to turn around and make a hasty run back to the Crankshaw's farm,' she said, spinning the car around and taking an alternative route so the car doesn't see us and start following us again. Millie is driving like a maniac and I hope she remembers there are four of us in this car not just her and I. I remind her of this in a stern voice as she clocks up wayyy past the speed limit. Whoa I just sounded like a responsible mother!

'I know what I'm doing,' Millie defended herself, 'you just go back to sleep.'

We approached the Crankshaw's farm with the park lights on, Matt's car is nowhere to be seen. Millie picked up her phone to call Matt again when he bangs on the window causing us both to scream.

I think I just peed myself a little.

'Jeppers Matt, where is your car?' Millie said, trying to locate her heart.

'Here!' he said, throwing Millie the two cameras from the front entrance, 'Damo and I hid da car under some branches, clever aye, you can't see it.'

'Where? Oh, over there,' Millie said, spotting the car in the long grass with a tree branch on top of it, 'okay well we'll keep an eye out while you and Damo go get the others, if we see an approaching car, I'll beep the horn.'

Matt looks like he just peed himself a little as well.

'There's a carton of rum in it for you both,' Millie said, sweetening the deal.

'Yeah fine, we'll do it, and not just cos you told us to do it for some cans of Bundy,' Matt stomped off with Damo who suddenly appeared out of the depths of the darkness. We watch as they disappeared up the long driveway towards the shed.

Millie switched on her interior light, 'oh will you look at this,' she said, turning the cameras over in her hands, 'smashed, deliberately smashed!'

'So do you think we will be able to get anything off it?' I said looking at Millie's facial expression which is crossing between really pissed off and really… well scary.

'Give it a go but I doubt it, wait till I track these fuckers down,' she seethed, 'destruction of property really pisses me off.'

I was just pondering if I should remind Millie of our trespassing when we heard a shrill piercing scream ringing out from the shed.

'Shit!' Millie said, throwing the cameras in the back seat and starting the car and heading towards the shed.

'You're seriously not going to go up there,' I panicked, hanging on as Millie sped up the drive towards the shed. 'Well I'm not going to fucken leave them there!' she screamed back, clearly the both of us are freaking out, 'get ready to open the back door for them to jump in!'

Clearly Millie and I are thinking the worst as she spun the car around and shined the lights into the shed as I ducked out of sight so I don't get shot at. Think I'll just close my eyes, bugger Matt, he can open his own door.

'What the hell,' Millie said in a puzzled manner, then started to laugh.

I poked my head up and opened one eye to see Marline holding Matt on the ground in a wrestling pose.

What the hell?

Millie and I tentatively get out the car to hear Matt groaning in pain as Marline had him in a hog-tied position on the ground. Damo appears from behind an old drum, clearly he just freaked out and hid.

'What are you doing here?' John said, appearing in the headlights looking slightly amused, causing Millie and I to jump.

'What are *you* doing here,' Millie questioned back, also slightly amused.

'Um… retrieving cameras,' she said in suspicious manner, 'what's your excuse? I thought you were bound by contract?'

'I'm off the clock,' he shrugged, 'so Marline and I thought we'd come up here, see if we could see anything, especially when Matt said he was run off the road.'

'So what, you're like an adrenaline junkie?' Millie asked.

'Yeah well it's not funny!' Matt exclaimed as Marline released her grip on Matt, 'do you know what it feels like when someone comes at you in da dark like that and crash tackles you,' Matt flips his body around to a sitting position, posed to punch anyone that comes near him.

'Sorry but I thought you were someone else,' Marline said with a grin on her face. 'But hey,' she continued, 'you've got a good set of lungs on you,' she giggled.

'Well you would scream if it happened to you too,' said Matt, red faced, pulling himself up from the ground.

'So did you get the cameras?' Millie asked John.

'I found one on the ground outside, but it doesn't look good,' he said, handing Millie a damaged camera, 'but no sign of the box.'

Despite John informing her of this Millie had a quick scout around by John's torchlight and questioned both Matt and Damo as to where they might have dropped the box in the first place. She looks really worried.

Matt informs Millie that he can't recall what happened to her stupid box as they were being shot at. Millie reminded him he screamed like a girl and Matt was just about to respond when the sound of motorbikes starting rung out in the distance. Matt and Damo run to the safety of Millie's car when single headlights appear at the old charred remains of the second shed in the distance.

'Everyone fall out,' John said as we all scurried back to our vehicles. John's van appeared from the side of the shed passing Millie's car as she started the engine as Matt and Damo curl up in fetal positions in the back seat. Millie reverses and follows John down the driveway, the dust from his vehicle impairing her vision. My heart is beating so fast I feel it's going to come out of my chest. And I don't dare look behind us.

We finally make it to the safety of the road. Millie was about to make the turn towards home when John did a u-turn in front of her and sped past us up the drive towards the shed again.

'What the hell?' Millie said, as we both looked behind us at John's dust. It doesn't appear that the motorbikes followed us out which means they are still up there.

'Okay so do we follow?' Millie asks, pondering this with a panicked look on her face.

'I vote no!' I said.

'Yeah me too,' Millie said, throwing the car back into gear and speeding off towards home.

'They'll be okay.' Millie said, trying to justify herself.

'Yeah it's their choice,' I said, also trying to justify myself.

No point asking Matt and Damo, I think they have gone back to the womb.

'Argh shit!' Millie examined, punching the steering wheel and turning the car around to go back. I so wanted to argue with her decision but I think I'll just curl up in the fetal position as well.

This Charming Dilemma

'Argh shit!' she exclaims again as three sets of headlights approach.

'It's them, the bikes!' I panicked, observing the single headlights. Millie stayed in the middle of the gravel road. Surely she's not going to play chicken.

'Um… Millie!' I said nervously as the headlights got closer.

Millie seems possessed, and I'm sure I just saw my life pass before my eyes.

'Millie!' I exclaimed, fear kicking in even more as the headlights got even closer as my foot pumps the imaginary brake on the passenger side.

'Shit!' Millie screamed, swerving as she realises the bikes weren't going to get off the middle of the road either. Millie hits the brakes as the car comes to a sliding halt, showering us in the dust of the gravel. The bikes speed past us as John pulls up beside us in his van.

Hang on… they don't look like motorbikes, but more like scooters! The sound of what I could only describe as overpowered electric lawnmowers faded into the distance as the dust cleared.

'Well that's weird!' said John.

14

'Is Matt Horton around?' the local policeman asked me from the other side of my desk at the office.

'Um… no,' I said, shaking my head slowly.

'Okay, his boss at the garage said he might be here, I was just inquiring as to why a car registered to him is parked in the long grass down Crankshaw Road with a tree branch on top?' I gave him my best bewildered look. 'Okay I'll try him at home, have a nice day,' he said.

I look at the piece of paper in my hand containing Jake's contact details but I am a bit hesitant to pick up the phone. I mean surely he doesn't need to know, but I do want him to know, I mean I would love nothing else than to be in a relationship with Jake, but not like this. I mean I want it to be a choice he makes, not because he feels he has to out of obligation.

Okay I'm over-thinking this, just pick up the damn phone.

I quickly punch the numbers into the office phone and hold my breath, okay this is it, just come out with it, remember, no expectations.

Oh great, it's a voice automation system. I finally pressed five for enquires when a male voice appeared on the line.

This Charming Dilemma

'T&G Mining.'

'Oh err, hi, I was just wondering, could I speak to a Jake Crankshaw or possibly leave my number for him?'

'Hold please,' he said as the sound of a political advert about how the industry contributes some of its profits to small communities and blah, blah. I think I need to slow my heart rate down as it's playing with the lump that has formed in my throat.

'You there?' the man's voice appeared on the other end of the line again.

'Yes,' I said, all poised.

'Jake Crankshaw finished up on our shutdown a couple of days ago, I can't give out his phone details due to his privacy conditions but I have an email address if you would like to contact him via email.'

He finished up a couple of days ago? To go where?

'Are you there?' the voice asked.

'Yes, yes, sorry, um… any idea where he would have gone?'

'No, I don't have that information, work finished here for his contact two days ago.'

'Okay, of course, um… yep email is fine thanks.'

I'm writing the email down with a slight tingle to my ear, lucky the guy is spelling it out as I can only concentrate on one letter at a time.

'Is there anything else I can help you with?' the man asks, wrapping up our conversation.

'No, thank you,' I said, about to hang up, I looked at the email address in front of me again.

'Oh, um… sorry but this email, it is <u>acrabobeopportunities</u>?'

'Yes that's right,' the man said.

'Okay, thanks,' I said disconnecting and picking up my mobile to text Millie.

Acrabobe, isn't that the mining company?

I text Millie asking her to spell the mining company as my brochure appears to be missing, well it's not missing, just can't be naffed to find it under this mountain of papers, but it sounds like the same name. Why would Jake's email have the same name?

Anyway I opened my email to compose a new one. I don't know how to write *Dear Jake, I'm pregnant and they are yours, yes yours because they are twins, yours truly, Lisa.* Well I could just write that but in case it isn't Jake's email and I give the bloke or lady on the receiving end of this email a bit of a soap opera read.

Dear Jake… no, too formal.

This Charming Dilemma

Hi Jake... better.

I really need you to contact me on some urgent business you need to know asap, as it's urgent, okay thanks. Oh in case you have forgotten... no... in case you deleted it... no can't write that either... okay my number is 042513395... better... it's urgent.

Regards Lisa... no, too formal.

Love Lisa... definitely not.

Lisa... better.

Okay close your eyes and hit send.

Millie's text comes back that yes it is indeed the correct spelling and I quickly send another message off to her telling her about Jake's email address.

The email flashed a message to inform me it was sent and now I guess it's in the fate of the electronic gods.

Matt obviously hasn't picked up his car, he and Damo were still asleep on the sofas when I left his morning, John was there filming normal activities around home before joining Daniel on an unusual photo shoot today. And after last night, we all agreed it was definitely scooters or small motorbikes we saw. John explained he had decided to confront whoever it was but didn't get the chance when they sped past him up the Crankshaw's driveway and down the road.

I did wonder if it could be Betty or Fran as they are the only ones that have scooters that I am aware of, but they definitely wouldn't be out at that time at night, Fran's normally in bed by 7.30pm and Betty has a hard time even attending CWA meetings after 6pm. But the more plausible explanation that John came up with, is that it's maybe kids and despite Matt's protests that eventually led to a sulky tantrum, possibly kids with air rifles.

My phone rung as I glanced at the CWA financial report that made its way from my car to my desk in amongst my bridal magazines and a packet of ready-made soup.

'Did you say that is Jake's email address?' Millie's voice said when I picked up the phone.

'Yeah, the contact number you gave me for Jake was the company he was working for, he left two days ago and that is the contact email they gave me.'

'acrabobeopportunities? As in two words, acrabobe then opportunities?' Millie asked again, clearly she is on the trail of something.

'Yeah and I have already flicked him an email, asking him to get in touch,' I said, glancing up to see Fran across the street parking her scooter.

'Wait I'll just Google this again,' said Millie as I continue to glance at Fran.

This Charming Dilemma

Betty has just joined her and I'm thinking I might need to close the blinds and lock the door as I have no doubt they are heading this way.

And they are both on the phone again.

I have a quick glance at the financial report in front of me, the outgoing expenses don't seem to itemise any phone activity, even though those two phones are owned by the CWA. In fact, I, as the president, am going to demand to see their phone activity statements. I mean seriously, they seem to be constantly on the phones, surely they are not talking to each other, and both Betty and Fran have landlines.

'Okay so I have a website,' Millie's voice appeared on the line again, 'it looks like an amateur website, something that has just been slapped together. It doesn't give away much, just says about an exciting opportunity and a form to register your interest for employment, which I am going to do,' said Millie with a sly tone to her voice.

I am listening to Millie but I also focused on Betty's scooter, it looks filthy, like it's got mud all up the tyres. The unusual thing about that is Betty is a clean freak and always seems to be washing it. Oh god and they are coming this way.

'There must be a mistake,' I said, watching Betty and Fran come closer, 'why the hell would Jake have an email address linked to a mining company, they have obviously made a mistake. Maybe they thought I said Jake Frankshaw, or I don't know, maybe there are two Jake Crankshaw's.'

'Yeah and maybe they thought you said Jake Wankshaw and thought, yes I know exactly who you are talking about,' Millie said in a sarcastic tone.

'That's not funny Millie, that's the father of my children.'

'Yeah but it fits, anyway I am going to put in a fake application and see what comes back.'

'Gotta go,' I said hastily hanging up as Fran and Betty make an entrance.

'Lisa dear,' Betty greeted, 'Fran and I were hoping you were here. Have you tried on the outfit yet dear? It's only three months until the big event. And well...' Betty said, looking at my waist line.

'Yes dear,' Fran added, removing her coat, even though it's almost 26 deg outside, 'if you're not busy can I see it on you to make some adjustments?'

I freak out at the thought of Fran seeing me in a two-piece considering my belly button is now protruding outwards.

'Um... no need,' I said, picking the outfit off the floor next to the bin where I left it last, 'I have just this second tried it on and it needs a little extending around the waist.'

'Tch told you, you shouldn't eat so much,' Betty said.

'Yes but by how much?' Fran said, pulling out her tape measure, 'I really think I need to measure you.'

Oh good lord no.

This Charming Dilemma

'Um, it's all good, I can do it later.'

'Nonsense, don't be embarrassed dear, we all put on a bit of weight at times, now come on, stand up.'

There is no way I am going to get out of this as I tentatively stand up, holding my breath and willing my belly not to move as Fran maneuvers the tape around my middle.

'Good lord you have put on the beef a little, look, even your bum and thighs are bigger since the last time I measured you,' she tutted, 'okay well I'll make some adjustments,' she said, writing down the measurements.

I let go of my breath.

'I know why you have put on weight,' Betty said, in a knowing way. I hold my breath again waiting for her to tell me she knows all about my condition and Jake and the fact that I am going to live my life a single mother.

'You're going to turn 40 soon, isn't that right dear, middle age spread, it happens,' she sighed.

'Yes, yes that's it,' I said, letting my breath go yet again, 'but speaking of outfits, since Ellen has decided to get married on the parade float, don't you think we need to rethink our dress?' I said, looking at the hideous outfit and wondering for the millionth time how the hell I am going to pull this off.

'No it's fine, Ellen is more than happy to have us in our knitted outfits, she said it will be the most unusual and wonderful wedding ever, in fact she is coming in shortly dear to discuss a few ideas,' Betty said.

I maneuver around Fran to sit back at my desk as she opens her tote bag to put my outfit back in. Hang on a minute, is that a camera box in Fran's bag?

'Yes so with these preparations,' Betty continued, taking a seat at my desk as Fran quickly zips her bag up, 'all the street float applications have been posted to the businesses and Maggie has managed to get some stallholders on board already, now I'm thinking we need to hire a bouncy castle for the kids and maybe have a sideshow ally,' she said, pulling out her folder from her satchel.

'Huh?' I said, pulling my thoughts back as I glance past Betty to observe the dirt on her scooter again, surely it wasn't Betty and Fran out at the Crankshaw's last night?

'So what do you think Lisa?' Betty said, holding up a piece of paper with a picture of a sheep wearing lace stockings

'Yeah, looks good,' I said, glancing at Fran's scooter that seems to be looking a little worse for wear too.

Fran's phone beeped as she exchanged a glance with Betty.

'Um is there somewhere private I can go?' Fran asked.

'You mean to the toilet?' I asked.

This Charming Dilemma

'Yes that's a good idea,' Fran said, hastily making her way through our kitchen facility area to the toilet out the back with her beeping vibrating.

'So shall I go ahead and order the mugs and stubby coolers with this logo?' Betty continued.

'Yes, yes,' I said, waving her request away, 'so… did you have a big night last night?' I asked Betty in a causal way.

'Lisa, what has that got to do with erotic sheep?' she scolded, 'so can you go ahead and order about two hundred of each?' she asked.

I know I should know better, I'm definitely not going to get any answers, innocent or otherwise, out of either of them while their brains are clearly focused on the Mardi Gras parade, but something is very fishy here. And why is Fran taking so damn long in the toilet! I glance at Fran's tote bag sitting next to the empty chair, actually… it's a good thing Fran is taking ages, if I can just distract Betty enough maybe I can get a quick look inside to confirm it is the same camera box, I mean it can't be a coincidence.

I can see Ellen heading this way in all her radiance, which is just perfect. Now just to get Ellen's presence to distract Betty. Ellen entered the shop with a smile as Betty greeted her like a long-lost daughter. My eyes are still glued to the tote bag.

Ellen settles in the chair next to Betty and starts rambling on about something,

I am kinda listening, considering it's me who is organising her wedding, but if I can just get Betty and Ellen to divert their attention for just a moment.

'Speaking of lemonade,' I said, interrupting Ellen as she shows Betty pictures of bridal wear she has flagged, 'why don't you show Ellen the stand?' I grinned, 'you know, since its famous and everything.'

'Oh I have already had a look,' she smiled, 'Rick showed me.'

Course he friken did.

'Now Lisa, we need a final count on the guest list,' Betty said, taking over, 'the truck is certainly not big enough to hold a lot of people.'

'Well I was thinking,' Ellen said, all coy again, 'could we have our official wedding on the parade float and maybe re-enact our vows in your gardens in front of family Lisa? It's just that some of our family might get a bit put-out if we didn't invite them all, I mean surely a parade float can't hold fifty people.'

Oh my god I can see a potential out happening here.

'Yes, yes it can hold fifty,' I smiled, 'and why should your family miss out on the actual official event,' I encouraged, an image of Jake attending popping into my head.

It also means I can get out of being parade queen.

'I agree,' said Betty, 'Lisa can ride in front on my scooter and the rest of us can walk beside the float.

This Charming Dilemma

Shit!

My phone rang again as Millie's name appears on the call screen, hmm spying the tote bag again I think I have an idea.

'Excuse me, um, important call,' I said, getting off my chair and handing Betty a copy of floral ideas to distract her while I make my way from behind my desk. Walking past the empty chair, I discreetly kick Fran's bag under my desk.

'Hello Lisa Collins um…' shit, I forgot for a moment where I am.

'Yeah, yeah it's me, okay, you sitting down?' Millie said.

'Not yet,' I said, making my way back to my desk and hooking Frans bag strap with my foot to pull it close towards me. Betty is still nattering to Ellen so I discreetly bend down to pretend I am scratching my foot.

'So I put the bogus application in and I have had an email back from Acrabobe Mining, an auto generated one telling me thank you for my interest, I will be in touch to discuss your application, blah, blah. So that pissed me off, so dug a little deeper and you will never guess whose name appears.'

'Um… I can't have that information now,' I said, looking at Betty and Ellen, as I slowly unzip the bag, 'maybe you could text it to me.'

'Maybe I could just tell you now,' said Millie.

'Yes you could, but discussions will have to be um… delayed… on it,' I said, 'and besides I may have some follow up information that might be of interest,' I said, moving the knitted garment aside with my finger.

Oh my god, it is the camera box, it's Sid's camera box!

'Okay whatever, but hurry home. Oh and Brendan called earlier, he wants to hold a meeting with us this afternoon at 4pm,' Millie disconnects before I had a chance to gasp at my findings, Fran was out at the Crankshaw's last night? No surely not, must be an explanation for it all, and why is she taking so damn long in the toilet?

Discretely I zip up the bag under my desk and kick it towards Fran's empty chair.

Shit I think I overshot the mark.

'Um, is Fran okay?' I asked Betty, 'maybe I should go and check on her.'

'No need dear, she'll be fine, just you know, too much prune juice.'

'Are you sure?' I said, pressing the issue, 'cos what if she is um… having trouble,' I said, getting up to move.

Betty also gets up. 'I'll go check dear,' she said making her way around Ellen.

'No, I insist,' I said, quickly maneuvering myself from behind my desk. I hastily make my way to the back room cutting in

This Charming Dilemma

front of Betty and picking up my pace. I can feel Betty gaining on me. I can almost feel myself break into a run, Betty is definitely going to chase me. The toilet door swings open just as Betty cuts me off, causing me to come to a sudden stop as her large frame blocks me.

'Oh Fran, we were just coming to check up on you,' Betty said, giving me a sweet smile. Hmmm what just happened here.

'Whose bag is this?' Daniel appeared, holding Fran's tote bag, 'I almost tripped over it!'

~　　~~~~~~~~

15

I'm back home and Millie has gone to get Amy from daycare. Goddammit, just as I had information now I have to wait to tell her my findings.

Daniel has also got the message about the meeting with Brendan along with Betty and Fran, not sure about Matt, I notice his car gone when I drove home, probably in hiding somewhere, sulking at the fact no one believes he was almost killed by stalkers.

I am still having a hard time believing Fran had Sid's camera box in her bag, I mean what would two old ladies be doing out at that time of night at a proposed mining site.

In fact, do any of them even have the ability to shoot a gun?

'Hi Lisa,' John appeared without camera in hand, 'Brendan is not far away,' he said taking a seat at the table next to Sid who has his earbuds in watching something on his tablet.

'Oh, so you have been talking to him?' I asked, knowing that John had been with Daniel all day and wondering what this is about. The pilot episode is due to be launched and I know Brendan had a meeting today with the executives so maybe he is going to announce he is going to throw a party.

This Charming Dilemma

Daniel also arrived looking pained as Betty and Fran crawl out of his car. I did leave Betty and Fran at the shop to discuss some parade business with Daniel about the permits he was organising so obviously they managed to convince him to give them a lift out here as well.

Millie also just arrived and I was about to go and greet her at the car to quickly tell her about the camera box in Fran's bag when Brendan pulls up beside her. And he doesn't look too excited.

'Hi Lisa,' he greets as Millie gets Amy out of the car seat, 'is everyone here, shall we get started?' he said, gesturing us inside.

'Yes, we will be there in a moment,' I said, waiting and willing him to just leave so I can tell Millie my findings, although I have to say, Brendan doesn't look too happy at all.

'Have I got something to tell you,' I said when Brendan was out of ear shot.

'Yeah well I have something to tell you too,' Millie said, handing Amy's daycare bag for me to carry inside, 'but you're not going to like it,' she said kicking the car door shut with her foot while balancing Amy. Sid ran out to take Amy from her as Millie gave him a grateful smile.

'Like it, why won't I like it?' I asked, curious.

'So what did you want to tell me?' Millie said, changing the subject.

'Oh yes, guess who has your camera box?' I said, getting all excited.

'Who?' asked Millie with a look of curiosity.

'Fran,' I said, driving the point home with hand gestures, 'I found it in her tote bag this afternoon at the office.'

'Fran has our camera box?' Millie said, her voice rising up a notch up from calm and tired.

'Ladies?' Brendan said, beckoning us inside, 'can we get started?'

We make our way inside and Millie instantly shoots Fran daggers as she takes her seat. Maybe I should have waited till after the meeting to tell Millie.

'Okay thanks guys,' Brendan said, taking a seat as Marline also appears from the sitting room while Sid straps Amy into her highchair. 'It won't take long but as you know I have been in a meeting with the executives, I have already spoken to my crew here and I am afraid to say… they have postponed the pilot episode till October.'

What!

'A decision was made to air another program in front of ours, which will run from now until September, but unfortunately it will mean filming will cease for now.'

I can feel the colour draining from my face as Daniel clicks his tongue, Betty and Fran comment on what a shame it is and

This Charming Dilemma

Millie, well Millie looks slightly relieved. Sid on the other hand looks ecstatic. Sid doesn't like the limelight.

'Don't they like it?' I said, trying to talk around the lump in my throat.

'It's not that Lisa, not at all. Look its simple economics, we have enough here to produce two or three shows after the pilot so there is no point filming any more until closer to the time of when the show airs, otherwise it's just money that is being spent with no revenue coming in.'

'But what about our Mardi Gras parade?' Betty said, ready to wind up.

'We will be back to film the parade day,' Brendan said, 'as that will be one of our features in the show but until then, the crew and I would like to take everyone here out to the Tavern tonight for dinner on us as a thank you, but we will be departing tomorrow morning and back in October.'

I feel like part of my world has tumbled, even though Brendan said its only temporary, I mean what if it's not. My whole environmental hero thing has come to a halt.

Silence fills the room as Brendan tentatively gets up from the table followed by John and Marline. I am so disappointed I can hardly move, I feel the tears welling up.

'Oh well,' Fran said, 'I suppose we can look forward to October when they will be back,' she said.

'What'd I miss?' Matt said entering the room still wearing the camouflage gear from last night, 'I would have been here but da copper told me I had to go and get my car.'

'Smashed any cameras lately Fran?' Millie said with a hint of venom to her voice.

Fran looks at her horrified. 'What are you talking about?' she spat.

'The camera box in your bag,' Millie said, her eyes flicking to Fran's bag.

Everyone, except me, is playing tennis with their eyes between the two. I'm just trying to locate the nearest exit.

'I don't know what you're talking about, you silly girl!' Fran said, getting up to leave.

'Really, well show me then,' Millie said, also rising from her seat.

Sid can obviously see something brewing as he takes Amy from her highchair and exits the room fast.

'I will do no such thing!' Fran spat, 'how rude of you.'

'Well if there isn't a problem then why the defensiveness?' Millie said, grabbing at Fran's bag.

I don't know what has gotten into Millie but she has got a hold of Fran's strap and she is not letting it go.

This Charming Dilemma

'Ladies, ladies,' Daniel soothed trying to calm the situation but getting met by Betty snapping and telling him to stay out of it.

'Let go young lady or I'll have you up for assault,' Fran seethed.

'And I'll have you up for destruction of property,' Millie snapped back as they play tug of war with Fran's homemade tote bag.

'It's not destruction of property because they were illegally there,' Fran screeched giving her bag a final tug and ripping it from Millie's hands.

'Arhhh so you were there!' Millie said, with one eyebrow raised, sporting a smug look on her face.

'Of course we were there,' Fran spat, reaching in her bag and throwing the empty camera box at Millie, 'but more to the point, what were you doing putting cameras up?'

'Trying to catch people like you,' Millie said stating the obvious.

'What's this about?' Daniel asked, trying to catch up.

'Millie and Lisa tried to get me and Damo to put cameras up at da Crankshaw's farm,' said Matt, 'and we were almost killed.'

'Killed?' Daniel asked bewildered.

'Yeah, shot at and den run off da road, and Millie didn't even say thank you.'

'You weren't shot at,' Betty scoffed, 'honestly you're a bigger drama queen then Lisa here, it was an air rifle Matt, we wouldn't deliberately shoot at you.'

Okay I think I have just stepped into the twilight zone.

'How did you come to own an air rifle?' Daniel asked Betty still with the bewildered look on his face.

'Oh it's Charlies', he keeps it locked up at my place, you know, safer then all those kids running around at his place.'

'Yeah that's probably a good idea,' Daniel nodded.

'Hang on, if you didn't mean to shoot at the boys then why were you trying to scare them off?' Millie said, trying to get the conversation back on track.

'Why were you putting cameras up?' Fran asked.

'Um... to get the facts of the mine,' Millie said with attitude.

'You're just being nosey,' Betty said, 'it's got nothing to do with you.'

'Um aren't you running a "Ban the Mine" campaign, or is that just a charade to cover what is really going on?'

Okay the tension in the room just went up a notch.

'You don't have the facts,' Betty scoffed.

'Maybe not,' shrugged Millie, 'but I find it a huge coincidence that the website recruiting workers for a purposed mine in

This Charming Dilemma

Taromeo is manned by none other than one of your ex CWA members.'

Betty and Fran suddenly go quiet.

'Ex CWA?' I said out loud, racking my brains, 'oh of course, Mrs Crankshaw.'

No wonder Jake's email is the same as the Company's name.

'No…' Millie said shaking her head with a look that tells me I am not going to like what I am about to hear.

Fran's phone beeps again followed by the faint sound of vibration. Fran jumps and quickly turns it off shooting a look at Betty.

'So did you want me to continue?' Millie asked, clearly wanting to spill everything.

Daniel is watching the room with interest and Matt… well Matt is picking his nose.

'Listen here, you nosey tart,' Betty said, standing up, her chair scrapping backwards, 'you think you know it all, you think it's all so easy out there, well it's not.'

'So you conspired together to make people in this town believe a company was going to build a mine and create opportunities.

When really it was a bunch of locals who think they might have coal underground and try to gain interest so investors will come in, coal or no coal.'

Daniel gasped at Millie's statement and looked to both of them for confirmation.

'Yeah so what, what is wrong with making a bit of money, it's not easy being on the pension.'

'Millie how do you know all this?' Daniel said, stepping in as Betty and Millie move closer to one another in a standoff.

'Well it wasn't hard, I put a phony application in to the mining site after Lisa got Jake's email address which happened to match the company that was promoting this flyer,' she said holding up the flyer promoting the mine.

'But hang on, weren't you two ladies against it?' Daniel asked, clearly confused.

'Well we had to create a bit of conflict with this town,' Betty confessed, 'after all, investors need to see a bit of risk involved otherwise they wouldn't see the potential.'

'Potential scam!' Millie mumbled… loudly.

'Why would you want Jake Wankshaws email?' Matt spat, 'he's a wanker Lisa, he did it wif my mum you know.'

I don't know how to answer Matt so best if I don't say anything.

This Charming Dilemma

'And then after a computer automated reply came through I got my nerd of a husband to dig a little deeper,' continued Millie, 'and well wouldn't you know, a Ms Pamela Horton was the creator of the site.'

'Pamela!?' I said, my blood suddenly running cold.

'Mum?' Matt exclaimed, 'you mean to tell me mum is still in touch with tosser Jake.'

Millie shoots me a sympathetic look as Betty continues to stand over her.

Okay I think I am going to be sick. Pamela Horton, Matt's mother, the one that ran off with Jake when we first went out together after Jake sold off his share of the farm to developers and Pamela embezzled funds from the CWA to finance their little projects together. It was only when Jake left her high and dry after her marriage broke down over the revelations that Pamela ended up in a metal health ward after having a nervous breakdown.

... Or did Jake sell off his share of the farm? And who to? This is getting confusing.

'Hang on, let me catch up,' said Daniel, rubbing his brow. 'Acrabobe Mining Company is actually a company run by Pamela Horton and Jake Crankshaw, and they have put a permit in for an open cut mine on the Crankshaw's old farm?' Daniel said, putting it into simpler terms.

'Yes,' said Millie, folding her arms in triumph and giving Betty a smug look.

'Well no prizes for guessing who burnt down the farm,' he mumbled.

'They were well compensated!' Fran scoffed.

Daniel located a chair and sat down at his realisation that the farm fire was no accident. And they got insurance, so that's fraud. He looks like he was about to faint.

'So how are you two involved?' he asked finding his voice again as Matt looks like he is disgusted with the whole world.

'Because they financed it from then on,' said Millie, looking all smug again.

'Oh you're a nasty tart,' Betty seethed, stepping away from Millie and fetching her phone from her bag.

'Well you should have come up with something a bit better then BFPC,' she said in a sarcastic tone.

'BFPC?' Daniel asked, probably afraid of the answer by now.

'Betty, Fran, Pamela, Crankshaw's,' Millie said stating the obvious.

'Really?' I asked, in awe of how Millie got hold of that information.

'No I just guessed,' Millie whispered from the corner of mouth, 'these old ladies can't help but talk.'

'So hang on, if you're financing the application and stuff now, where the hell are you getting the money from?'

This Charming Dilemma

Daniel asked, winding up at the obscureness of it all, 'I mean you ladies, no offense, couldn't budget two pennies, that is why you keep coming to me for budget advice!' he exclaimed even louder.

Betty and Fran didn't answer. Stunned silence filled the room until the sudden shrill of Betty's phone ringing broke the tension. Hang on a minute, the phone calls?

No surely not.

The whole CWA financial sheet is flashing in my eyes and images of Betty and Fran on their phones. Oh my god and the day Fran left her phone at the office, the calls I thought were telemarketers. And oh my god, Matt thinking someone was "doing it" behind the CWA shed, when Fran disappeared… on her phone!

'You're financing the potential mine with phone sex?' I said in horror, feeling dizzy.

Betty and Fran looked at the beeping phone in horror, Millie, reading their expressions, lunges for the phone. Betty intercepts Millie but misses her as Millie picks up the phone.

'You bitch!' Fran screams, lunging for Millie as the vibrating phone flies across the room and now Fran is pulling at Millie's hair.

'Ewwww, ewwww!' Matt exclaims, looking like he wanted to peel his own skin off, 'me… I mean Damo, rung dat number cos Munta dared him too at a party one night. And it was a nana!'

The room explodes into chaos as Millie and Fran continue to fight. Betty is screaming at them both, while Matt is rocking back and forth moaning in disgust. I fall into the seat beside a bewildered and stunned Daniel, wondering what the hell just happened. I look up to see Brendan, Marline and John standing in the door-frame with shocked expressions as they take in the scene in front of them.

Brendan starts shaking his head.

'It's a shame we had stopped filming,' he sighed.

~~~~~~~~~~
~~~~~~~~~~

16

3 months later.

I adjusted my headset and tuned in.

'Lisa dear!' Betty shrilled through my ear piece, causing me to flinch. 'Is this thing working?'

It's the morning of the Mardi Gras parade, and I cannot believe the day is here.

'It would be better if you were standing away from me,' I whispered with all the patience I could muster.

'Okay, roger that dear,' she said, shouting at the two-way radio, causing me to flinch again.

It hasn't been an easy few months since Brendan and the cameras left, I seem to be growing at rapid speed and it's became increasing hard to conceal, well, my body. My current body temperature is on par with a fiery inferno. And I still have just over six weeks till due date.

Shit, six weeks, better start thinking about a nursery.

And maybe telling my parents.

But can't concentration on that now, I have a parade and a wedding to get through today.

Luckily Betty and Fran are being reasonable these days since the night of the big revelations. No one has really spoken about it since, even Matt has sworn off anything to do with phones after discovering Betty and Fran were running a phone sex business to finance a company that tricked investors in believing there is a pending mine happening on the old Crankshaw's farm. No one really came forward to say it was Jake who burnt down the farm but there is no doubt it was him that helped mastermind the whole thing. It seems the Crankshaw's, along with Jake and Pamela, Matt's mother and Jake's old lady lover, got tired of the farming game and sought to make some money. Apparently they recruited Betty and Fran after they realised they could use the CWA supposedly not-for-profit lemonade stand, to filter the funds. Betty decided to get on board with the investment and for some bizarre reason, came up with the concept of the phone sex business. Apparently Fran was getting up to forty calls a day and has never seen so much money. No wonder she knitted so fast, pent up frustration. But after seizing the CWA iphones and destroying the sim cards, well poor old Fran has taken up popping bubble wrap instead. Apparently she is addicted to it now.

I never got a reply email from Jake but after finding out he is still having relations with Pamela, I decided not to pursue it. Which is fine because Daniel has been fantastic, he has even accompanied me to three doctor's appointments now and seems to be more excited about this than I am. He still can't believe I haven't told my parents but as I reminded him, life gets busy and it's not that I don't want to tell my parents, or Matt, or the CWA ladies, it's just that, well John is back with

This Charming Dilemma

the camera to film the parade so still have a slight chance to woo the producers, okay I no longer have an outlet to be an environmental hero and I haven't worked out a new plan as to how I am going to make an impact, but I am sure a solution will present itself.

The mining permit was denied by the council due to not meeting the required guidelines, and after the local council put out a small press release in their newsletter stating that, well it kind of died and the Crankshaw farm has been brought by a development company that is going to divide it up into lifestyle blocks. Well that's the rumour.

'Let's run through this again,' I said as the CWA ladies stand around in their erotic knitwear looking, well, ridiculous.

Thank god I managed to get out of wearing Fran's hideous knitted garment as Fran got sick and tired of having to modify it to fit, and since Betty has insisted that we stick to celery and carrot sticks instead of cakes and scones at all CWA functions, everyone is now blaming me since I am the one overweight and Betty is making everyone eat the healthy food. After trolling through clothing sights, I have finally found an outfit that conceals, well my whole self. Even though Matt keeps asking me why I am wearing a tent.

'Fran... you're riding the scooter yes? Betty, you're behind Maggie here whipping her with this,' I instructed, handing her a horse whip I borrowed from the local pony club, 'Gloria, you are... fire twirling and Mary, where is Mary?'

'Oh she is just helping Matt dear,' Fran said, adjusting her knitted stocking. Honesty, I hope the parade viewers are blind as it's not going to be a pretty sight.

Poor John is having a hard time containing himself and Marline, well we lost Marline's composure a long time ago.

Thank god the sun is behind the clouds as it's terribly warm for October and I have been feeling a bit off colour since I got up this morning. And I have been to the toilet what feels like about a million times today but I'm sure it's just nerves.

'Why do I have to wear dis?' Matt appeared, wearing a sheep costume and walking like the Michelin man.

That's it, we have now lost John's composure too.

'Because I can't!' I hissed.

'Oh dats right, cos you're too fat.'

'No because I am the celebrant,' I smiled.

Apparently after Fran gave up trying to modify my garment it was decided that I could wear a sheep costume as the parade mascot, but after it was discovered I couldn't wear it due to size, and the fact that all the colour drained out of Ellen's face of the thought of a sheep joining her and Rick in matrimony, I managed to convince Matt to wear it for me. And its only costing me a bottle of rum, a box of Australian's finest ale and a life time of Matt reminding me of the time I made him wear a sheep costume.

This Charming Dilemma

'It's so unfair Lisa, you need the exercise more,' he said from the depth of his woolly head gear.

'Okay so everyone is ready,' I said focusing on the parade float and of course the bride to be. Ellen will be joining us when the float gets to parade central, where she and her father will join Rick and the rest of the guests who will be getting on the float shortly.

Sid and Millie are back at the house doing the final preparations for the reception and I have to say the place looks great with the big white marquee standing proud on the pristine lawn. I have so far managed to avoid Rick during the planning but when Rick and Ellen popped round last night, Millie convinced me to come out of my bedroom after I decided to hide in there to avoid awkwardness, by telling me I have to fucken see him at some stage as I am organising his fucken wedding, I finally went out and said hi. And you know what, it wasn't awkward, even after Ellen commented on how lovely the house was and Matt dropped into the conversation that Rick probably did it with me in every room of said house.

'Lisa,' Daniel said, making an appearance, 'I know you're busy, but I need to talk with you quickly.'

'Yep just give me a sec,' I said struggling to get up on the float to do a final check before the guests arrive. My back is really starting to ache, it started last night after I tried to hide in my closest when Rick arrived so I think I have pinched a nerve or something, but it seems to be getting worse.

Even though we are in the back streets with the other floats, the vibe coming from the town is buzzing, there are people everywhere and every business in town has pulled out all stops today.

The wedding guests are starting to gather at the base of the float as I struggle to get back off. I am really not feeling that great, but considering this is my first wedding in public, no wonder I'm feeling like I have a bowling ball in the pit of my stomach.

'Are you sure you're up for this?' Daniel asked all concerned as I flinched at yet another pain rippling through my back, 'you don't look good.'

'Oh it's fine,' I scoffed, 'just nerves… and a sore back.'

'I do have a back up celebrant,' Daniel said, with another hint of concern.

'Pff, that's not needed, its fine,' I scoffed.

'Okay well I just wanted you let you know that…'

'Excuse me?' an elderly man interrupted, 'is this the wedding float.'

'Yes it is Uncle Charlie,' Daniel said, giving me a look to tell me he is losing his marbles, 'here, I'll help you up.'

Daniel escorts the old man onto the float as the guests arrive one by one,

This Charming Dilemma

some look happy to be getting on the back of a makeshift truck, others, well… they look like they would rather be wearing Betty's knitted corset and suspenders.

'Lisa dear!' Betty's voice rung out through my earpiece, I really wish that woman would speak away from the mouthpiece.

'What is it Betty?' I said back into the mouthpiece as Daniel escorts more guests onto the float. Matt is standing in the front of the float in his sheep costume.

'Rick is here with Jake, they want to know if they can come up?'

Jake! Jake has arrived.

A searing pain ripped through me causing me to double over. I really must find a toilet before the parade starts as it feels like I want to pee my pants.

'You okay?' asked Daniel again.

'Yep' I breathed through the pain, 'I just um… need the toilet.'

'Okay, well let me get the rest of these people up and I'll help you,' Daniel said.

'Hi Lisa,' Jake's voice appeared as I tried to straighten up.

And there he is. It's like the past has just walked up and is standing in front of me, shit now Rick is here. Yep definitely in my face.

'Oh Jake… hi,' I said with all the enthusiasm I could muster, especially when another back spasm hit, 'um… fancy meeting you here, I didn't know you were coming.'

'You didn't know I was coming to my brother's wedding?'

'Lisa dear!' Betty's shrill voice rang through my ear piece again as Jake moved off, 'we are about to get started, Ellen is waiting to board down the road.'

Fran starts her scooter while the other ladies gather at the front of the float, Betty pushes a disgruntled Matt to the front of the pack.

Oh my god I really do need the toilet.

'Um attention, attention,' I spoke through my mouthpiece to the crowded float, 'if you would all like to take your um… places, we're about to move off. Remember we are on a moving vehicle so no um… shenanigans.'

The last of the guests settle behind the barrier that has been disguised with lace and silk and I am trying to get back off to go to the toilet. I feel like I am going to wet my pants. The police car sounded his siren to start and the float started to move off.

Shit!

Daniel takes his place beside Rick as his best man and I adjust my head piece and take my place at the alter.

This Charming Dilemma

The wedding music rings out as we start to proceed down the main street of the town, in the distance I can see Ellen's car waiting. The streets are lined with people and the atmosphere is buzzing. The idea is, Ellen gets on in the middle of the parade with her father and the ceremony starts then.

Which is all very nice but I wish this thing would go faster, I don't know if I can hold my bladder.

I scan the faces in the crowd and try my best to not look at Jake who is standing right in my line of vision, now I am thinking about if I should take him aside later and tell him, but every time I think about it, visions of Pamela appear. Great, now I am even more nervous. Daniel is looking at me with concern, and even though the sun is behind the clouds, I can't stop sweating.

Sounds of laughing and wolf whistling ring out as Betty and the rest of the CWA ladies show off their knitted gear. Matt should be dancing around handing out balloons to the kids but instead he looks like an old wether, no manhood, dragging his woolly bones down the street. He'd better pick his game up.

I lean forward to tell Daniel that I really, *really* need the toilet and he has to delay the float somehow when it came to a sudden stop causing my body to jerk forward with the sudden movement.

Shit I just wet my pants!

Daniel is looking at me in horror as the splash hit the ground. I can hear the crowd's cheers as Ellen gets on the float and the wedding song gets even louder.

I glance at Jake and his eyes divert to the waterfall coming out from underneath my dress. Okay act normal, so far its only Daniel and possibly Jake that has noticed.

I clear my throat as Ellen is escorted up on the float and makes her way towards Rick, now with everyone focused on the bride I look down to get a better look at the mess at my feet. There seems to be a lot of liquid there. Unless... nah surely not, I still have six weeks to go, it's too early, it must be nerves... and a weak bladder, although I still feel like I desperately need to pee...

The music fades and Ellen is looking every bit the fairy tale character she is. I feel a pang of jealousy mixed with happiness as I see Rick's face all happy and loved up.

'Ahem... thank you all for coming.' I said, my voice changing as another spasm hit, gee this back pain is really going to town since I peed myself. Great, now I feel constipated too.

'If there is anybody that can give due reason as to why this couple can't be married then... ow... then just... ow, shit. Just come forward alright!' I snapped, letting out a slow breath.

'Um Lisa are you okay?' Daniel whispered as Ellen and Rick look at each other.

This Charming Dilemma

'Yep all good,' I said holding my hand up to say it's all good. Crap how many pages long is this ceremony. And why are we moving.

'Um the float's not moving,' Daniel mumbled.

Shit did I say that out loud.

'Sorry,' I whispered to Ellen who smiled sweetly back at me.

My script in front of me is becoming blurry and I'm finding it hard to concentrate.

'Okay, we'll just skip this part when it goes on about marriage being a sacred commitment because I'm sure you two probably have figured it out by now and we'll just get to the vows. Okay so now we will do the vows.' I said the last bit louder, willing them to not question the fact I just skipped about ten minutes forward.

The vows seem to be taking forever and I feel like my eyes are popping out of my head trying to contain this pain.

Oh shit they are done.

'Now with the um... farrk, giving and taking... I mean, receiving, of the rings.'

I take another outward breath as rings are exchanged and look out to the crowd. I can vaguely see Matt in his sheep costume.

'Lisa dear!' Betty's voice rang into my ear piece, 'stand up straight!'

Daniel is giving me a wide eyed stare. Oh that's right I am meant to say something here. 'Repeat after me, with this ring I… oh god, mother of mercy!'

I collapse to the ground as Daniel steps forward in time to catch me. 'Right that's it,' he said, 'I think I need to call…'

'Another celebrant,' I interrupted, willing him not to say ambulance, 'I just need to sit down.'

'Is everything okay?' Rick said with alarm as I fall on to my back in relief.

'I think she might be in labour,' Daniel whispered.

'No, no, not the case, not that at all,' I smiled, breathing through another intense spasm and getting to my feet, 'just a bad back and a touch of nerves, okay so where was I, oh yes so repeat after me, with this ring I thee wed…'

Ellen looks a bit freaked as she repeats my words. Slipping the ring onto Rick's finger and glancing at me sideways. I can hear murmurs coming from the crowd.

'Rick your turn,' I said, willing this to be over as Rick quickly slips Ellen's ring on.

'So with the power invested in me… oh fuckity fuck, I now… oww, oww, oww… pronounce you man and wife. Now where is that bastard Jake Crankshaw!' I screamed out as another wave of pain hits. Then cue the music as Daniel initiates cheers from the bewildered crowd.

This Charming Dilemma

'Just pretend all is normal,' he whispered to Ellen and Rick as they looked at me in horror as I sit on the floor of the parade float trying not to moan.

I can hear the faint cheers of the crowd as the float starts to move again towards its final destination as confetti is been thrown everywhere.

'What's going on?' Jake's voice appeared as I try to act like I'm just a normal person sitting on the floor… in pain.

'This is all your fault!' I spat at Jake.

'It's my fault what?' Jake asked confused.

Daniel pulls out his phone. 'We really need to get you to the hospital.'

'What's wrong with her?' Jake asked, 'and why is it my fault?'

'Oh just back pain,' I said, breathing through another round of pain. I mean really, is this a good time to tell Jake I am having his babies.

'It's my fault you have back pain?' Jake asked.

'No you idiot, she's pregnant,' Daniel snapped, placing his phone back in his back pocket, 'okay the ambulance is going to meet us at the end of the parade, think you can hang on?'

'Oh yes I'm fine,' I said, 'just let me push.'

'Why is it my fault she's pregnant,' Jake said as I gripped his arm causing him to flinch as I dug my nails into him.

Okay well I guess I have no choice but to tell Jake now, thanks to Daniel telling him I'm pregnant, I mean, shit I was going to wait until the right time presented itself...

'Because it's yours,' I groaned.

'Mine?' Jake said with an odd look on his face.

'Actually I wouldn't be so sure about that,' Daniel said taking his jacket off and placing it on the ground between my legs.

'What do you mean?' I puffed, sounded like I had just run a marathon.

'Jake wasn't the only one... um involved,' Daniel said choosing his words carefully.

Jake scoffed at Daniel. 'What you? I thought you batted for the other team.'

'Oh, no it's definitely not Damo's,' I groaned, 'I'm having twins remember.'

Even though I am feeling really uncomfortable and want to rip the head off everyone right now. I can still see the colour drain from Jake's face.

'Twins?' he said cautiously.

'You didn't sleep with Damo,' Daniel said, clutching my hand as another wave came over me.

'I didn't? But Damo told me I did,' I said closing my eyes and drifting off as my body seems to be calming itself down.

This Charming Dilemma

'Damo was wrong,' Daniel said in the midst of the calm I am feeling right now, 'Damo passed out in the front doorway, it wasn't his bed you woke up in remember?' he said his voice fading out. Okay, false alarm the calm is slowly fading and pain is returning. God I really want to push.

'Not long now,' Daniel reassured as I can feel the rocking motion of the float coming to an end.

'God Lisa what are you doing? You were meant to play Thunderstruck after da wedding was finished, I even had it ready for you to hit da play button and everything!' Matt's whining voice appeared, as I scrunched my eyes fighting the urge to push. In fact someone needs to remove my underwear.

'You're not supposed to climb all the way into the sheep Matt,' said Jake amused.

'Shut up wankshaw,' Matt spat back.

'Quick Matt take off that costume,' Daniel said as I start pulling at my underwear. I had a sudden flashback of Millie saying how your dignity goes out the window when you're in labour. Well it's true cos I don't fucken care. I just want my entire body naked so I can go sit in a nice ice pool in Antarctica.

'But I only have undies on underneath this,' Matt moaned.

'It's okay you've got nothing to show off anyway,' Jake teased.

'Right that's it wankshaw, I've had enough of you!' Matt said, tearing off the costume and crash tackling Jake out of my sight.

'Lisa dear!' Betty's shrill voice also appears, I look up and all I can see is a crowd of faces looking down at me, 'what are you doing down there? You were supposed to play some rock music after the wedding so we can get dancing, what's going on?'

'She's in labour,' Daniel said, throwing the sheep costume over my legs.

'Pfft she can't be pregnant, she doesn't even have a boyfriend!'

Okay I'm pushing.

I can feel two strangers merge upon me so I can only presume they are ambulance paramedics. A sense of relief came over me as they instructed me to push again. Damn straight I'll be pushing because right now, apart from wanting to punch Matt and Jake in the face, that's all I want to do.

'Well, well,' Millie appeared, taking my other hand, 'we do know how to put on a show,' she said.

I really want to punch Millie as well but I think I'll deal with that later, right now everything feels like it's on fire.

Okay now it's fine, it's all good... shit, what's that.

This Charming Dilemma

I open my eyes to find a baby, on my chest. Oh my god, it's a real baby.

'It's a boy,' said Daniel, all gooey as I can feel Millie's tear stained cheek on my forehead.

Well that was easy, wonder what all the fuss is about.

'Is dat a baby?' Matt appeared, looking a little frazzled in his underwear, 'but I fought Millie was da one that could be preggo.'

'Well I'll be damned,' Betty said, 'fancy you being pregnant all this time.'

I stare at the little bundle as a rush of intense contentment comes over me, in fact if anyone comes near this baby at the moment I will rip their heads off.

Shit the urge to push is coming back.

'Okay, let's go again,' the paramedics said as Daniel wraps up my little bundle and takes him off my chest.

Grrr he better not take him far.

I grab Millie's hand with force as she yells in pain and calls me a bitch. I think Matt is standing at my feet with a full view because he actually looks like he is going to throw up. Actually that's an idea, I'll push and aim at Matt.

The pain sears through me before a slight relief takes over again before another baby appears on my chest.

'And this one's a girl,' the paramedic said, documenting the time, 'two minutes and ten seconds apart.'

Daniel places my boy beside her and we all stare in awe at the tiny things in front of us.

I glance around but I can't see Jake anywhere, only Daniel, Millie, Matt, and Betty, well it's an odd family but I guess it is what it is.

Can't help but feel I'm missing someone though.

'Lisa?' a familiar voice rung out as I look up to see my parents hovering over me with an extreme look of horror on their faces.

Shit, I knew I was missing someone.

~　　~~~~~~~~

17

I can't believe I'm a mother.

We finally made it to hospital where I have been asleep for a total of twenty five minutes over the past 24 hours. It's also taken that long for my parents to recover from the fact that they have become sudden grandparents.

Everyone clapped and cheered as the three of us were escorted off the float to the waiting ambulance, even John was there and unbeknown to me, he got the whole lot on film, including the bit where Matt crash tackled Jake to the ground and gave him a few punches for sleeping with his mum and the bit where Marline had to come and rescue Matt when Jake got the upper hand and pinned Matt to the ground.

The twins arrived early and despite their early entrance which I learned later was very lucky to have happened straightforward and naturally, they came in weighing around five pounds each, thank god they weren't any bigger and I swear I am never ever doing this again.

Jake was here earlier and despite him asking me what I wanted from him, I decided my answer was nothing. We are still unclear as to who actually conceived the twins whether it was Daniel or Jake, odds aren't on Jake as he is an identical twin which doesn't run in families I'm now told, it doesn't really matter because the real dad, the one who will be an actual father to them both is not ever going to be Jake anyway, but Daniel.

Daniel told me about the night, we all got a little worse for wear after the B&S ball. It wasn't Damo I has well... relations with that night, but in fact Daniel, I know I should be mad, but Daniel couldn't remember much either, he never told me of his suspicions due to the fact he didn't want to ruin our working relationship, and yes Daniel is still gay, he was just "caught in the moment", well that's the way he put it, and even though I'm pretty sure the universe planned it this way, I think it's best to say those days of alcohol induced blunders are well and truly over.

But Daniel has offered to step up to the father role and I couldn't be happier. We're still not going to live together, well for now, due to the fact that Daniel can't live with my unkempt house-keeping ways and I wouldn't be able to cope with his show home OCD anal retentive habits, but it's going to be just fine. Mum and dad have offered to stay for what I imagine to be an eternity, dad has gone out this morning and brought two bassinets for when we arrive home, Millie and I have also decided to let mum fuss over the babies room and paint it whatever colour she likes, it's the least I can do since I have denied them of a chance to get used to the fact they have become grandparents.

Ellen and Rick sent their regards. Their wedding reception was a huge hit thanks to the fact that Millie, Sid, Betty, and Fran took over the fort. I offered them a chance to do the

This Charming Dilemma

ceremony all over again when I am back on my feet, they weren't too upset and said its fine, it's all signed and it's a wedding they will never forget!

The festival was a huge success and the town loved the erotic knitted theme and now the talk around town is that it should be an annual event. Hmmm, we'll see. John and Marline are more than happy with the film they received. Marline even likened it to The Bold and The Beautiful, not sure how I should take that.

Matt reckons he has sworn off Marline now, after she keeps teasing him about being a big girl and doesn't stop beating him up. He said he doesn't need a girl bringing his manhood down.

'Oh good, you are awake,' Daniel said coming in carrying some treats, two giant teddy bears and a box of vitamins for me. The twins are sleeping peacefully on my chest, I haven't wanted to put them down for twenty-three hours now, the hour I had to was when I had a shower and the bitch midwife made me go to the toilet against my will, where I swear I peed shards of glass. I'm sure Daniel planned his role in his mind all along, as he has even got the builders in to give him quotes on building an extended area at the office to accommodate a nursery and play room. Love Daniel, he is so thoughtful and he looks so proud and I am ecstatic with the whole situation.

'Sup?' Matt also made an appearance followed by Millie, Sid, and Amy.

Matt has only just forgiven me for not telling him I was pregnant when he wanted to sign me up for Weight-Watchers or enroll me for the Biggest Loser. And after I informed him it's okay he doesn't need to fill the father role of Jake Wankshaw, and that it's Daniel who wants to take that role, a sigh of relief came over him but he has promised to be the twins bodyguard until they both turn 21. I mean how sweet is that, children with their very own spotted youth following them everywhere.

'So what are der names?' Matt asked as Millie takes one and Daniel takes the other.

I haven't given thought to any names but as I look around at the weird situation in front of me I am trying to think of any names that would describe how bizarre my life and the situation has become. I mean yes Daniel and I are obviously going to have a platonic relationship based on co-parenting but you know what, I'm okay with that. I mean who needs to do the whole conventional marriage and babies thing. Sooo overrated. From now on I am Lisa who doesn't do things normally.

'How about Will and Grace like on da TV?' Matt suggested. Daniel and I shoot alarmed glances at each other while Millie gives Sid a look of awkwardness. Its sooo unconventional but you know what... it fits.

In fact it's... it's perfect.

Will and Grace it is then.

18

Four months later.

'Hurry up it's starting!' Betty called out as we are all gathered around a television at CWA headquarters for the launch of Betty and Fran's new show.

Yes Betty and Fran's new reality show.

After a meeting with the producer Daryl Loft, and director Brendan, I have decided not to pursue a career as a celebrity reality television star. I mean it really is overrated and who needs it anyway. Business is going well and thanks to Ellen spreading a good word about my dedication to the ceremony even whilst in labour, I have more than enough weddings and christenings and stuff to keep me busy in-between feeding and burping.

Will and Grace are nearly four months old and they are just the best babies ever, okay so they have already started a tag team where one will sleep while the other is wide awake and I feel like a constant milking machine and not to mention, have changed a zillion nappies, but I wouldn't change it for the world. Daniel is an awesome father, he even stayed up with me all night one night when Grace was sick. Yep I can honestly say I am truly blessed.

Did I mention I haven't slept in four months.

My parents are still here and I really do think they are overstaying their welcome just a tiny bit. Although have to admit, it's been a little bit of a blessing, especially as far as Sid was concerned, there are some days where the washing was too overpowering for him and he hid under the bed at the very thought of it, so Millie thought the kindest thing to do for him was to send him to Conspiracy Camp for a week to give him some Sid time. He is due back next week and Millie said they think they have found a panther type creature that escaped from a secret government Lab out in the middle of the Australia desert, so it sounds like he is having a good time.

It didn't take a lot of editing to turn the show into the Betty and Fran show, I mean after all, they seemed to be behind every situation I was involved in. It was a suggestion put forward by me to Brendan and then Brendan to Daryl, to hold off, and change the focus. And even after Brendan found out about the time they were investigated for accidentally selling homemade eye pillows stuffed with marijuana he still thought it was a great idea and it works well as they also do cooking demos and show people how to crochet stuff. In fact there are already plans to extend the show on tour around Australia on their scooters with the erotic knitwear promoting health and keeping the spirit of the old girl alive, as Fran puts it, and besides Betty said it's definitely a better way to earn a living then phone sex, or scamming investors to invest in a mine that wouldn't have happened.

'Ohh here it goes,' Fran said, taking a seat as the last advert comes on signaling the start of the show.

This Charming Dilemma

'How exciting!' squealed Maggie as the lights are dimmed and credits roll. Millie and I exchange glances as an image of Jake appears across the screen.

I haven't thought about him much since the day at the hospital, I did hear he and Pamela have taken the share of the sale of the farm and are now up north somewhere, probably trying to think of their next money-making scheme. I really feel I have dodged a bullet there, even though it took me a couple of goes to learn it. The Crankshaw's farm is to become a housing estate containing exclusive lifestyle blocks and a 18 hole golf course, in fact it's perfect as it is going to complement our B&B.

Ever since the Mardi Gras parade, the whole place seems to be on the move, even Daniel is thinking of turning his place into an accommodation outlet, then him and I get a place together with the kids.

Yes did I mention I have kids. Still getting used to that.

Mum and Dad are ecstatic I didn't parade myself on national television, in fact Mum said that's the most grown-up decision I have made since giving birth to the twins. They weren't so hot on the names to begin with and yes they are still getting used to the fact I am co-parenting with someone who I will obviously never have an intimate relationship with. But who cares.

'Hey dats me,' Matt said as he and Damo appear in suits looking like idiots. In fact it's well edited, you wouldn't even think I was involved at all.

Sounds of hooting and laughing ricochets around the hall as the show goes on, I have to say, I am so pleased it's not me on there.

Millie is now working from home as a private investigator, she still has training to do so she's not out following people around or anything, just mainly following up on insurance fraud and missing person cases, stuff like that.

And it's great because now Millie doesn't care what I do. I mean she cares, but ever since the twins were born, she has ceased any lecturing about well... anything, even when I made the papers after my unusual birth Millie convinced me to send my story into That's Life magazine. Okay so I may have decided not to be a television celebrity but I guess a wee bit of a celebrity status even if it was just for the month of December, is okay.

'You know,' Millie whispered, leaning over as I watch the footage of the Mardi Gras parade and remember back to that special day, 'Brendan is thinking about a real life Will and Grace series,' she suggested, raising an eyebrow at me.

A tiny surge of excitement came over me at the thought of an actual show staring me and Daniel, but you know what, I don't need to showcase that to the world. After all I have my own private dramas happening here every day amongst the very people in this room and that is really all the drama I need.

***************************End**********************

This Charming Dilemma

Good-buy Lisa

Well as this is the end of the journey for Lisa and the Charming series, I would like to thank those who helped me get started, those who waited patiently for the next book and those people who encouraged me to keep going.

Look out for exciting new titles in 2020/2021

Follow me on Facebook/Sharon Gartner Author